Crowley

Dugdale & Hotten
v
Rose Dugdale ?

SEXUALITY, MAGIC AND PERVERSION

Also by Francis King

RITUAL MAGIC IN ENGLAND
ASTRAL PROJECTION, MAGIC AND ALCHEMY
(*Editor*)
THE REBIRTH OF MAGIC (*Macdonald*)

FRANCIS KING

SEXUALITY, MAGIC
AND PERVERSION

LONDON
NEVILLE SPEARMAN

Sexuality Magic and Perversion © 2002 Feral House

All rights reserved.

ISBN: 0-922915-74-1

Feral House
P.O. Box 13067
Los Angeles, CA 90013

www.feralhouse.com
info@feralhouse.com

10 9 8 7 6 5 4 3 2 1

First printed in Great Britain © 1971 Neville Spearman Publishers, Ltd.

First printed in the United States of America © 1972 Citadel Press, Inc.

CONTENTS

Part One: A Witch, a Pornographer and Oriental Sex Magic
Chapter 1 A Dildo for a Witch 3
2 Pornography, Edward Sellon and Indian Tantricism 10
3 The Real Tantricism—Buddhist and Hindu 30
4 Chinese Sexual Alchemy 37

Part Two: The Occidental Background
Chapter 5 Primitive Fertility Cults 40
6 The Great Mother Falls on Evil Days 54
7 Masses—Black, White and Amatory 65
8 Priapus Rediscovered 75

Part Three: Sexuality and Magic in the Modern World
Chapter 9 Templarism and Sex Magic 91
10 Enter Baphomet 101
11 Saturn-Gnosis, Sex Magic, and Planetary Aspects 115
12 The Bishop and the Boys 122
13 Sexual Magic in the United States 142
14 Magicians, the Orgasm and the Work of Wilhelm Reich 158
15 A Whip for Aradia 163
16 The Future of Sexual Magic 169

Appendices:

Appendix A The Dildo in History 173
B Robert Graves, Witches and Islamic Mysticism 175
C Copulating with Cleopatra 177
D Another Sex-Magic Ritual 186
E Ralph Chubb, Boy Love and William Blake 190
F Crowleyanity in Switzerland 194

Selected Bibliography 199
Index 205

ILLUSTRATIONS

		opposite page
1	Drawings of nineteenth-century coffer lids	20
2	The last degeneration of Priapus as the ithyphallic god of the witches	21
3	The Guibourg Mass	52
4	J. K. Huysman	53
5	Bishop C. W. Leadbeater	84
6	A pen and ink sketch by Crowley	85
7	Leah Hirsig	116
8	Erotic painting in the *Chamber of Nightmares* at the Abbey of Thelema, Sicily	117
9	Crowley, *circa* 1925	148
10	Crowley in O.T.O. insignia as *Baphomet*	149
11	Crowley in old age	149
12	The Prophet Vintras	180
13	Peladan	181

ACKNOWLEDGEMENTS

My thanks to G.A.D. for her invariable kindness and encouragement. To Liz Miller for her typing, patience and German translations. To Gerald Yorke for the loan of documents. To Timothy d'Arch Smith for information. To Messrs. Jonathan Cape for permission to quote an extract from Aleister Crowley's *Confessions* and to Messrs. Peter Davies for permission to quote an extract from Miss June Johns' *King of the Witches*.

PART ONE

A Witch, a Pornographer
and Oriental Sex Magic

CHAPTER ONE
A Dildo for a Witch

The title of this chapter may require some explanation, but I have no doubt that a substantial number of my readers will be aware that a dildo (alternative spellings are dildoe and dildol) is an imitation penis, and that, while the use of such an artificial aid to sexuality may seem to show a level of erotic sophistication verging on depravity, its history extends back almost as far as that of Mankind itself.

Enough, for the moment at any rate, of the dildo![1]

The witch of my chapter heading requires a more detailed explanation. She was not the traditional hag, complete with cat and broomstick, nor did she display any noticeable tendencies to either bewitch cattle, fly up a chimney on a broomstick, or turn milk sour. She was only twenty-three years of age, quite pretty, and a rather good viola player. I had first met her at a concert, but it was only after I had known her for some time and she had discovered that I was mildly interested in the more obscure aspects of occultism and magic, past and present, that she told me that she was not only a witch, but quite an important witch, the High Priestess of one of the covens of the contemporary witch-cult.

I was fascinated. It was not that Marian (for so I will call her) was a witch—I had already met several, most of them living on one variety or other of welfare hand-out—but that she was the first witch I had met who seemed to have charm and to be not only reasonably intelligent but a real personality in her own right; the most pronounced character-trait of the other witches I had met had been an inordinate and inexplicable fondness for the sweet white wines of Spain and Cyprus. One

[1] See Appendix A—"The Dildo in History".

night Marian got very drunk on sherry—a drink to whose effects witches seem peculiarly susceptible—and told me the extraordinary story of the perverse sexual rite by which she had been initiated into the degree of High Priestess. It was this story that first aroused my interest in the complex interconnections between sexuality, religion and magic, and I think it worth recounting in some detail. Before doing so, however, it is best that I should briefly explain the origins of the contemporary witch-cult.[2]

In England there are a considerable number of groups of witches, known as covens. I estimate that there are between two and three thousand active witches who are members of such groups. The cult now seems to be enjoying a mushroom growth in the U.S.A., where at least one small business has found it worthwhile to specialise in the production of athames (ceremonial knives), scourges, and the other impedimenta of what its practitioners refer to as "the craft". Without exception all the cult members I have met have believed, or at least pretended to believe, that their magical-sexual-religious rites are of immemorial antiquity, the remnants of the Great Mother worship of Stone-Age Europe, now at last able to re-emerge into the open after enduring an underground existence during long centuries of Christian persecution.

It would be nice if this was so, but alas, it isn't! With one or two dubious exceptions all the covens of the modern witch-cult owe their existence to the activities of Gerald Gardner, an eccentric Englishman who died in 1964.

Gardner, whose relations seem to have been even more eccentric than he himself—his father used to strip naked every time it rained, go into the garden and sit on his clothes until the rain stopped, while one of his uncles spent a fortune on building places of worship for various Protestant denominations—had been born in the North of England but had spent much of his life in the Far East until his retirement from the Malayan customs service in 1936. He combined a taste for dabbling in the messier fringes of occultism with a considerable although unscholarly, acquaintance with the whole field of English and Manx folklore. Indeed, from March 1946 until his death he was a member of the Council of the Folk Lore Society, although it is probable that his fellow-members of that august body were somewhat embarrassed by

[2] A more detailed examination of the origins of this movement is made in Chapter XXI of my *Ritual Magic in England* (Neville Spearman, 1970).

his habit of plagiarising from long-dead folk-lore collectors, as they certainly were by his mysterious assumption (*circa* 1950) of the degrees of M.A., Ph.D. and D.Litt.! These sudden academic honours were certainly not conferred by any recognised university. At first I thought that they had been obtained from a degree-mill known as the Temple Bar College (Seattle), with which some of Gardner's associates had been mixed up in the early 'forties. I found, however, that by order of the Federal Trade Commissioners this institution had been closed down in July 1947, some years before plain *Mr.* Gardner blossomed out as *Dr.* Gardner. Gardner's degrees were almost certainly obtained from one or other of the bogus Universities associated with the strange ecclesiastical underworld of the *episcopi vagantes*.

In 1954 Gardner published *Witchcraft Today*, not as bad a book as one might have expected, for the publisher's reader, an occult scholar of real distinction, had insisted on the deletion of the more rubbishy passages. The book's basic theses were four in number; (a) that Margaret Murray had been right in her assertion that the mediaeval witch-cult had enjoyed a real existence, and had not been a mere fantasy of the Inquisitors, (b) that this cult was the "Old Religion", the still surviving faith of prehistoric man, (c) that this secret religion had survived into the present century (Gardner claimed to be in touch with hereditary witches and implied that he himself was a member of a coven) and (d) that the magical-religious practices of the cult involved the worship of a horned God and a great Mother-goddess by rites involving both flagellation and sexual intercourse. These simple, but quite unproven assertions, were padded out with a good deal of rather meaningless flim-flam about the Order of the Garter, the Knights Templar and their alleged homosexual practices etc. etc.

One of the most notable personality characteristics of the majority of occultists is their overpowering credulity, their capacity to believe six impossible things before breakfast. Someone has only to announce the existence of a mysterious book, or an even more mysterious occult fraternity, and there will always be those who are prepared to produce the required article or organisation—usually for a suitably large fee. For example, no one had heard of any alchemical writings of the early English St. Dunstan until the Elizabethan magician Edward Kelly stated that he had found a strange red powder of projection and *The Book of St. Dunstan*, describing how to use this same red powder for the purpose of transmuting base metals into gold, in the ruins of Glastonbury

Abbey. Nevertheless, within fifty years of Kelly first making his claim to this discovery no less than half a dozen alchemical tracts had been printed, all of them differing one from another and each claiming to be the sole authentic *Book of St. Dunstan*. Again, the American horror-writer H. P. Lovecraft invented a completely imaginary grimoire (text book of magic), entitled the *Necronomicon*, which became almost a fixed feature of the plots of the many stories he churned out for *Weird Tales* and other pulp magazines of the 'thirties. For some reason unknown to me many occultists became convinced that such a grimoire really existed; sure enough, a forged *Necronomicon* was produced, its contents pilfered from a much older forgery, the *Fourth Book* of the pseudo-Agrippa, but put into an Egyptian-cum-Arab form, and I know of at least one would-be Magician who has paid forty guineas for this literary-occult curiosity.

It is not surprising, therefore, that after Gardner had loudly proclaimed the existence of a network of covens practising traditional witchcraft such a network actually came into existence. In fairness to both the witches and Gardner however, it must be admitted that there were almost certainly at least two pre-Gardnerian covens in existence before 1954, one in St. Albans and the other in the New Forest. I think it most unlikely that their origins go back before 1900, however, and that in all probability they came into existence *after* 1921 and the publication of Margaret Murray's *Witch Cult in Western Europe*.

Gardner himself seems to have been well prepared for a rebirth of the witch-cult and to have made suitable contingency-plans many years before. For as long ago as 1943/4 he had employed Aleister Crowley, at a suitably large fee, to compose rituals that could be used in a new, Gardnerian witch-cult. There seem to have originally been four of these rituals:[3] the first one designed to be used at a Spring-festival to be held on either March 21st or April 30th, the other three for initiation rituals into the cult. The latter included both ordinary and sado-masochistic sexual components, for the first-degree ritual involved scourging—the would-be witch was told that he or she had "to suffer in order to learn", and the third-degree ritual had sexual intercourse between a couple while surrounded by the other members of the coven as its so-called "Sacrament of Life".

The cult rapidly grew, but not all those who desired to consider

[3] Later on other rituals were composed. They are markedly inferior in form and content to the original four and are clearly not of Crowley's manufacture.

themselves as witches shared Gardner's voyeuristic and masochistic preoccupations, and a gradual process of evolution led to the emergence, on the one hand, of groups of the utmost respectability, some of which even went so far as to eschew the traditional nudity, and, on the other hand, of covens which emphasised sexuality even more than Gardner himself. For a time Gardner managed to act as a sort of unitary centre and to keep these diverging trends in some sort of co-operative relationship with one another. After his death in 1964, however, the evolutionary process seems to have accelerated and today the cult is more segmented than ever before. At the present time there are at least five competing splinter movements (each, inevitably, claiming the sole orthodoxy) varying from one with an almost puritanical attitude towards sex, and largely concerned with traditional ritual magic, to another which incorporates almost every variety of sexual perversion, from anilinctus to zoophilia into its rituals.[4]

It was into one of the more extreme of the sexually inclined covens that "my" witch, Marian, had been initiated. It will be remembered that the first-degree "Gardnerian" rite involved scourging. In many covens this "suffering in order to learn" has become symbolic, no more than a few token flicks administered by either the High Priest (to female candidates) or the High Priestess (to male candidates). Exactly the opposite process had taken place in Marian's coven; at her initiation she had been stripped, tied up so tightly that her circulation had been impeded, and heavily beaten on the back, buttocks and even breasts by not only the Priest but by each member of the coven. This heavy scourging was continued until Marian was bruised and bleeding—she told me that she had been so badly scarred that it had become impossible for her to wear a low-cut dress.

Marian's admission to the third degree—by which she became a High Priestess in her own right—was even more traumatic an experience. She had expected to undergo ritual sexual intercourse with the High Priest, but she found that the High Priestess, who seems to have been the dominant figure in this coven, had decided that she herself would "initiate" Marian with the aid of a dildo. The High Priestess justified this plan with the argument that a sodomitical interlude between the High Priest and a young male initiate had "reversed the physical plane polarities of the Chiefs" and that to restore the balance it was essential

[4] The ritual patterns and sexual practices of the more heavily sexually orientated covens are examined in detail in a later chapter of this book.

A DILDO FOR A WITCH

that she herself should play the male part in what she primly referred to as "an act of lesbian love-making". "Love-making" is hardly the term I would have chosen to describe what actually took place. For the dildo used was very old, unlubricated, and made of wood. Marian found the experience extremely unpleasant, suffered great pain, and eventually had to have medical treatment in order to remove splinters from her vagina. Nevertheless, there were clearly masochistic elements in Marian's psychological make-up, for it was apparent that she extracted a certain amount of emotional stimulation and fulfilment from telling me this unpleasant story. I wondered whether Marian and the other members of her coven were simply sado-masochists, using witchcraft as a means of living out their own pathetic fantasies, or whether, just possibly, they were something more, whether, in fact they were following the ancient and almost forgotten tradition of using pain and sex as a means of achieving ecstasy—ecstasy in the full sense of God-intoxication.

Over the next three months I had many conversations with Marian. As time passed, and she became aware that I was a reasonably sympathetic listener, she told me more and more about her coven's beliefs, the sado-sexual techniques used by its members, and, most important of all, what those techniques were designed to achieve.[5] Almost against my will I gradually came to the conclusion that these people were no ordinary "bunch of perverts", out for kicks, but were (however misguided their beliefs might be), genuinely striving to transcend the limits of ordinary consciousness and to reach what Hindus call *samadhi*—that Union in which subject and object become one.

Marian's revelation fascinated me. I began to devote a good deal of puzzled thought to the complex interconnections between sexuality, religion and western occultism and decided to undertake a brief study of the subject. As I read books, letters and manuscripts my puzzlement grew. For, from my knowledge of present-day sexual magic, I knew that there was present in western occultism an underground strain of the oriental sexual-religious-magical philosophy known as Tantricism, and I had always assumed that this had ultimately derived from Aleister Crowley and the *Ordo Templi Orientis*[6]—but to my surprise I found what seemed to be a Tantric element in western occultism before

---

[5] A detailed examination of these beliefs and techniques is made in the chapter of this book entitled "A Whip for Aradia".

[6] Dealt with in a later chapter of this book.

Crowley was even born! I found it, for example, hinted at in the allegedly Rosicrucian writings of Hargrave Jennings.[7] I determined that my first task must be to trace down the source of these first faint echoes of Bengali and Tibetan sex-magic and I decided to start with Hargrave Jennings, whom I knew had both been obsessed by sex and friendly with several dubious scholars, anyone of whom might have been the link for which I was looking.

I approached Timothy d'Arch Smith, a bibliographer whose knowledge of the more obscure byways of Victorian literature is unequalled, and asked him for his help.

"Do you by any chance know", he asked me, "whether Jennings was friendly with a pornographer named Edward Sellon?"

I replied that I not only thought it possible but was fairly sure that such a friendship had existed; for in a copy of an anonymously written, wretchedly illustrated, Victorian pornographic novel—the property of a private collector with whom I was acquainted—I had seen Hargrave Jennings' bookplate. An MS note on the flyleaf of the same volume, presumably written by Jennings himself, conveyed the information that the illustrations were by a certain Captain Edward Sellon, now deceased, and that the writer of the note had known him well.

"There," said Timothy, "is almost certainly your connecting link. Have a look at Sellon's *Annotations on the Sacred Writings of the Hindus* and see if it gives you any clues."

Taking Timothy's advice I went along to the library of the British Museum, where I found Sellon's own copy of the *Annotations*, a splendid volume in which he had bound up many of his own watercolours and drawings along with the printed sheets.

As I read I began to find that the material before me was oddly familiar; I soon felt sure that I had previously read parts of it, or at least something very similar to parts of it. I turned to Jennings' book *Phallicism, Celestial and Terrestrial*. To my astonishment I found that the sixth and fifteenth chapters of it had been lifted bodily, without the benefit of quotation marks, from Sellon's *Annotations*!

Timothy d'Arch Smith had been quite right; Sellon was the man for whom I had been looking, the man whose writings had first brought Tantricism to the attention of occidental occultists.

[7] Dealt with in Part Two of this book.

CHAPTER TWO

Pornography, Edward Sellon and Indian Tantricism

In a later chapter I shall show how Richard Payne Knight and Thomas Wright were responsible for the birth of a dilettante interest in the Priapic worship and sexual magic of ancient and mediaeval Europe; but it was that extraordinary personality Edward Sellon—soldier, coach-driver, fencing-master and pornographer—who first created any widespread interest in the sexual practices of Indian Tantricism. I use the phrase "widespread interest" of course, in only a comparative way; a small minority of English and French scholars seem to have had an interest in the sexual aspects of Indian religion as early as the eighteenth century, and Sellon's real achievement was to extend this interest and to give both the (admittedly tiny) sexually-emancipated minority of the middle-classes and sexually-orientated occultists some awareness of the sexual-religious-magical tradition of left-handed Tantricism. Sellon's *Annotations Upon the Sacred Writings of the Hindus* did not appear until 1865, the year before his death, but his life illustrates so well both the oddness of character and the contempt for the generally accepted nineteenth-century social *mores* that were probably essential for anyone undertaking a serious study of Tantricism at that period, that I think it worth while recounting it in some detail before examining the *Annotations*.

Sellon was born in 1818 and was "the son of a gentleman of moderate fortune whom I lost when quite a child".[1] Sellon adds that as a conse-

---

[1] This and the succeeding quotations come, unless otherwise indicated, from Sellon's posthumously published pornographic autobiography *The Ups and Downs of Life*. I have been unable to obtain access to a copy of the first edition (1867) and have been forced to rely upon (a) a wretchedly printed continental

quence of this early bereavement he was "designed from the first for the army" and, when still only sixteen years of age, he went to India where, on October 27th, 1834, he was gazetted as an Ensign in the 4th Madras Native Infantry. Sellon seems to have enjoyed his ten years in India, taking a more than average interest in native social, religious, and sexual life—particularly the latter. He wrote:

"I now commenced a regular course of fucking with native women. The usual charge for the general run of them is two rupees. For five, you may have the handsomest Mohammedan girls, and any of the high-caste women who follow the trade of a courtesan. The 'fivers' are a very different set of people from their frail sisterhood in European countries; they do not drink, they are scrupulously cleanly in their persons, they are sumptuously dressed, they wear the most costly jewels in profusion, they are well educated and sing sweetly, accompanying their voices on the viol de gamba, a sort of guitar, they generally decorate their hair with clusters of clematis, or the sweet scented bilwa flowers entwined with pearls or diamonds. They understand in perfection all the arts and wiles of love, are capable of gratifying any tastes, and in face and figure they are unsurpassed by any women in the world.

"They have one custom that seems singular to a European, they not only shave the Mons Veneris, but take a clean sweep underneath it, so you glance at their hard, full and enchanting breasts, handsome beyond compare, and fancy you have got hold of some unfledged girl. The Rajpootanee girls pluck out the hairs as they appear with a pair of tweezers, as the ancient Greek women did, and this I think a very preferable process to the shaving.

"It is impossible to describe the enjoyment I experienced in the arms of these syrens. I have had English, French, German and Polish women of all grades of society since, but never, never did they bear a comparison with those salacious, succulent houris of the far East."

As well as all these commercial sexual transactions Sellon seems to have devoted a considerable amount of effort to seducing such married

edition (c. 1900) which had both been heavily cut and had added to it, by some semi-literate hack, a great deal of extremely filthy and boring homosexual material and (b) extracts printed by Pisanus Fraxi (Ashbee) in his *Index Librorum Prohibitorum* (1877).

and unmarried European women as were available and to writing *Herbert Breakspear*, a sentimental novel with an Indian setting.[2]

On the whole Sellon seems to have taken pleasure in almost all his Indian experiences—even his duel with a fellow-Englishman, inevitably, over a woman, does not seem to have caused him undue distress—and it is in every way understandable that, when he came home to England on leave in 1843, he was surprised and annoyed to find that his mother had not only selected a suitable prospective bride for him but had more or less arranged the marriage. He seems to have had a healthy Victorian respect for money, however, and cheered up when he discovered that his mother's choice was not only good looking but the heiress to a fortune, resigned his commission[3] and got married.

The first few months of married life were spent in Paris, and seem to have gone well enough, but on the couple's return to England early in 1845 Sellon was shocked to discover that his wife had very little capital of her own and, still worse, that his parents-in-law were only prepared to make an allowance of a beggarly £400 a year! Feeling thoroughly cheated Sellon abandoned his wife and returned to live with, and no doubt on, his mother at her home in Bruton Street, London. The separation lasted two years, but Sellon kept himself fully occupied by keeping a mistress at "a little suburban villa" and by seducing his mother's fourteen year old parlour-maid, "a sweet pretty creature" who had "received a pretty good education, and was not at all like a servant, either in manners or appearance".

After their reconciliation Sellon and his wife continued to live with his mother but soon began to have violent disagreements. The worst of these, which led to Sellon being confined to bed for a month, was precipitated by the young Mrs. Sellon's discovery of the affair between her husband and Emma, the previously mentioned "sweet pretty creature". On this occasion it seems to have been Mrs. Sellon who first took refuge in violence, for she gave her husband, as he himself said, "such a tremendous and violent box on my right ear as nearly to knock me out of my chair". Sellon goes on to record his reactions:

[2] This, the only literary production of Sellon that would not have been out of place in a Victorian drawing-room, was not published until 1848. From internal evidence it is nevertheless clear that at least a first draft of the novel must have been completed as early as 1842.

[3] According to Sellon's own account this resignation took place in 1844, shortly before his marriage. Curiously enough, however, his name still appeared in the East India list as late as 1847.

"I very calmly flung the remainder of my cigar under the grate, and seizing both her wrists with a grasp of iron, forced her into an armchair. 'Now you little devil,' said I, 'you sit down there, and I give you my honour, I will hold you thus, till you abjectly and most humbly beg for mercy, and ask my pardon for the gross insult you have inflicted on me.'

" 'Insult! think of the insult you have put upon me, you vile wretch, to demean yourself with a little low bred slut like that!' and struggling violently, she bit the backs of my hands until they were covered with blood, and kicked my shins till she barked them.

" 'I say, my dear,' said I, 'did you ever see Shakespeare's play of Taming the Shrew.'

"No answer.

" 'Well, my angel, I'm going to tame you.' She renewed her bites and kicks, and called me all the miscreants and vile scoundrels under the sun. I continued to hold her in a vice of iron. Thus we continued till six o'clock.

" 'If it is your will and pleasure to expose yourself to the servants,' said I, 'pray do, I have no sort of objection, but I will just observe that John will come in presently to clear away the luncheon and lay the cloth for dinner.' A torrent of abuse was the only answer.

" 'You brute,' she said, 'you have bruised my wrists black and blue.'

" 'Look at my hands, my precious angel, and my shins are in still worse condition.'

"By and by there was a rap at the door, 'Come in,' said I. John appeared—'Take no notice of us, John, but attend to your business.'

"John cleared away the luncheon and laid the cloth for dinner. Exit John.

" 'Oh, Edward, you do hurt my wrists so.'

" 'My ear and face are still burning with the blow you gave me, my hands are torn to pieces with your tiger teeth, and will not be fit to be seen for a month, and as to my shins, my drawers are saturated with blood,' said I.

" 'Let me go! let me go directly, wretch!' and again she bit, kicked and struggled.

" 'Listen to me,' said I, 'there are 365 days in the year, but by God! if there were 3,605, I hold you till you apologise in the manner and way I told you, and even then, I shall punish you likewise for the infamous way you have behaved.' She sulked for another half hour, but did not bite or kick anymore. I never relaxed my grasp, or the sternness of my countenance. My hands were streaming with blood, some of the veins were opened, her lap was full of blood, it was a frightful scene.

"At length she said, 'Edward, I humbly ask your pardon for the shameful way I have treated you, I apologise for the blow I gave you, I forgive you for any injury you have done me, I promise to be docile and humble in future, and I beg—I beg,' she sobbed, 'your forgiveness.'

"I released her hands, pulled the bell violently, told John to run immediately for Dr. Monson (the family physician), and fell fainting on the floor. I had lost nearly a pint of blood from the wounds inflicted by the panther. When I recovered my senses, I was lying on the sofa, my hands enveloped in strapping plaister and bandages, as were also my shins. Emma and my wife knelt at my feet crying, while Monson kept pouring port wine down my throat. 'Could you eat a little,' said he kindly.

" 'Gad, yes,' said I, 'I'm awfully hungry, bring dinner, John.'

"They all stared, it was ten o'clock; however, dinner was served, though sadly overdone, having been put back three hours. John had only laid covers for two, presuming my wife and I would dine tête-à-tête. I told him to bring two more. Monson and my wife raised their eyebrows—'Doctor, stay and dine with us, call it supper if you like; Emma, I desire you to seat yourself.' She made towards the door. 'Augusta,' said I, addressing my wife, 'persuade Emma to dine with us, I will it.'

" 'You had better stay,' said my wife, with a sweet smile. Emma hesitated a moment, and then came and sat beside me."

Dinner duly took place—and a very odd dinner it must have been, for Dr. Monson, who seems to have been almost as eccentric a character as his patient, took it upon himself to lecture Mrs. Sellon on the wickedness of losing one's temper with one's husband. No doubt neither Mrs. Sellon nor her husband gave Dr. Monson's discourse the full attention it deserved, for while it was being delivered Sellon was otherwise occupied; he describes himself as having:

". . . one of my bandaged hands up Emma's clothes while he was saying this, and was feeling her lovely young cunny. It was nuts to crack for me. Dr. Monson gone, I rang the bell, 'John, you and the servants can go to bed,' said I. John cast an enquiring glance at Madam and Emma, bowed and retired.

"I asked Emma for my cigar-case, as for Augusta, I did not notice her. I lit a cigar, and drawing Emma on my knee, sat before the fire and smoked. 'You can go to bed, Augusta,' said I, as if she was the servant and Emma the wife, 'I shall not want you any more.' The humbled woman took her candle, and wishing us both good night, went to bed.

" 'Oh, Edward,' said poor little Emma, 'what a dreadful woman she is, she nearly killed you, you nearly bled to death! Dr. Monson said two of the great veins at the back of each hand had been opened by her teeth, and that if she had not given in when she did, you would have bled to death.'

" 'But here I am all alive, my sweet.'

" 'But you won't have me tonight, mind.'

" 'Won't I though!'

" 'Now, Edward! pray don't, you are too weak!'

" 'Then this will give me strength,' said I, and I drank at a draught a tumbler of Carbonell's old Port. I made her drink another glass, and then we lay down on the couch together. I fucked her twice, and then in each other's arms we fell asleep.

"It was six o'clock the next morning when I woke up. I aroused Emma and told her I thought she had better go to her own room, before the servants were about; my hands were very painful, so arranging with her when and where she should next meet me, I went up stairs to bed. My wife was fast asleep, I held the candle close to the bed and looked at her, she was lying on her back, her hands thrown over her head. She looked so beautiful, and her large, firm breasts rose and fell so voluptuously, that I began to be penetrated with some sentiments of remorse for my infidelities. I crept into bed and lay down beside her. I soon fell asleep. I might have slumbered some two hours, I was aroused by being kissed very lovingly. I was sensible that a pair of milky arms clasped me, and that heaving breast was pressed to mine. I soon became aware of something more than this which was going on under the bed-clothes. I opened my eyes and fixed them upon the ravisher! It was Augusta. She blushed at being caught, but did not release me. I remained passive in her arms. My hands I had lost the use of; inflamation had set in in the night, I felt very feverish, in an hour more I was delirious; I became alarmingly ill."[4]

Throughout his illness Sellon was nursed by the two women, but upon his recovery he rather ungraciously dismissed the maid and entered upon another brief period of domesticity with Augusta. This ended when, almost inevitably, yet another cast-off mistress reappeared upon the scene. Shortly afterwards Sellon's personal circumstances became ever more difficult, for his mother's income was sharply reduced as a consequence of the embezzlement of a large part of her capital by that standby of Victorian novelists, a defaulting solicitor. For the first time in his life Sellon became in real need of money and took a job as driver of the mail-coach that ran between London and Cambridge.[5] He seems to have been surprisingly successful at his new occupation, earning about three hundred pounds a year and holding down the job until the opening of the London–Cambridge railway made mail-coach and driver alike redundant. Comparatively unworried by this setback Sellon set up as a fencing-master in London—it is clear from contemporary references to this phase of his life that he was a competent, possibly even a brilliant, swordsman.

Somehow or other Sellon's wife traced him to his fencing-rooms—he could never discover how—and yet another reconciliation took place. Augusta seems to have decided that her husband was better removed from the temptation of London and whisked him away to "a charming cottage she had ... in a remote hamlet, not a hundred miles from Winchester" where for three years the couple enjoyed a quiet rural existence. Sellon himself seems to have been puzzled as to how he endured the boredom of country life for so long, but I suspect that he did not greatly care where or how he lived as long as someone else was meeting the bills. In any case Mrs. Sellon took good care to provide for her husband's needs, both sexual and sporting. He noted approvingly:

[4] When reading this account for the first time I was inclined to dismiss it as fiction but on comparing it with the surviving examples of Sellon's pornographic fantasies I found that the style was so markedly different that I became confident that Sellon was telling the truth—although possibly embroidering it.

[5] This choice of career is not as odd as it may appear at first sight. Young bloods of the period prided themselves on their ability to handle a four-horse team in much the same way that their present-day equivalents are proud of driving an Alfa-Romeo or an E-type Jaguar car.

"Augusta would strip naked, place herself in any attitude, let me gamahuche[6] her, would gamahuche in her turn, indulged all my whimsies, followed me about like a faithful dog—obtained good shooting for me in the season, and a good mount if I would hunt."

This rustic idyll—a strange mixture of Ovid and Virgil—was brought to an end by the birth of a son. Sellon was completely devoid of normal paternal feeling and his morbid jealousy of his infant rival was comic in its fury:

"... matters became worse, everything was neglected for the young usurper. My comforts all disappeared and at length I became so disgusted, that I left her ... going up to town ..."

For some months Sellon enjoyed the delights of London, occupying himself with gambling and a complex series of fornications, but he was then compelled to return to his wife by an elderly relative, a wealthy nobleman, from whom he hoped one day to inherit something. Sellon's angry description of the circumstances leading up to this forced reconciliation makes extremely amusing reading, although it was clearly not intended to do so! He wrote:

"But in six months this woman began to feel certain motions of nature, which told her there were other joys besides the pleasure of spoiling her breasts to give suck to her brat, and she wanted to see her spouse again. She was virtuous, was this woman, so ought to have been a crown to her husband ... but let that pass.

"She came up to Town, and called on the Earl. She was all pathos and meekness, of course. She told her 'sad tale'. My relative was moved, a 'woman in tears' is more eloquent with some people, than 'the woman in white!' I received from my relative a very peremptory letter from this man; it would not do to offend him; I consented to live with her again."

In the circumstances it is, perhaps, not surprising that this, the last attempt at cohabitation did not long endure. The final rupture came when Augusta found her husband engaged in teaching some young

---

[6] Gamahuche was the most commonly used nineteenth-century word for oral-genital contacts. It survives in abbreviated form, as the vulgar expression "gam". I cannot trace any etymological relationship with the colloquial American term "gams"—meaning legs—which seems to be derived from the Italian.

school-girls what he chose to call, with untypical coyness, hide-and-seek.

Once more in London Sellon supported himself by teaching fencing, by acting as guide (and, one is inclined to suspect, as pimp) on continental tours, and by writing hack-pornography for Dugdale and Hotten, England's leading publishers of obscene books and prints. While the literary quality of these last-mentioned effusions is not particularly high it does seem to be a little better than the general run of nineteenth-century pornography. The following extract from *The New Epicurean or The Delights of Sex Facetiously and Philosophically Considered in Graphic Letters Addressed to Young Ladies of Quality*[7] is typical:

> "But Phoebe was not listening; she had seated herself on a truss of hay, and with her eyes fixed on the again stiffening pizzle of the Stallion, had fallen into a reverie. I guessed what she was thinking about, so seating myself by her side, I stole a hand up her clothes, she trembled, but did not resist, I felt her firm plump thighs, I explored higher, I toucher her feather; soft and silky as a mouses skin was the moss in which I entwined my fingers. I opened the lips, heavens! Could I believe my senses. She was spending, and her shift was quite wet. Whether it was accident or not, I cannot say, but she had dropped one of her hands on my lap.
>
> "My truncheon had long been stiff as iron; this additional aggravation had such an effect that with a start, away flew too material buttons, and Jack sprang out of his box into her hand. At this stage she gave a little scream, and snatching away her own hand, at the same time pushed away mine, and jumping up, began smoothing down her rumpled clothes, and with great vehemence exclaiming: 'Oh, la, fie, sir: doantee doantee, Oh I'm afeard' etc., etc.
>
> "But I was not going to lose such a chance, and began to soothe her and talk, until at length we got back to the same position again. I grew more bold, I kissed her eyes, and her bosom; I handled her lovely buttocks; I frigged her clitoris—her eyes sparkled; she seized upon that weapon which had at first so frightened her and the next minute I had flung her back on the hay, and was frigging away at her maidenhead, but she made a terrible outcry and struggled most

[7] According to the title page this book was *Printed for Thomas Longtool, Rogerwell Street*. The real publisher seems to have been J. C. Hotten. The extract I give comes from pp. 21-2 of the second edition (1870?).

violently. Fortunately Mrs. Jukes had a convenient attack of deafness, and heard nothing; so that after a good deal of trouble, I found myself in possession of the fortress, up to the hilt. Once in, I knew well how to plant my touches, and ere long a soft languor pervaded all her limbs, pleasure succeeded pain. She no longer repulsed me, but sobbing on my shoulder, stopped now and then to kiss my cheek.

"Her climax came at length, and then she threw all modesty aside; entwined her lovely legs around my back, twisted, wriggled, bit, pinched, and kissing me with ardour, seemed to wake up to the new life she had found."

As for Sellon's continental tours, the financial and sexual complexities of the last of them, described in the following letter dated March 4th, 1866, are probably typical of them all:[8]

"You will be very much surprised no doubt to find that I am again in England. But there are so many romances in real life that you will perhaps not be so much astonished at what I am going to relate after all.

"You must know then that on our trip to the continent (Egypt it appears was a hoax of which I was to be the victim), we were to be accompanied by a lady! I did not name this to you at the time, because I was the confidant of my friend.

"On Monday evening I sat for a mortal hour in his brougham near the Wandsworth Road Railway Station waiting for the 'fair but frail', who had done me the honour to send me a beautiful little pink note charmingly scented with violets, in which the dear creature begged me to be punctual—and most punctual I was I assure you, but alas! she kept me waiting a whole hour, during which I smoked no end of cigars.

"At length she appeared, imagine my surprise! I! who had expected some swell mot or other, soon found myself seated beside the most beautiful young lady I ever beheld, so young that I could not help exclaiming, 'Why my dear you are a mere baby! how old may

---

[8] This letter was printed in full by Ashbee in *Index Librorum Prohibitorum* (1877). As this book is now virtually unobtainable (only 250 copies were printed), however, I feel that the letter is worth reproducing in full, particularly as it so well illustrates Sellon's peculiar outlook on life. A condensed version of the *Index* has recently been published as a paperback in the United States, but the letter I reproduce was excluded from it.

I be permitted to ask?' She gave me a box on the ear, exclaiming, 'Baby indeed! do you know sir, I am fifteen!!' 'And you love Mr. Scarsdale very much I suppose?' said I as a feeler. 'Oh! comme ça!' she rejoined. 'Is he going to marry you at Vienna, or Egypt?' I asked. 'Who's talking of Egypt?' said she. 'Why I am I hope my dear, our dear friend invited me to accompany him up to the third Cataract, and this part of the affair, you I mean my dear, never transpired till half-an-hour before I got that pretty little note of yours.' 'Stuff!' she said, 'he was laughing at you, we go no farther than Vienna!' 'Good!' said I, 'all's fair in love and war' and I gave her a kiss! She made no resistance, so I thrust my hand up her clothes without more ado. 'Who are you my dear?' I enquired. 'The daughter of a merchant in the city who lives at Clapham,' said she. 'Does your mother know you're out?' I ejaculated. 'I am coming out next summer,' said she. 'That is to say you were coming out next summer,' said I. 'Well I shall be married then you know,' said the innocent. 'Stuff!' said I in my turn. 'How stuff?' she asked angrily, 'do you know he has seduced me?' 'No my angel, I did not know it, but I thought as much—but don't be deceived, a man of Mr. Scarsdale's birth won't marry a little cit like you.' She burst into tears. I was silent. 'Have you known him long?' she asked. 'Some years,' said I. 'And you really think he won't marry me?' 'Sure of it, my dear child.' 'Very well, I'll be revenged, look here, I like you!' 'Do you though! by Jove!' 'Yes,' and,—I give you my word I was into her in a moment! What bliss it was! None who have not entered the seventh heaven can fathom it! But alas! we drew near the station, and I only got one poke complete. She pressed my hand as I helped her out of the Brougham at the Chatham and Dover Station, as much as to say 'you shall have me again'. Scarsdale was there to receive her. Not to be tedious, off we started by the Mail, and duly reached Dover, went on board the boat, reached Calais, off again by train. Damned a chance did I get till we were within ten or twelve versts of Vienna. Then my dear friend fell asleep, God bless him! The two devils of passengers who had travelled with us all the way from Calais had alighted at the last station—here was a chance!! We lost not an instant. She sat in my lap, her stern towards me! God! what a fuck it was, 'See Rome and die!' said I in a rapture. This over we were having what I call a straddle fuck, when lo! Scarsdale woke up! I made a desperate effort to throw her on the opposite seat, but it was

1. Drawings of coffer lids which nineteenth-century antiquarians supposed to be evidence of the sexual heresies of the Templars (see chapter 9)

2. The last degeneration of Priapus as the ithyphallic god of the witches (from a seventeenth-century broadsheet, *The Merry Pranks of Robin Goodfellow*).

no go, he had seen us. A row of course ensued, and we pitched into one another with hearty good will. He called me a rascal for tampering with his fiancée, I called him a scoundrel for seducing so young a girl! and we arrived at Vienna! 'Damn it,' said I as I got out of the train with my lip cut and nose bleeding, 'here's a cursed piece of business.' As for Scarsdale who received from me a pretty black eye, he drove off with the sulky fair to a hotel in the Leopoldstadt, while I found a more humble one in the Graben near St. Stephen's Cathedral, determined, as I had £15 in my pocket to stay a few days and see all I could. But as you will find in Murray a better account of what I did see than I can give you, I will not trouble you with it. I got a nice little note the next day from the fair Julia appointing a meeting the next day at the Volksgarten. How she eluded the vigilance of her gallant I don't know, but there she was sure enough in a cab—and devilish nice cabs they are in this city of Vienna, I can tell you. So we had a farewell poke and arranged for a rendezvous in England, and the next day I started and here I am, having spent all my money!

"So there's the finish of my tour up the Nile to the third Cataract, to Nubia, Abu Sinnel (sic), etcetera. It is very wrong I know, I deplore it! but you also know that what's bred in the bone, &c., so adieu, and believe me
"Yours very truly
"E. SELLON."

A month later Sellon shot himself in his room at Webb's Hotel in Piccadilly. Before doing so he wrote an excessively sentimental and gloomy poem entitled *No More*,[9] which concludes:

> *For I am in the cold earth laid,*
> *In the tomb of blood I've made.*
> *Mine eyes are glassy, cold and dim,*
> *Adieu my love, and think of him*
>   *No More.*
> *Vivat Lingam*
> *Non Resurgam*[10]

---

[9] This poem, which is not indecent, was for some unknown reason reproduced in *Cythera's Hymnal or Flakes from the Foreskin* which, according to its title page, was published in 1870 by the Oxford University Press. The date may be correct!
[10] Long live the penis, it will not rise again.

So ended the life of Edward Sellon, pornographer, soldier, coach-driver, and, as will be seen from the extracts from his writings which follow, the man responsible for introducing a Tantric strain into the occultism of the West.

Sellon's interpretation of Tantricism was crudely materialistic, for while he seems to have had a fair knowledge of the practical techniques of the cult it does not appear that he had any real understanding of its underlying philosophy. Here he was very much a man of his own time, interpreting the subtleties of Hinduism in accordance with the vulgarly anthropomorphic conceptions of deity that were familiar to him from the writings of theologians of the evangelical school. He wrote:

"As the Saivas are all worshippers of Siva and Bowanee (Pavati) conjointly, so the Vaishnavas also offer up their prayers to Laksmi-Nayarana. The exclusive adorers of this Goddess are the Sactas.

"The cast mark of the Saivas and Sactas consists of three horizontal lines on the forehead, with ashes obtained, if possible, from the hearth, on which a consecrated fire is perpetually maintained. The adoration of the Sacti[11] is quite in accordance with the spirit of the mythological system of the Hindus in Bengal, at least three-fourths are Sactas, of the remaining fourth, three parts are Vaishnavas, and one Saivas.

"Independently of the homage paid to the principal Deities, there are a great variety of inferior beings, Dewtas, and demi-gods of a malevolent character and formidable aspect, who receive the worship of the multitude. The bride of Siva, however, in one or other of her many and varied forms,[12] is by far the most popular goddess in Bengal and along the Ganges.

[11] *Sactya Rites among Mussulmans.* According to Buckingham, "Between Zohaub and Kermanshah there are a people called Nessereah, who, like those of the same name in Syria, pay divine honours to the Pudendum Muliebre, and hold feasts resembling ancient mysteries of Venus." (Sellon's Note.)

[12] In alluding to Bhavani (Pavati) as distinguished by a variety of names implying Nature, and among others using that of Shacti, Paolino in his *Voyages*, p. 327, gives an account of the Magna Mater of the Hindus. "She changes," he says, "and transforms herself into a thousand shapes, and appears sometimes as a man and sometimes as a woman. Her votaries paint the Medhra" (in Bengal called yoni), "which is represented by two side strokes, and a red one in the middle" (on the forehead). "This mark represents the womb of Bhavani," in its conventional form.—*Paolino's Voyage to Malabar.* (Sellon's Note.)

"The worship of the female generative principle, as distinct from the Divinity, appears to have originated in the literal interpretation of the metaphorical language of the Vedhas, in which Will, or purpose to Create the Universe, is represented as originating from the Creator and co-existent with him as his bride, and part of himself. We read in the Rig-Veda the following—

" 'That divine spirit breathed without afflation, single, with (Swadha) her who is sustained within him, other than her nothing existed.' Again, 'First, desire was formed in his mind, and desire became the original productive seed.'[13] The Sama-Veda also, speaking of the divine cause of creation, says, 'He felt not joy, being alone. He wished for another, and instantly the desire was gratified. He caused his body to part in twain, and thus became male and female. They united, and human beings were produced.[14]

"Prakriti,[15] the mother of gods and men, one with matter, the source of error, is identified with Maya or delusion,[16] and co-existent with the Omnipotent, and his Sacti, his personified energy, his bride. According to Wilson, 'these mythological fancies have principally been disseminated by the Puranas, and were unknown anterior to those writings'. The whole subject is given *in extenso* in the Brahma-Vaivaartta Puran (a Purana which is not considered orthodox), under the head of Prakrita Khanda, in which the legends having reference to the modifications of the female principle are narrated. It is further stated in this Puran, that Brahma, having determined to create the universe, became androgynous, male and female; the right half having the sex and form of a man; the left, that of a woman. In his images he is sometimes thus represented, and is then termed Ardnari. 'This is Prakriti of one nature with Brahm; illusion, eternal, as the soul so is its active energy, as the faculty of burning is in fire.'[17]

[13] As. Res., viii. 393. (Sellon's Note.)
[14] Idem, viii, 426. (Sellon's Note.)
[15] "Prakriti is inherent Maya, because she beguiles all beings"—As. Res., xvii. (Sellon's Note.)
[16] On the base of Minerva's statue at Sais, whom the Egyptians regarded to be the same as Isis, a goddess who bears so striking an analogy to the Hindu Prakriti or nature, there was this inscription: "I am everything that has been, that is, and that shall be: nor has any mortal ever yet been able to discover what is under my veil."—Plutar. de Iside et Osiride, s. ix. (Sellon's Note.)
[17] Thus in the Kuma-Puran, c. xii., we read, "His energy, being the universal

"In another passage of the Sama Vedha it is said that Krishna, being alone invested with the divine nature, began to create all things by his own will, which became manifest in Mula-Prakriti . . .

"Although the adoration of the Sacti is authorised by some of the Puranas, the rites and formulae are more clearly set forth in a voluminous collection of books called *Tantras*. These writings convey their meaning in the similitude of dialogue between Uma (or Siva) and Pavati.

"The followers of the *Tantras* profess to consider them as a fifth Vedh, and attribute to them equal antiquity and superior authority.[18] The observances they prescribe have in Bengal almost superseded the original Ritual, but the question of their date is involved in considerable obscurity. From the practices described in some of the Puranas, particularly that of the Diksha, or rite of initiation, from the Agni Puran, from the specification of formulae, comprising the mystical monosyllables of the Tantras, in that and other similar compilations; and from the citation of some of them by name in different puranas, we must conclude that some of the Tantras are prior to those authorities.

"The Tantras are too numerous to specify them further, but the curious reader will find them under the heads of Syama Rahasya, Anandra, Rudra, Yamala, Mandra, Mahodahi, Sareda, Tilika, and Kalika-Tantras.[19]

"Although any of the goddesses may be objects of the Sacta worship, and the term Sacti comprehends them all, yet the homage of the Sactas is almost restricted, in Bengal, to the consort of Siva. The Varnis, or Vamacharis, worship Devi as well as all goddesses. Their worship is derived from a portion of the Tantras.

---

form of all the world, is Maya, for so does the Lord, the best of males, and endowed with illusion cause it to revolve. That Sacti of which the essence is illusion is omniform and eternal, and constantly displays the universal shape of Mahesa." (Sellon's Note.)

[18] Thus in the Siva Tantra, Siva is made to say, "The five scriptures issued from my five mouths, and were the East, West, South, North, and Upper: these five are known as the paths to final liberation. There are many Scriptures, but none are equal to the Upper Scripture." Kulluka Bhatta, commentating on the first verse of the 2nd ch. Menu, says, "The Scruti is twofold, Vaidika and Tantrika, that is Tantra." (Sellon's Note.)

[19] Vide the Sanscrit copies of the Tantras in the British and Indian Museums. (Sellon's Note.)

"According to the immediate object of the worshipper is the particular form of worship; but all the forms require the use of some or all of the five Makaras[20]—Mansa, Matsya, Madya, Maithuna, and Mudra—that is, flesh, fish, wine, women, and certain mystical gesticulations with the fingers.[21] Suitable muntrus, or incantations are also indispensable, according to the end proposed, consisting of various unmeaning monosyllabic combinations of letters, of great imaginary efficacy.[22]

"When the object of worship is to acquire an interview with, and control over, impure spirits, a dead body is necessary. The adept is also to be alone, at midnight, in a cemetery or place where bodies are burnt. Seated on the corpse, he is to perform the usual offerings, and if he do so without fear or disgust, the Dhutas, the Yoginis, and other male and female demons become his slaves.

"In this and many of the observances practised, solitude is enjoined, but all the principal ceremonies comprehend the worship of Sacti, or POWER, and require, for that purpose, the presence of a young and beautiful girl, as the living representative of the goddess.[23] This worship is mostly celebrated in a mixed society; the men of which represent Bhairavas, or Viras, and the women, Bhanravis and Nayikas. The Sacti is personified by a naked girl, to whom meat and

[20] They are enumerated in the Syama Rahasya. "Mudra and Maithuna are the fivefold Makara which takes away all sin." (Sellon's Note.)
[21] Here Sellon slipped up badly. While in ordinary language *Mudra* means mystical finger gestures in the "twilight" or "intentional" language of Tantricism it means kidney-beans or some parched grain attributed with aphrodisiac qualities.
[22] "It is the combination of H and S called Prasada Mantra, and described in the Kularnava."—Wilson, As. Res. (Sellon's Note.)
[23] The female thus worshipped is ever after denominated Yogini, i.e., "attached". This Sanscrit word is in the dialects pronounced Jogi or Zogee, and is equivalent to a secular nun, as these women are subsequently supported by alms. The word from custom has become equivalent with Sena, and thus is exactly the same as Duti or Dutica (doo-ty-car). The books of morality direct a faithful wife to shun the society of Yogini, or females who have been adored as Sacti.

The Sacti system bears a striking affinity with Epicureanism. It teaches Materialism and the Atomic system of chance. (Compare the Ananda Tantram, c. xvii. with Lucretius, lib. iii.)

The worship of women and the Sacta h'oma vidhi are grounded on passages in the Veda which orthodox Brahmins regard as of doubtful authority. (Vide Rig Vedam, Bk. ii. c. viii. sections 13, 14, 2nd attham, 8th pannam, ricks B. 14, which contain the Sucla Homa Mantram, &c.) (Sellon's Note.)

wine are offered, and then distributed among the assistants. Here follows the chanting of the Muntrus and sacred texts, and the performance of the Mudra, or gesticulations with the fingers. The whole terminates with orgies amongst the votaries of a very licentious description.[24] This ceremony is entitled the SRI CHAKRA, or PURNABI-SHEKA, THE RING or full Initiation.[25]

"This method of adoring the Sacti is unquestionably acknowledged by the texts regarded by the Vanis as authorities for the impurities practised.

"The members of the sect are sworn to secrecy, and will not therefore acknowledge any participation in Sacta-Puja. Some years ago, however, they began to throw off this reserve, and at the present day they trouble themselves very little to disguise their initiation into its mysteries, but they do not divulge in what those mysteries consist.

"The Culanava has the following and other similar passages: the Tantras abound with them:

" 'Many false pretenders to knowledge, and who have not been duly initiated, pretend to practise the Caula rites; but if perfection be attained by drinking wine, then every drunkard is a saint; if virtue consists in eating flesh, then every carnivorous animal in the world is virtuous; if eternal happiness be derived from the union of the sexes, then all beings will be entitled to it. A follower of the Caula doctrine

---

[24] Wilson, on Hin. Sects. vol. xvii., As Res. (Sellon's Note.)

[25] Ward, on the Vaisnavis, p. 309.
The leading rites of the Sakti Sodhana are described in the Devi Radhasya, a section of the Rudra Yamala. It is therein stated that the object of worship should be either "A dancing girl, a female devotee, a courtesan, Dhobee woman, a barber's wife, a female of the Brahminical or Sudra tribe, a flower girl, or a milkmaid. Appropriate muntrus are to be used. She is to be placed naked, but richly ornamented with jewels and flowers, on the left of a circle described for the purpose, with various muntrus and gesticulations, and it is to be rendered pure by the repetition of different formulas, being finally sprinkled over with wine by the peculiar mantra.

"The Sacti is now purified, but if not previously initiated, she is to be further made an adept by the communication of the Radical Mantra whispered thrice in her ear, when the object of the ceremony is complete. The finale is what might be expected, but accompanied throughout by muntrus, and forms of meditation very foreign to the scene."—Wilson, As. Res., vol. xvii. 225, on Hin. Sects. (Sellon's Note.)

is blameless in my sight if he reproves those of other creeds who quit their established observances. Those of other sects who use the articles of the Caula worship shall be condemned to a metempsychosis during as many years as there are hairs of the body.'

"The Kauchiluas are another branch of the Sactas sect; their worship much resembles that of the Caulas. They are, however, distinguished by one particular rite not practised by the others, and throw into confusion all the ties of female relationship; natural restraints are wholly disregarded, and a community of women among the votaries inculcated.[26]

"On the occasions of the performance of divine worship the women and girls deposit their julies, or bodices, in a box in charge of the Guru, or priest. At the close of the rites, the male worshippers take each a julie from the box, and the female to whom it belongs, even were she his sister, becomes his partner for the evening in these lascivious orgies.[27]

"Dancing formed an important part of the ceremonial worship of most Eastern peoples. Dancing girls were attached to the Egyptian temples and to that of the Jews. David also, we are told, 'danced before the Lord with all his might'. And to every temple of any importance in India we find a troup of Nautch or dancing girls attached.

"These women are generally procured when quite young, and are early initiated into all the mysteries of their profession. They are instructed in dancing and vocal and instrumental music, their chief employment being to chant the sacred hymns, and perform nautches before the God, on the recurrence of high festivals. But this is not the only service required of them, for besides being the acknowledged mistresses of the officiating priests, it is their duty to prostitute themselves in the courts of the temple to all comers, and thus raise funds for the enrichment of the place of worship to which they belong.

---

[26] This sect appears in the Sankara Vijaya as the Uchchishtha Ganapati or Hairamba sect, who declare that all men and all women are of one caste, and that their intercourse is free from fault.—Vide Ward's Works, vol. ii. 5, on the above subject.—Wilson on Hin. Sects, vol. xvii. (Sellon's Note.)

[27] Yet these Sacteyas (or adorers of Sacti) look upon all but themselves as "pasu iana", mere brutes! (Sellon's Note.)

"Being always women of considerable personal attractions, which are heightened by all the seductions of dress, jewels, accomplishments and art, they frequently receive large sums in return for the favours they grant, and fifty, one hundred, and even two hundred rupees have been known to be paid to these syrens in one night. Nor is this very much to be wondered at, as they comprise among their number, perhaps, some of the loveliest women in the world.

"It has been said already that among the classes from which a medium for Sacti is selected, is the courtesan and dancing-girl grade; they are indeed more frequently chosen for this honour than the others before enumerated. A Nautch woman esteems it a peculiar privilege to become the Radha Dea on such occasions. It is an office indeed which these adepts are, on every account, better calculated to fulfil with satisfaction to the sect of Sacteyas who require their aid, than a more innocent and unsophisticated girl.

"The worship of Sacti (as already observed) is the adoration of POWER,[28] which the Hindus typify by the Yoni, or womb, the Argha or Vulva, and by the leaves and flowers of certain plants thought to resemble it. Thus in the Ananda Tantram, c. vi., verse 13, we find an allusion to the Aswattha, or sacred fig-tree (the leaf of which is in the shape of a heart, and much resembles the conventional form of the Yoni, to which it is compared) . . .

"In Ananda Tantram, cap. vii. 148, and other passages, reference is made to Bhagamala. She appears to be the goddess who presides over the pudendum muliebre, i.e., the deified Vulva; and the Sacti is thus personified.

"In the mental adoration of Sacti a diagram is framed, and the figure imagined to be seen inside the Vulva. This is the Adhamukham, or lower face, i.e., the Yoni, wherein the worshipper is to imagine (mantapam) a chapel to be erected.[29]

"All the forms of Sacti Puja require the use of some or all of the five—Makaras,[30] Mansa, Matsya, Madya, Maithuna, and Mudra—

---

[28] In Egypt we learn that Typho sometimes bore the name Seth, "by which they mean the Tyrannical and overbearing POWER, or, as the word frequently signifies, the POWER that overturns all things, and that overleaps all bounds."—Plutar. de Iside et Osirides, xxxvi. (Sellon's Note.)

[29] Ananda Tantram. (Sellon's Note.)

[30] They are enumerated in the Syama Rahasya. "Mudra and Maithuna are the fivefold Makara, which takes away all sin." (Sellon's Note.)

that is flesh, fish, wine, women, and certain mystical twistings or gesticulations with the fingers.

"Such are some of the peculiar features of the worship of POWER (or Gnosticism)[31] and which, combined with the Linga Puja (or adoration of Phallus), constitutes at the present day one of the most popular dogmas of the Hindus."

Such was Sellon's description of Tantricism. As far as the *Facts* of Tantric worship were concerned it was not too far from the truth, but Sellon's failure to arrive at any faint conception of the inner philosophy of Tantricism completely invalidated his interpretation of the cult.

---

[31] Simon Magus is supposed to be the founder of Western Gnosticism, he it was who corrupted the Nicolaitanes (vide Apocalypse, ii. 6, 15). They held sensual pleasure to be the true creed.

In the *Foreign Quarterly Review*, p. 159, 580, the following passage occurs: "The grand object of the magic of the Christians in the middle ages was to obtain the command over the services of demons: such were the pursuits of witches. But these were always looked upon as criminal. The belief that men possess the power to control spirits was not peculiar to the Gnostick Christians. The liturgies of the Roman and Greek churches contain several rules on these subjects."

The Memoirs of Scipio di Ricci, of Pistoja, reveal some remarkable facts, plainly demonstrating that Sacteya ideas had found their way into the monasteries and convents of Italy in the latter part of the last century. (Sellon's Note.)

CHAPTER THREE

The Real Tantricism—Buddhist and Hindu

In pre-Communist Tibet a strange story was told about the fifth Dalai Lama. The "Fifth", who died *circa* 1680, was unique among Dalai Lamas in that he was a libertine, a rake and a notorious womaniser. Until recently the love-songs he wrote were still popular with the common people of Tibet and, in Lhasa, certain houses, where tradition averred that he had held assignations with one or other of his mistresses, were marked with a mysterious red sign and were the subject of a furtive and unofficial veneration.

The story runs that the Dalai Lama was on one of the upper terraces of his palace. He was being subjected to the reproaches of his advisers, who found his sexual immorality little to their taste.

"Yes, it is true that I have women", he admitted "but you who find fault with me also have them, and copulation for me is not the same thing as it is for you."

He then walked to the edge of the terrace and urinated over it. With the force of gravity the stream of urine flowed down from terrace to terrace, finally reaching the base of the palace. Then, miraculously, it re-ascended the terraces, approached the Dalai Lama, and re-entered the bladder from whence it had come.

Triumphantly he turned to those who had been abusing him: "Unless you can do the same", he said, "you must realise that my sexual relations are different from yours."

The inner meaning of this curious tale is illustrated by another story, this time told of Marpa, who flourished in the eleventh century A.D. and was the teacher of Tibet's great yogi Milarepa. Marpa wished to ensure that a married disciple of his should become the father of a child intended to be the physical vehicle of incarnation of a great lamaistic teacher. To this end Marpa first gave a special initiation to both the disciple and his wife, following which the couple retired, separately, for a prolonged religious retreat during which various rituals were conducted and the Bodhisattvas were invoked and asked to give their blessing to the operation.

At the end of the retreat a further initiation was given to the two, after which they retired into the private oratory of Marpa. Here Marpa sat on a throne with his own wife, the semi-divine Dagmedma, by his side, and at his feet lay the newly-initiated couple, writhing in silent copulation. When orgasm had been achieved the sperm was received by Marpa into a shallow bone dish, the brain-pan of a human skull—a type of bowl still used in certain Tibetan rites—and mixed with certain magical herbs, following which it was drunk by the disciple and his wife.

Both these stories reflect the sexo-yogic practices of Buddhist Tantricism and they also illustrate the major non-theological difference between Buddhist Tantricism on the one hand, and Hindu and Jaina Tantricism on the other. For while ritual sexual intercourse (in either actual or symbolic form) is the central religious act in all Tantric cults, there is one considerable variation between Hindu and Buddhist technique; in Hindu rites the sexual act ends in the male practitioner ejaculating his semen into the vagina of the female, while in Buddhist rites the semen is retained by the male and no ejaculation takes place. Thus one Buddhist text instructs the adept that he should "place the *Vajra* in the *padma* but should retain the *bodhicitta*". This sentence is a good example of the code in which most sexo-yogic treatises are written; the literal meaning of *vajra* is thunderbolt, that of *padma* is lotus, and *bodhicitta* means mind of enlightenment, but here the words mean, respectively, penis, vagina and semen. A variation of this technique of seminal retention has sometimes been used. In this variation ejaculation did take place but the semen was then re-absorbed by the male through the urethra. To the western reader such a practice may seem to have been physiologically impossible, but there is some evidence that this improbable feat has been achieved and certainly the technique was taught in several treatises on hatha-yoga, the novice being instructed to learn the required muscular control by sucking either water or milk up his urethral canal. It is, of course, true that semen re-absorbed in this way would have entered the bladder and not, as at least some Tantric adepts seem to have believed, the testicles. It seems likely that the Fifth

Dalai Lama was, rightly or wrongly, supposed to have been trained in this technique and that the story of his miraculous urination was a symbolic presentation of seminal re-absorption.

The origins of Tantricism are shrouded in uncertainty. The name itself is derived from the *Tantras*, literary works expounding various systems of esoteric Buddhism and Hinduism. These treaties deal with almost every aspect of esoteric religio-magical thought; there are *Tantras* dealing with astrology, with the construction of the mystic diagrams known as mandalas, with the preparation of ritualistic ingredients, etc. etc.[1] In spite of the heterogeneous nature of their contents the form of the *Tantras* usually follows a rigid literary convention. They almost always begin with a conversation between two deities; one asks the other a question, the other refuses to answer, the first again begs to be told the answer to his or her question. Eventually the enquiring deity gets its way and the *Tantra* assumes the form of an answer to the question that has been asked—before this, however, there is usually a good deal of oriental flim-flam, with the god saying that the information he is about to give has never before been divulged, that it is only being given now because of the veneration and admiration with which he regards the questioner, and so on.

Scholars have been, still are, and probably always will be, divided on the question of whether Hindu Tantricism grew out of Buddhist Tantricism or *vice versa*. The older view, now held by only a minority of scholars, was that Buddhism had come into contact with Tantricism or some similar cult and that from a blending of philosophical and theological concepts derived from the former and sexo-yogic techniques derived from the latter had come into existence Vajrayana Buddhism —the oldest school of Tantric Buddhism—which although it was eventually extinguished in its Indian motherland, successfully survived in Tibet. The more modern, and now generally accepted theory is that all Hindu schools using sexual polarity symbolism were originally derived from Buddhism.[2]

In any real sense the problem is insoluble. Perhaps, as has been

---

[1] In spite of the low repute in which orthodox Hindus hold the *Tantras*—they generally regard them as being not only heretical but "dirty"—actually erotic passages only make up some six to seven per cent of the total bulk of Tantric texts.

[2] For an interesting variant of this latter theory see chapter eight of Agehananda Bharati's brilliant *Tantric Tradition*.

THE REAL TANTRICISM—BUDDHIST AND HINDU

suggested by Sh. Dasgupta, neither Buddhist nor Hindu Tantricism grew out of the other—although there seems little doubt that the oldest Buddhist *Tantras* are chronologically earlier than the oldest surviving Hindu *Tantras*—but that both grew out of a religious, sexo-yogic cult of ancient India, this cult manifesting as Tantric Buddhism when in contact with Buddhist philosophy, and as Saiva and Shakta Tantricism when associated with the religious speculations of the Saivas and Shaktas.

The philosophy of all schools of Tantricism sees both the universe, the macrocosm, and man himself, the microcosm, as being made up of two opposing aspects—male and female, static and dynamic, negative and positive[3]—and holds that the existence of these opposites in a state of duality is the source of all sorrow, pain, change, and suffering. The object of all religious endeavour should be, so it is believed, liberation from this duality and a return to a state in which the two opposing principles are united in a state of absolute non-duality.

Hindu Tantricism has called the male, that is to say the negative, passive, principle, *Shiva*, and the female, dynamic principle *Shakti*. In the human body (which, as in western occultism, is regarded a microcosm, a universe in miniature) the two principles are regarded as being particularly associated with two of the chakras—the centres of psycho-spiritual force which are of such importance in the esoteric physiology of Yoga. *Shiva* is regarded as dwelling in the Sahasrara chakra, the "thousand-petalled lotus" supposedly situated at the crown of the head, while *Shakti* is associated with the Muladhara chakra which is believed to lie over the perineum and the base of the spine. Liberation from duality can only be achieved, so it is believed by enabling *Shakti*, often symbolised as a coiled serpent, to uncoil herself, to rise up through the psychic centres, and to unite herself with *Shiva* in the thousand-petalled lotus.

The theory of Tantric Buddhism seems to show considerable similarity. The male principle—here seen as the active, phenomenal, aspect

[3] There is an important divergence between the Buddhist and Hindu *Tantras* regarding the nature of the principles. Hindu *Tantras* regard the female as being the active principle, while the Buddhist *Tantras* assign this role to the male. Mysteriously enough, Tibetan Buddhist iconography seems to disregard its own philosophical outlook, for in the famous *yab-yum* icons (which show a god and goddess in sexual intercourse of a yogic nature) the female clearly in energetic motion, sits astride the male, the latter in a position which makes movement impossible.

of the polarity—dwells in the head, and only by uniting it with the female principle of voidness, residing in the navel and solar plexus, can non-duality be achieved and liberation attained.

It is not, however, the theory of the various Tantric schools that is important, but their sexo-yogic practice, and in this the various schools show a remarkable resemblance to one another; just as, in the western world, the mystical practices of George Fox, the Quaker, and Madame de Guyon, the Catholic, were almost identical in spite of their theological differences, so the sexo-yogic practices of both Hindu and Buddhist Tantrics are essentially the same,[4] in spite of the fact that the former believes in the existence of some sort of "real", eternal ego, while the latter does not. In the last analysis it is only the nature of the actual psycho-spiritual experiences undergone by Tantric practitioners that are of any real importance, and we are forced to regard these as identical, at least until the unlikely event of a Hindu Tantric being converted to Buddhism (or *vice versa*) and reporting a change in the experiences undergone by him. The *only* fundamental difference between Hinduism and Buddhism is that the first has an ontology, the second has not.

The central core of Tantric religious practice is sexual intercourse—either actual or symbolic. Those who use the rites in which physical copulation takes place are termed followers of the left-hand path, those whose union is only symbolic are referred to as followers of the right-hand path. A good deal of nonsense has been talked about these terms,

[4] On both sides of the Buddhist/Hindu fence claims have been made that members of their own faith do not indulge in sexual practices involving actual physical copulation. Certain Hindu pandits, for example, have claimed that *all* the *Tantras* dealing with physical intercourse are to be interpreted symbolically and that those who think otherwise are immoral, evil and "dirty". It is a pity that this sort of nonsense has received the support of some western scholars who should have known better; thus Evans-Wentz, who displayed an extremely puritanical attitude towards Tantricism—no doubt a hangover from his early years as a member of the Theosophical Society—so far forgot that moral detachment which is so integral a part of the equipment of Scholarship as to refer to "those hypocrites who follow the left-hand path in Bengal and elsewhere". Even Lama Anagarika Govinda has claimed that physical sexuality plays no part in Tibetan Tantricism—a statement that, in its literal meaning, is quite simply untrue. Agehananda Bharati has made the ingenious suggestion that by "physical" the Lama meant "consciousness of physical" in which case the statement is probably correct, for there is some evidence to show that the advanced Tantric adept engaged in copulation is more or less unaware of what is happening on the physical plane.

"left-hand" and "right-hand", by western occultists who, following H. P. Blavatsky's erroneous interpretation of them, have endeavoured to endow them with some moral significance—the transition from "left" to "sinister", and from thence to "evil" is an easy, and misleading, one for the European to make. In reality the terms have no moral significance whatsoever. They simply express the plain fact that in rites culminating in physical sexuality the woman practitioner sits on the left of the male, while in those in which the copulation is merely symbolic she sits on his right.

The preliminaries to the sexual rites of Hindu Tantricism are very similar to those of more orthodox Hindu worship, but these preliminaries are followed by a type of religious observance that is as shocking to an orthodox Hindu as is the Black Mass to a believing Roman Catholic. "I shall proclaim left-handed practice, the supreme religious observance of Durga", says one Tantric text, and goes on "following which the adept gains magical powers speedily in this Kali-Yuga. The rosary should be made of human teeth, the goblet of a man's brain-pan, the seat of the skin of an adept, the bracelet of a woman's hair. The sacrificial ingredients are to be saturated with wine, one must have sexual intercourse with another's wife, no matter what her caste may be. Thus is left-handed practice, which bestows all magical powers, described, O benign Goddess."

At times the *Tantras* are even more outspoken. Thus one of them says that "he who but once offers a hair of his *Shakti*[5] in the cemetery becomes a great poet, a Lord of the Earth and goes forth mounted on an elephant". A commentary upon this passage explains "hair" as meaning a pubic hair with its root which after male ejaculation has been soaked in semen. Another recension of the same *Tantra* advocates the physical consumption of semen by the male operator from the vagina of his partner.

The five "sacraments" partaken of by the practitioners of Tantric rites are usually known as the five Ms. They are *matsya* (fish), *mamsa* (meat, often beef, in normal circumstances completely forbidden to Hindus), *madya* (any alcoholic beverage), *mudra* (this word usually means ritual gesture, but in Tantric terminology it refers to kidney beans or any parched grain believed to have aphrodisiac qualities), and *Maithuna* (sexual intercourse). The participants in the rite also take hemp (i.e. *cannabis indica*, which contains more of the essential alkaloid

[5] That is to say, the female partner in ritual sexual intercourse.

than *cannabis americana*, the American variety of the same plant from which marijuana is derived) but as a preparation for the ceremony, not as part of it. Probably this is done because, as Agehananda Bharati has suggested, unless under the influence of some hallucinogenic drug pious Hindus would find it quite impossible to break through traditional taboos and partake of the five Ms.[6]

After the orthodox preliminaries are concluded comes the consumption of the first four Ms (alcohol, meat, fish and the "aphrodisiac" parched grain). While this consumption takes place the practitioners concentrate on the thought that it is not they as ordinary individuals who are eating and drinking the forbidden substances but the Goddess residing in them as the coiled-up Serpent Power. Simultaneously they mentally repeat their personal mantras, for each Tantric practitioner has his own specific mystic word, given to him by his teacher at the time of his first initiation into the cult.

The ritual sexual intercourse begins with the male practitioner drawing a triangular diagram—symbolic of the Goddess and the Serpent Power which is her aspect in the human body—upon his couch. For some time the practitioner worships the Goddess, mentally projecting her image into the triangle he has drawn, and then he calls his female partner. After various ritual purifications he lays her upon the couch and then, visualising himself as the god Shiva and the woman as the wife of Shiva, "offers the father face to the mother face"—i.e. copulates, all the time repeating various traditional mantras (there is a special one for each stage of intercourse, including a special one designed to be recited at the moment of orgasm) and mentally concentrating upon the idea of using the senses as a means of sacrificing to the Goddess.

Such is left-handed Tantric practice—as one *Tantra* says "with alcohol, meat, fish, *mudra* and women, so should the great initiate worship the Mother of the Gods".

---

[6] In spite of many statements to the contrary made by present-day puritanically inclined devotees of Transcendental Meditation and other syncretistic religious cults of oriental origin there is no doubt whatsoever that many early Buddhists and Hindus used psychedelic drugs as one of the many means of inducing ecstatic mystical states. It is probable that the *soma*, the divine drink of Vedic literature, was an infusion of the hallucinogenic mushroom *amanita muscaria*. In reality almost the only difference between genuine mystical states and drug-induced ecstasy seems to be that the effects of the latter are only temporary while those of the former are permanent.

CHAPTER FOUR

Chinese Sexual Alchemy

There is some resemblance between the theoretical aspects of Tantricism and the ancient Indian Siddha cult. The main emphasis of this latter movement is on a psycho-physical yogic process designed to achieve spiritual development through an intense physical development supposedly leading to a vast extension of the life-span or even actual immortality. The cult, which in somewhat altered form survives at the present day, holds that "death may be either put off *ad libitum* by a special course of re-strengthening and revitalizing the body so as to put it permanently *en rapport* with the world of sense, or be ended definitively by dematerialising and spiritualising the body, according to prescription, so that it disappears in time in a celestial form from the world of sense, and finds its permanent abode in the transcendental glory of God".[1] This immortality is to be achieved by "drinking" the "nectar" dripping from the "moon" in the thousand-petalled lotus, the *chakra*, or psycho-spiritual centre, believed to be situated above the head.[2]

It is probable that the Siddha cult evolved out of ancient Indian alchemy, which, like later western alchemy, was not purely a primitive chemistry but was an amalgam of a physical *praxis* with mystical techniques and speculations having some similarity with those of Tantricism. According to Dr. V. V. Raman Shastri (op. cit.) there was an

[1] From Dr. V. V. Raman Shastri's *Doctrine and Culture of the Siddhas in The Cultural Heritage of India* (Vol. II), as quoted by Shashibusan Dasgupta in *Obscure Religious Cults*.
[2] And, of course, roughly equivalent to the Kether of the microcosmic Tree of Life in the Qabalistic system taught by Mathers and Aleister Crowley.

ancient vernacular tradition that the Siddhas were "a band of death-defying theriacal and therapeutic alchemists indebted in all respects to Bhoga, a pre-Christian Taoist immigrant from China, who, in his methods of keying up the body of impure matter through *reverberation* and *projection* to the pitch of practically cancelling demise, merely sought to promulgate the lesser athanasic precepts of Lao-tse, since the vital objective of the Tao-Teh-King is the transfiguration of the immortalised ethereal body into a permanent garment of celestial virtue, in order to fit it to associate to eternity with the Tao".

It seems probable that the name (Bhoga) of this legendary alchemist was a corruption of the Chinese *Bo-yang*, one of the titles of Lao-tse, to whose authorship the alchemical classic *Tsan-tung-chi* ("Doctrine Regarding the Three Similars")[3] was falsely attributed. Whether or not this was so, it is in any case likely that there was a certain amount of truth in the traditional belief that the doctrines of the Siddhas had a Chinese origin, for a sexo-yogic alchemical school putting great emphasis on the prolongation of life survived in China proper until the Communist takeover in 1949, and at the present time it still has living adepts in Hong Kong and amongst the overseas Chinese of South-East Asia.

The date of the origin of alchemy in China is uncertain, but it was clearly very early, tradition averring that it was first practised in the fourth century B.C. by a certain Dzou Yen, a magician whose miracles included ripening millet in a cold climate by playing music on a set of warm pipes.

As early as 144 B.C. an imperial edict forbade the manufacture of alchemical gold—on the ground that unsuccessful experimenters turned to robbery and murder in order to regain the wealth they had squandered—but the prohibition does not seem to have extended to the search for the pill of immortality; for only eleven years after the prohibition the Emperor gave a friendly reception to an alchemist who claimed to have discovered the secret of eternal life by worshipping the Goddess of the Stove.[4]

---

[3] Significantly, this work deals with the preparation of the "pill of immortality"—the Elixir of Life.

[4] Dubs describes the Chinese Goddess of the Stove as "a beautiful old woman clad in red garments with her hair done up in a knot on top of her head"; as the divine being in charge of cooking and the preparation of medicines it was natural enough that she should also take charge of alchemy.

The Chinese alchemical obsession with long life is illustrated by a story told of the same Bo-yang who wrote the previously mentioned *Doctrine of the Three Similars*. The tale, which comes from a collection entitled *Lives of Immortals*, tells how the alchemist, accompanied by three disciples and his pet dog, went up into the mountains in order to prepare a magical medicine.[5] Having finished his manufacture of the pill of immortality he announced his intention of administering it to his dog; he did so and the creature immediately fell dead. Bo-yang turned to his disciples, saying, "The dog has died. Seemingly the medicine has not fully achieved the Divine Light. What shall we do?" The disciples replied by asking him whether he himself would be prepared to take the elixir. "Certainly," he said, "I should be ashamed to return to the world admitting that I had failed to obtain immortality. To live without taking the elixir would be as bad for me as to take it and die." Saying this he inserted the pill in his mouth and instantaneously expired. One of his disciples, a certain Yu, still retained a faith in the elixir, took it—and met the same fate as his master. The other two disciples, less credulous than their fellow, decided not to take the medicine, arguing that a few more years of mortal existence were preferable to a recipe for longevity that led to instant extinction; they left the mountain with the intention of subsequently returning with coffins for Bo-yang and Yu. As soon as they had gone Bo-yang revived from his seeming death and gave other pills—this time the genuine elixir—to the dog and the faithful Yu. Both were immediately restored to life and all three then "went the way of the immortals"—but not before meeting a woodcutter and giving him a letter addressed to the two doubting disciples telling them what had happened and pointing out that they had missed their chance of eternal life. The account concludes with the hardly surprising statement that the two "were filled with regret".

An early text lays down the pre-conditions for achieving success in the practice of alchemy; the practitioner must fast for a hundred days, he must not be born under unfortunate planetary configurations, he must learn the art orally, from a Taoist master—books are only for beginners—he must worship the gods in a fitting manner and, above all, he must not be a civil servant. In spite of the semi-magical, semi-

---

[5] Mountains were popular with Chinese alchemists; one text affirms that transmutation can only be achieved on a *large* mountain—no other mountain will suffice.

religious conception of the nature of alchemy that underlies these rules there is no doubt that at this early stage of the evolution of Taoist alchemy the manufacture of the elixir was still supposed to be achieved by a manipulation of physical substances. The nature of the substances used was decided by the application of the theory of the two opposites, Yin and Yang.

Yin and Yang were supposedly the two manifest aspects of the one eternal reality;[6] from their action and interaction came the elements that made up the phenomenal world. Yang was considered to be fiery, active, male and solar in its nature while Yin was watery, passive, female and lunar. It was believed that vitality and longevity were essentially Yang in nature and therefore it was particularly upon supposedly Yang substances—such as gold, mercuric sulphide and sulphur[7]—that alchemical experimentation was concentrated.

By the end of the sixth century A.D. *physical* alchemy in China was in a state of decline; by the end of the first millennium it was all but extinct. From it, however, using much of its chemical terminology and many of its theoretical concepts evolved a number of closely related schools of interior psycho-spiritual alchemy in which the *ting* (the cauldron), the furnace, the lead and mercury that were to be transmuted into the gold of immortality, were all considered as component parts of the human practitioner of the art. At least one, and probably all, of these Taoist alchemical schools was largely concerned with sexuality and the generative process.

There is a curious dichotomy in both the Indian and Chinese attitudes to male sexuality. On the one hand sexual potency—indeed sexual athleticism—is regarded as being a desirable male attribute; the popular Indian press is full of advertisements for aphrodisiacs and tonics designed to increase or restore virility; one brand of tonic heads its advertisements with the words *Become a Bed Breaker!*, another (very popular with all classes of the population) has printed on its labels the stern injunction *Reserved for Maharajahs and Very Rich Men*. On the other hand, semen is regarded as something very precious, something that must not be wasted, and many men worry that they may be

---

[6] And, of course, still are by some—perhaps more in the west than in the east; for the surprisingly successful contemporary cults of "Zen cooking" and "macrobiotic food" are based on the belief that all foods can be divided into Yin substances and Yang substances.

[7] Other minerals used were arsenic (!), alum, mica and calcium carbonate.

suffering from a quite imaginary disease called spermatorrhoea—an involuntary leakage of semen supposedly leading to physical and mental debility or even to death. This conception of semen as concentrated life-force, loss of which should at all costs be kept to a minimum, is not peculiar to the Far East but seems to be a widespread human belief, emanating from the deepest levels of the unconscious, and it is only in the last few decades that it has ceased to be part of the popularly accepted sexual wisdom of the west. In the last century one treatise, *A Second Inquiry Into a Frequent Cause of Insanity in Young Men*, described the evil effects produced by frequent masturbation and the consequent loss of the magical fluid.[8]

"The pale complexion, the emaciated form, the slouching gait, the clammy palm, the glassy or leaden eye and the averted gaze indicate the lunatic victim to this vice.

"Apathy, loss of memory, abeyance of concentrative power and manifestation of mind generally, combined with loss of self-reliance, and indisposition for or impulsiveness of action, irritability of temper, and incoherence of language, are the most characteristic mental phenomena of chronic dementia resulting from masturbation in young men."

Some Victorian physicians even believed that an excessive loss of semen would be produced by sexual intercourse two or three times a week. Acton, a genito-urinary surgeon of some eminence, reported the case of a fellow medical practitioner who had been afflicted in this way;

"There was general debility, inaptitude to work . . . in fact, he thought he was losing his senses. The sight of one eye was affected . . . he married seven years ago, being then a hearty, healthy man, and it was only lately that he had been complaining. In answer to my further inquiry, he stated that since his marriage he had had connection two or three times a week, and often more than once a night! This one fact, I was obliged to tell him, sufficiently accounted for all his troubles. The symptoms he complained of were similar to those we find in boys who abuse themselves. It is true that it may take years to reduce some strong, healthy men, just as it may be a long time before some boys are prejudicially influenced, but the ill effects of excesses are sooner or later sure to follow."

The teachers of Chinese sexual alchemy have been (and still are) quite as convinced of the evil effects of the loss of semen as were the Victorian proto-sexologists; some have even been of the opinion that

[8] It was a popular belief that "a drop of semen equals an ounce of blood".

the mere production of the fluid in the body leads to harmful results—thus a chapter of one text urges abstention from onions, leeks and garlic on the grounds that they are aphrodisiac and encourage the production of "generative fluid" while another section of the same instructional work argues that the untimely deaths of elderly people occur because they have allowed themselves to continue enjoying sexual intercourse, thus letting the "generative fluid" leak away and leaving them with no "vital resistance" against infection. In spite of the crudeness of such physiological conceptions it would be unfair to dismiss Taoist alchemy out of hand, for beneath the primitive biological beliefs and terminology is concealed an extremely subtle psycho-spiritual philosophy and technique designed to harness and transform the forces of the libido in order to attain adeptship—the "manufacture of the elixir of immortality".

Chinese sexual alchemy conceives of semen as a physical product of what it calls "generative force"—the "essence of procreation" which has some resemblance to the libido of the depth-psychologists and more to the orgone energy of Wilhelm Reich.[9] The first step in the process of manufacturing the pill, or elixir, of immortality is the prevention of the generative force from following its usual course (i.e. the production of semen) by the "lighting of the inner fire". This is done by a type of regulated and deep breathing[10] very similar to the *pranayama* of Indian Hatha Yoga. The breathing in brings pressure to bear on the generative force, which is situated in a crucible (i.e. a centre of psychic force more or less identical with an Indian *chakra*) in the lower abdomen, and causes it to rise up a psychic channel associated with the spine to the top of the head. The deep expiration of the breath then brings the force down through the (psychic) channel of function at the front of the body back to the crucible from whence it came.[11] The process of circulation is continued until the generative force is considered sufficiently purified to be ready to be transmuted into *lead*—which in this connection means something like the *prana*, vital energy, of Yoga—and then it moves up from the crucible, or psychic centre, in the lower abdomen to that situated in the solar plexus, where the transmutation takes place.

[9] See Chapter 14, "Magicians, The Orgasm and the Work of Wilhelm Reich".
[10] That is to say a breathing so deep that it affects all the muscles of the lower abdomen.
[11] This technique has a remarkable similarity to an occidental magical process described by Regardie in his *Art of True Healing*.

It must be emphasised that in the process briefly described above sexual excitation as such is not avoided; however, ejaculation *is* avoided and the force of sexual excitation is supposedly taken to be used in the creation of lead (vitality). Indeed, a total lack of *any* sexual excitation is considered to make the alchemical processes quite impossible of achievement; the Taoist master Chang San Feng said that in the case of elderly people who felt no spontaneous sexual arousal the practice of masturbation was a useful means of stimulating the generative force. He recommended that after the elderly male practitioner of alchemy had achieved an erection by this means he should commence the deep breathing exercises and visualisation of the circulation of the force and continue this process until the penis ceased to be tumescent—this cessation of erection being regarded as evidence that the alchemical agent (the generative force) had successfully been transferred to the psychic centre in the solar plexus.

After the successful transmutation of the generative force into lead (*prana*) the next stage is to raise the lead from the solar plexus crucible to the psychic centre associated with the head (supposedly situated in approximately the same position as the pineal gland) where it is to be transmuted into mercury (i.e. spiritual force) by yet another series of exercises involving deep breathing and the visualisation of orbiting streams of force.

The Taoist alchemical texts inform the student that, when this has been achieved, nocturnal emissions—the much-dreaded spontaneous loss of semen and the "magical" type force associated with it—will cease; he is warned, however, that when he has reached this happy state "prenatal vitality" will escape from the bowels in the form of wind. The breaking of wind is regarded as desirable when the wind is merely noxious gas evolving from decomposing food in the stomach and intestines, but the would-be alchemist is warned not to break wind if the "wind" is really "pre-natal vitality" and detailed instructions are given to him as to how this occurrence can be prevented. They involve placing the right middle finger on the "dragon centre" (the end of a psychic channel supposedly terminating in the palm of the left hand), simultaneously placing the left middle finger on the "tiger centre" (a similar psychic channel terminating in the palm of the right hand), raising the tongue to the palate,[12] contracting the anus and taking

---

[12] This touching of the palate with the tongue is a component part of several Chinese alchemical processes. One text urges it as a means of increasing the flow

seven deep breaths. This procedure, students are assured, will spread vitality throughout the body and eliminate the tendency to break wind.[13]

In Taoist alchemy the eyes are regarded as positive (yang) and the rest of the body as negative (yin). Therefore when the vital force has been raised to the psychic head centre it is by rolling the eyes in a particular manner that the practitioner achieves the "inner copulation" that supposedly leads to the manifestation of spirit. This rolling of the eyes is performed in cycles of sixty—thirty-six times from left to right and then twenty-four times from right to left (in Taoism thirty-six is a yang number and twenty-four is a yin number). Each revolution of the eyes is done slowly, being accompanied by a full inspiration and expiration of the breath.

When spirit has manifested in the head centre it is driven down to the crucible in the lower abdomen (sometimes referred to as "the water centre") in order to be "fixed" and stabilised. When this has been done the *mercury* (i.e. stabilised spirit) is enveloped by *lead* (vitality) which has previously been purified by being vibrated in a continuous ascent and descent of the psychic channel that links the psychic water centre with the psychic fire centre situated in the heart. The united lead and mercury form what is sometimes referred to as the immortal embryo.

The alchemist now begins to practise "immortal breathing", often referred to as the self-winding (i.e. automatic) wheel of the law. This is done by accompanying every inspiration of the breath with the stream of force entering the body at the heels and travelling up to the brain and accompanying every expiration of the breath with a visualisation of the same force travelling down from the brain and out through the trunk. This leads to the production in the head centre of a divine food which nurtures the immortal seed situated in the water centre. The alchemical process is completed; all that remains is the quickening of the immortal embryo with spirit—another complex set of exercises enables this to take place—and the alchemist becomes ready to undertake the final stage of the work.

When the immortal seed has been nurtured to maturity—this is in-
of saliva (regarded as "the most precious thing that preserves our physical strength") which is then retained until the mouth is full and then suddenly swallowed; it then is believed to enter the centre in the lower belly and be transformed into generative force—the subtle analogue of semen.

[13] More or less the same process is recommended for those who are situated some way from their lavatory and are inconvenienced by a need to visit it. I would have thought that even a long walk was less trouble!

dicated by six signs[14]—the alchemist is ready to prepare the elixir of immortality. Guarding himself against destroying all that he has previously achieved (such destruction comes if the alchemist indulges in any one of the "seven passions", the "ten excesses", or the "nine unsettled breaths") he gathers together the "four essentials of alchemy"—utensils, money, friends and a suitable place. The utensils are simple enough; a round wooden "bun", covered in cotton, used to block the anus, and a clothes peg to put upon the nostrils. The money is required for the mundane purpose of purchasing food, the friends (who must also be alchemists) are required to attend to the physical needs of the practitioner and "to pinch his backbone when required". The ideal place is an ancient Taoist temple on a mountain, far away from either cities or graveyards; "it is advisable to choose an ancient abode where previous masters have realised immortality so that it is free from disturbing demons and the practiser can enjoy spiritual protection from his enlightened predecessors" said Chao Pi Ch'en.

Having reached to his temple the alchemist concentrates on the lower abdominal (water) centre and "shakes the six sense organs" (nose, ears, eyes, tongue, mind and penis). This "arouses the immortal seed" in the testicles and it tries to move out through the penis. This exit, however, has already been shut by the exercises previously performed by the alchemist and the immortal seed now moves towards the anus; here its escape is prevented by the previously mentioned wooden bun. The whole object of the exercise is to cause the immortal seed *to travel up the spine*. When the alchemist feels the seed approaching the coccyx he "opens" the spine by (1) pressing a finger hard on the base of the penis, (2) rolling his eyes, (3) sucking in a deep breath, (4) thrusting his tongue against his palate, and (5) stretching the small of his back.[15]

---

[14] They are (1) and (2) the hearing of the dragon's hum in the right ear and the tiger's roar in the left ear (it is supposed that the filling of all psychic channels with force leads to a continuous noise, audible to the alchemist alone); (3) a golden light is seen in the head centre; (4) fire is felt blazing in the water centre; (5) the back of the head is felt to vibrate; and (6) the penis retracts in upon itself. The Taoist master Chao Pi Ch'en gave a quick method of deciding whether or not the seed is mature; one sits in a dark room looking at the flame of an oil lamp, rolls one's eyes nine times from left to right and then shuts them. If one sees a white light surrounded by sparks the seed is mature, if, on the other hand, one sees a dark circle (also surrounded by sparks) maturity has not been attained.

[15] This fivefold sequence is referred to as "the five dragons upholding the holy one".

Simultaneously one of the companion alchemists pinches the base of the backbone and the immortal seed passes through the first "gate of the spine". The immortal seed then passes up the spine through two other gates (at each of which the five dragons sequence is again practised) to a psychic centre situated at the back of the head.

Immediately the immortal seed has reached the head the practitioner begins an eye-rolling sequence—thirty-six revolutions from left to right and twenty-four revolutions in the opposite direction—all the time gazing at the inner light that now manifests itself. At this stage another danger manifests itself; there is now a risk that the immortal seed will drain out through the nose! The clothes-peg is brought into play, fulfilling the same function for the nostrils that the wooden bun did for the anus. The immortal seed, prevented from escape via the nostrils, now moves down into a psychic cavity situated above the nostrils and (physically) manifests itself in the form of saliva. Under no circumstances must this saliva be spat out. Instead it is passed down the body into the lower abdominal centre. There it remains; the alchemical operation is complete. Immortality has been achieved and the alchemist has only to develop his (immortal) potentialities and to appear in countless "transformation bodies".[16]

My summary of Chinese alchemical techniques has been brief and, inevitably, inadequate; and whilst all the points of this account of sexual alchemy have ultimately been drawn from Chinese sources it is certain that some aspects of my interpretation would be challenged by Chinese Taoists, such as Charles Luk (Lu K'uan Yu), who are still working within the alchemical tradition. Those of my readers who desire to make a wider and deeper study of this tradition would be well advised to study Charles Luk's *Chinese Meditation* and *Taoist Yoga*—both published by Rider and Co.

[16] It will by now be obvious to the reader familiar with Jungian depth-psychology that the Secret of the Golden Flower, so misunderstood by C. G. Jung and Richard Wilhelm, was a secret of sexual alchemy.

PART TWO

The Occidental Background

CHAPTER FIVE

Primitive Fertility Cults

Our contemporary technological western civilisation is the first human society which has not had to be preoccupied with the problems of fertility. For modern storage and transportation techniques have ensured that a crop failure or a cattle pestilence in one area can be swiftly compensated for by an inward movement of food from another area.[1] In Europe and North America drought, flood and hurricane are no longer inevitably followed by famine, pestilence and death, and it is difficult for an inhabitant of these technologically advanced regions of the Earth to conceive of an environment in which the failure to reproduce of either one's plants or one's animals means, quite simply, physical extinction. Nevertheless, this has been the human situation throughout most of history (and all of pre-history), and, to some extent at least, is still the condition under which the majority of the world's population live today.

It is not, therefore, surprising that both fertility symbolism and rituals designed to promote fertility have played a major part in the magical and religious culture of all agricultural societies. Whilst it is always dangerous to make cultural generalisations it is reasonably true to say that all primitive fertility religions share four common characteristics; they are (a) a conception of the importance of duality and "pairs of opposites" in the process of reproduction, (b) a belief that the nature

---

[1] It is interesting to note that several authorities have claimed that in the Bengal famine of 1942 there was an actual *surplus* of food in the Indian sub-continent as a whole; the famine was caused not so much by a food production failure as by the inadequacies of the Indian railway system—there was simply no means of moving enough food from areas of food surplus to areas in which the crops had failed.

of time is cyclical rather than linear, (c) a philosophical picture of nature as being both personal and hierarchic, and (d) a belief in cause and effect.

The first of these shared characteristics—that of the importance of duality—requires little explanation; it must have been at a very early stage of man's intellectual development that he realised that both male and female elements were necessary for successful human reproduction. Inevitably enough, the idea of fertility as a product of duality was extended, firstly, from humanity to other animate beings and, secondly, from the world of animate beings to the world of inanimate objects. Thus fire was seen as male, water as female, while fire itself was seen as the child of its parents—the two sticks which were rubbed together in order to produce it—and in at least some still-spoken primitive languages the horizontal soft stick against which the upright hard stick is rubbed is referred to as "the woman" while the hard stick itself is known as "the man". The gods were also seen as male and female; crop fertility was often conceived of as the result of the copulation of the "sky father" with the "earth mother".[2] As a consequence of this divine duality the later evolution of fertility religions often produced a situation in which it was considered vaguely improper for a man to worship a god or a woman to worship a goddess, for such a worship of a deity of one's own gender violated the principle of sexual polarity. According to the classical writer Macrobius the essential sexual duality was often maintained by transvestism; thus at the shrine of Aphrodite in Cyprus female worshippers dressed as men, while the priests of Hercules at Coos only sacrificed when clad in female garments. Interestingly enough, in the corrupt ritual magic of the Middle Ages the whole concept of polarity became reversed—the magician had to be of the *same* sex as the force he or she invoked; Maimonides, the mediaeval Jewish philosopher and theologian, described a magical text-book in which it was laid down that when a man invoked Venus he should wear a woman's vest and that when a woman invoked Mars she should don the arms and armour of a man.

The second characteristic of fertility-based religion—the belief that

---

[2] This conception of the gods as male and female was sometimes complicated by the existence of hermaphroditic gods who were not sexually neuter but combined within themselves male and female principles. It is significant that one of the Old Testament names of God, Elohim, is formed from a masculine singular followed by a feminine plural.

time is non-linear—arose from the fertility cycle itself. Time was conceived of not as a linear progression from point A to point B but as a circle ending in its own beginning; western man sees time as an evolutionary ladder with himself standing on its topmost rung; his primitive ancestors saw time as a serpent biting its own tail. This cyclical conception of time was a necessary product of fertility itself; for all those who have lived in close contact with nature have inevitably become aware of the cyclical pattern of the reproductive process. In temperate climates producing one crop a year the nature of the seasonal pattern was apparent; seed germinated in the spring, the plants grew in the summer, ripened in the autumn, died in the winter, and then, in the spring, the whole cycle began again with fresh life springing from the "dead" husks of the old. Even in non-temperate climates, where the progression of the seasons was by no means so easily observed, man became aware of similar cyclical patterns—the alternation of "dry" and "monsoon period", the return of the "heliacal rising" of some star, or the complexities of the lunar cycle. This last, which requires extremely sophisticated observation,[3] was of particular interest because of the supposed correlation between the twenty-eight day "full moon to full moon" cycle and the menstrual cycle of the human female.

For technological urban man it is easy to see the fertility cycle as a mere series of easily explained natural phenomena but primitive man conceived of it as a product of the personalised and hierarchic structure of nature itself; for nature was regarded as having some features in common with humanity, as being approachable by and communicable with mankind, and as being hierarchic, in that it was made up of a hierarchy of spiritual entities extending downwards from the "sky father" and the "earth mother" to the minor godlets of springs, trees and rivers.

The fourth characteristic of all fertility cults—a belief in the law of cause and effect—was a necessary corollary of and depended upon, the second and third characteristics I have previously described. The fertility cycle was not seen as an event that "just happened", but as being caused by (and its continuance depending upon) the benevolent intervention of the many non-human entities who made up the hierarchy of nature. Thus either crop-failure or the sterility of man and/or beast

[3] Professor Thom has shown, if not conclusively, at least with a very high degree of probability, that many of the megalithic structures of neolithic Britain were sophisticated lunar observatories.

were never considered to be the result of "natural disasters", instead they were seen as the results of supernatural powers deliberately withholding the gift of life.

From the belief in supernatural forces as the causative factors in the fertility cycle sprang much of primitive magic and religion,[4] for the function of both these was largely the affecting of nature by either placating or manipulating the beings that controlled it.

The overall symbolism of primitive fertility cults was often directly derived from the act of human copulation; the "sky father"[5] and other gods were represented as ithyphallic (i.e. with erect penis) and the "earth-mother" was often shown as being grossly pregnant, enormously full breasted, and with exaggerated vaginal labia. The sacred copulation of the god and goddess was frequently considered as being the original act of creation that had given birth to the universe, and this "heavenly marriage" was re-enacted each year, not only by the gods, but by human beings, thus ensuring the renewal of fertility. Homer referred to the time when ". . . Demeter, yielding to her desire, lay with Iasion in the thrice ploughed fallow land" and magically orientated acts of sexual intercourse performed on the freshly ploughed land were the culminating point of many fertility festivals; thus in Sparta, the "Corn King" copulated with the "Spring Queen" and in Orissa a similar annual event survived well into the seventeenth century.

The primitive fertility religions survived in the civilisations of the ancient and classical world. Thus the Osiris of the Egyptians, the

---

[4] There are grave doubts as to whether the distinction between religion and magic is a meaningful one. Some anthropologists have conceived of a "religious rite" as one that relies on the intervention of supernatural powers outside the worshipper himself and of a "magical rite" as one that relies only on the powers of the magician himself. It is doubtful whether under this definition, there has *ever* been a *purely* magical or *purely* religious ritual; even the rites of mediaeval sorcery must be considered by this definition, as being essentially religious rather than magical in nature.

[5] While the pattern of a male sky deity whose function was seen as the fertilisation of the "earth-mother" was an extremely common one it was not universal. In ancient Egypt the polarity was reversed, and the sky deity was the goddess Nuit, who, thousands of years later, was to come to occupy a position of great importance in Aleister Crowley's religion of Thelema. The reader will remember that a similar polarity reversal (between Hindu and Buddhist Tantricism) was described in the third chapter of this book.

3. The Guibourg Mass—from a nineteenth-century history of sorcery.

4. J. K. Huysman—his cat was subjected to magical attacks—see Appendix, "Copulating with Cleopatra".

PRIMITIVE FERTILITY CULTS

Bacchus of the Romans and the Hermes[6] of the Greeks were all phallic gods; similarly there were sexual elements in the Mysteries of Isis and there is some reason to suppose that the Mysteries of Eleusis *may* have involved (a) a veneration of the male and female sexual organs, and (b) a ritual copulation between priest and priestess.

There was another, and darker, side to fertility religions, particularly to those in which the female principle of the earth mother was dominant. The giver of life was also the giver of death, the womb of the earth which gave birth to animal and plant had another function as the grave into which all men ultimately descended. Persephone spent half her life in the underworld and Ishtar also went down into that same shadowy half-world. It is this dark, sterile aspect of the religion of the Great Mother that may have survived in the witch-cult of the Middle Ages.

[6] The caduceus (that is to say the winged staff with intertwined serpents) of Hermes was very probably a stylised penis. Similar visual euphemisms were common in ancient iconography; thus the bodily figure of a phallic god was often used as the symbol of his penis, frequently such a god would be shown standing on a vesica-shaped boat, the latter symbolising the vagina of the goddess. Sellon stumbled on this fact and, with the over-enthusiasm that was so typical of him, claimed that just about every mythological boat was a vagina in disguise. Accordingly, he asserted that the word *Argo*, the name of the boat in which sailed Jason and his companions in the quest of the Golden Fleece, was etymologically connected with the Indian word *argha* (vagina), and that the Hebrew Ark of the Covenant, the sacred container holding the Tables of the Law, was a symbolic vagina containing a dried penis! He wrote that "there would also now appear good ground for believing that the ark of the covenant, held so sacred by the Jews, contained nothing more or less than a phallus, the ark being the type of the *argha* or Yoni" (in *Proceedings of the Anthropological Society*, Vol. I, 1865).

CHAPTER SIX

The Great Mother Falls on Evil Days

Thessaly was the home of Hecate, goddess of childbirth, abortion, poison and witchcraft. Originally she was probably an Asiatic goddess but the Greeks had naturalised her, and, while it can hardly be said that they had taken her into their hearts, they were certainly afraid of her, In Samothrace her worship was amalgamated with that of those extraordinary deluge-gods the Kabiri, and in Caria her worship was carried on by eunuch priests, a fact which seems to provide some link between Hecate and the Asiatic goddess Cybele, whose devotees showed their love of their Lady by self-emasculation.

By the fifth century B.C. Hecate had become identified with both Artemis, the chaste moon-goddess, and with "Diana the many-breasted"—yet a third Greek deity associated with the moon. The later pagans rationalised the existence of three separate moon-goddesses by arguing that the moon was the symbol of femininity and thus had three aspects; Artemis, corresponding to the young, chaste girl, Diana, symbolising the fertile mother, and Hecate, the woman who had passed the menopause, sterile, cold and dark. Nevertheless, originally Hecate was not a lunar deity, and it is probable that the identification with Artemis was made because both deities were associated with the canine world—Artemis had a pack of hounds, while the black dog was sacred to Hecate and the appearance of such a hound was popularly supposed to be a herald of her appearance—and with wild nature.

The terrifying nature of the worship of Hecate is illustrated by the following invocation of her: "Come infernal . . . Bombo, goddess of the broad roadways, of the crossroad, thou who goest to and fro at night, torch in hand, enemy of the day, friend and lover of darkness, thou who dost rejoice when the bitches are howling and warm blood is spilled, thou who art walking amid the phantom and in the place of tombs, thou whose thirst is blood, thou who dost strike chill fear into mortal heart, Gorgo, Mormo, Moon of a thousand forms, cast a propitious eye upon our sacrifice."

The connections made in this invocation between darkness, witchcraft and crossroads are of great interest, for they have survived to the present day in the darker side of the Voodoo religion of Haiti.

As I have said, Thessaly was the home of Hecate, and its women enjoyed a popular reputation for witchcraft throughout the Hellenistic world and were even supposed to have the power of "drawing down the moon" from the heavens.[1] For this reason Apuleius, when he wrote his *Metamorphoses*—a tract in favour of Isis-worship disguised as a romance—automatically sent Lucius, his marvel-seeking hero, there:

"Extremely desirous of becoming acquainted with all that is strange and wonderful I called to mind that I was in the very heart of Thessaly, celebrated by the unanimous consent of the whole wide world as the land where the spells and incantations of magic are, so to speak indigenous . . ."

The cult of Hecate and Greek beliefs about witchcraft spread to Rome where, perhaps, certain dark cults, remnants of Etruscan magic, already enjoyed a shadowy existence. Thus Horace described an incantation at which a black lamb was torn to pieces, while still living, as a sacrifice to Hecate, and belief in Black Magic was so widespread that when Antinous, the favourite of the Emperor Hadrian, was accidentally drowned in the Nile it was popularly rumoured that he had been sacrificed as part of a magic spell designed to lengthen the Emperor's life-span.

It is a curious fact that when a religion is in a state of decline, either permanent or temporary, it is the least pleasant part of the religion that shows the greatest capacity for survival. Thus, today, many of those who have completely lost their faith in such traditional beliefs as the redemptive death and triumphant resurrection of Jesus Christ retain a

---

[1] J. W. Brodie-Innes, an Edwardian novelist who was also an occultist and a member of the Hermetic Order of the Golden Dawn, wrote a story in which this extraordinary feat was carried out by a Scottish witch of the seventeenth century. Certain English members of the contemporary witch-cult who are familiar with the story have claimed to be able to do the same thing. Even more surprising, some of them have actually found those who are credulous enough to believe them!

lurking fear of the Christian Devil and his minions. There are a lot of agnostics who avoid walking under ladders, looking at the new moon through glass, or spilling salt! The pagan cults of the Graeco-Roman world were no exception to this rule. Long after the bright gods of Olympus had been forgotten the darker gods still held their place in the hearts of the rural populace of the more out-of-the-way parts of Europe. Even if Apollo and his fellows were remembered at all, their colours had faded into sombre hues, and in their transformed forms they bore more resemblance to Priapus and Hecate than to their Olympic originals.

This transformation of gods into devils had begun almost immediately after Constantine had made Christianity the official religion of the Empire in 313 A.D. and was continued under his successors. Thus, in 354, Constantius issued a ukase against nocturnal sacrifices "henceforth, let all such abominations cease"—a law that was clearly ineffective, for in 381 Theodosius promulgated a similar law, a clear indication that night-meetings and sacrifices to the gods were still being secretly conducted in the abandoned Temples of the old faith.

It may be that from such secret meetings, from such invocations of the old gods against the usurping Galilean, and from the desperation of conservative rural folk who had seen their ancient faith humiliated and almost destroyed by the new, sprang the mediaeval witch cult with its adoration of the sexual principle—if, indeed, such a thing as the mediaeval witch-cult ever existed!

There are four main schools of thought regarding the European witchcraft of the Middle Ages. The first, the traditional one, more or less accepts the truth of the charges made by the Church against sorcerers and witches. That is to say, it accepts the existence of a principle of spiritual evil, called the Devil, Lucifer, or Satan, and believes that it is at least theoretically possible for a human being to enter into relations with that evil principle, to co-operate with it, and even to enter into formal alliance with it by means of a pact. "We have made a covenant with Death and with Hell we are at agreement" has always been a favourite Old Testament text with this school of thought. In modern times the late Montague Summers has been the most notable exponent of this point of view; with the aid of his considerable, although sometimes shaky, scholarship he was always prepared to defend the behaviour and beliefs of the mediaeval inquisitors, however loathsome the former, however improbable the latter.

THE GREAT MOTHER FALLS ON EVIL DAYS

The second school of thought is that which will be always associated with the late Margaret Murray, a professional Egyptologist who also dabbled in anthropology and mediaeval history. The thesis of Dr. Murray was almost breath-taking in its simplicity; indeed, it was its very simplicity that made it so attractive to the intellectuals of the 'twenties and 'thirties, a period when simple answers—Adler's psychology, Varga's interpretation of Marx's economics, Roger Fry's aesthetics—were much in vogue.[2]

Dr. Murray held that witchcraft, which she preferred to call "the Dianic cult", could be traced back to the prehistoric cults of, firstly, the Great Mother, principle of fertility and fecundity, and, secondly, that of the Divine King "who", in Frazer's words, "slew the slayer, and shall himself be slain". She contended that this Dianic cult was a highly organised religion, with its own priests, festivals and meeting places; that it could "be traced back to pre-Christian times and appears to be the ancient religion of Western Europe"; and that it was, at certain times, a very real and dangerous rival to Christianity itself.

Dr. Murray supported her thesis with a good deal of evidence extracted from the confessions of witches themselves, confessions, it is worth remembering, that had often been extracted under torture and were therefore only too likely to have reflected the prejudices of the torturers.[3] At first sight much of this evidence is extremely convincing (for example "the persistence of the number thirteen in the Covens,

---

[2] It is true, of course, that at the present time we seem to be entering a similar era. Hence, no doubt, the popularity with the young of the poetry of Corso and Ted Hughes, the "novels" of William Burroughs, and, most worrying of all, the pseudo-radicalism of the sinister racialism of Fanon. Margaret Murray's books, never completely out of fashion, are clearly due for a great revival!

[3] Since the Moscow trials of the 'thirties, in which so many of the Old Bolsheviks confessed to almost every possible crime—an actual *majority* of the Bolshevik Central Committee that had made the October Revolution were capitalist agents if the evidence given at the trials was to be believed—we have all grown considerably more sceptical about evidence extracted under torture. There is a remarkable similarity between, for example, a young German girl of the sixteenth century confessing that, naked, she had attended the Sabbath and there indulged in every variety of perversion and some of the confessions produced at the Moscow trials. One remembers that one of the Moscow accused confessed, in a fervour of self-recrimination, to having met and plotted with Trotsky at the Hotel Bristol in Copenhagen although, in reality, the hotel had been burnt down some years before; this is very like the fervent repentance displayed by some accused witches for impossible supernatural crimes to which they had confessed.

the narrow geographical range of the domestic familiar, the avoidance of certain forms in the animal transformations") but further examination shows that Dr. Murray was highly selective in her choice of material. Thus, while she accepted as truth all those points in the confessions of accused witches that supported her own theoretical point of view, she completely disregarded all those supernatural elements in the same confessions that might have either, on the one hand, validated the theological conclusions of the prosecutors or, on the other hand, shown that the confessions resulted from delusion, imposture, or the promptings of the torturers. In spite of this Dr. Murray was prepared to accept certain supernatural components of the confessions—e.g. animal transformations—when they could both be given a naturalistic explanation and used to support her own "Dianic" thesis.[4] Again, Dr. Murray's use of evidence was lacking both in scientific method and a sense of history. She argued, for example, that the extraordinarily limited number of personal names occurring among women accused of witchcraft was an indication that such names as Agnes, Alice, Isabel and Mary were "witch names", conferred on the children of members of the witch-cult. An examination of various baptismal records, however, shows that these alleged "witch names" occurred almost as frequently among the general population as they did amongst those accused of witchcraft—what variation there was is insufficient for any statistical significance to be attached to it. In fact Dr. Murray appears to have had something of an obsession about personal names, arguing that the mere existence of the name Christian was proof that another, non-Christian, religion existed in the same society. In the same way, I suppose, it could be argued that the fact that some little girls are from the very moment of birth, named Virginia presupposes that there exist other little girls who, from the moment of birth, are *not* virgins!

---

[4] Here I must once again draw an analogy from the strange intellectual underworld of Marxist sectarianism. The Trotskyists class the Soviet Union as "a degenerated workers' state with socialist foundations and a degenerate, bureaucratic superstructure". At the time when the Soviet Union seemed ahead in the space race, having just launched Sputnik I, I heard a Trotskyist arguing that this proved that there was "a socialist foundation to the Soviet Union's economy". Years later, when the U.S.A. had triumphantly beaten Russia to the Moon I heard the same Trotskyist contending, while in argument with an orthodox Communist that this American success showed "that there were bureaucratic deformations in the Soviet economy". This method of reasoning shows a surprising resemblance to that of Margaret Murray.

As for Dr. Murray's belief that such individuals as Gilles de Retz and even St. Joan of Arc were "Divine Kings" (incarnate deities who arranged their own sacrificial deaths as a sort of primitive agricultural fertility rite and "who, like the early Christian martyrs, rushed headlong on their fate, determined to die for their 'faith'") one can only say, firstly, that there is not the slightest shred of evidence for it and, secondly, that it depends on the theory of the Divine King as put forward by J. G. Frazer—a theory that is no longer taken seriously by anthropologists in the form that it was put forward by the Seligmans and Frazer himself.[5]

The third attitude towards European witchcraft—that the whole thing was a mixture of madness, imposture and folly—was first put forward in the sixteenth century by the Kentish squire Reginald Scot in his *Discoverie of Witchcraft*. It grew popular with the rationalistic, deistic intellectuals of the following century and by the year 1900 was almost universally accepted. This theory has a great deal more to be said for it than the followers of Margaret Murray would admit, and I am quite sure that it explains much of the evidence given at the trials which occurred during what Trevor-Roper has called "the European witch craze of the sixteenth and seventeenth centuries". In spite of its undoubted attractions this theory has one devastating drawback; it completely fails to explain the remarkable similarities between *some* of the practices described in evidence given at the European witch-trials and witchcraft techniques definitely known to either be used or have been used in the primitive cultures of such widely separated areas as Lapland and Haiti.

The fourth interpretation of the nature of the mediaeval witch-cult —and the one to which I myself subscribe—is a compromise between the rationalistic explanations of the nineteenth-century historiographers and the ultra-credulous theorising of Margaret Murray and her followers.[6] It discounts all the allegedly supernatural elements of occidental

---

[5] The fundamental error of Frazer and the Seligmans was that they overestimated the magico-religious aspects of sacral kingship and underestimated the political. It seems highly improbable that the senile and incestuous Major Weir— another of Margaret Murray's candidates for incarnate godship—could ever have been regarded as a Divine King. For a penetrating criticism of the Frazerian theory of sacral kingship see, E. E. Evans-Pritchard *The Divine Kingship of the Shilluk of the Nilotic Sudan* (C.U.P. 1948) and the symposium *The Sacral Kingship* (Leyden 1959).

[6] A fifth theory of the nature of the witch-cult—a theory charming in its

witchcraft as being the result of fraud, hysteria, imposture and abnormal psychological states.[7] On the other hand it also rejects the idea that an organised anti-Christian religion could have survived in Europe throughout the entire period from the fall of the Roman Empire to the end of the seventeenth century—the extinction of the Albigensian heresy and the rapid decline of fifteenth-century Lollardry are indications of the extreme improbability of such a survival. The witch-cult is seen to have been not an organised counter-religion (except, perhaps, for very limited periods during times of acute social and political breakdown) but as a survival of magical and other pre-Christian folk practices *without the survival of pre-Christian "theology"*. Just as the twentieth-century agnostic often ensures the baptism of his children for purely social reasons, having no belief in the doctrine of baptismal regeneration and continuing to conduct his or her personal life in conformity with the now dominant hedonistic philosophy of the permissive society, so the mediaeval "witch" cured a sick child by passing it through the symbolic hole in an upright prehistoric megalith and yet, quite sincerely, attended Mass on a Sunday and regarded herself as a good Catholic. The worship of the fertile Mother must have been performed by individuals or by very small groups of devotees. Nevertheless, in view of much of the evidence given at the witch-trials it would be futile to completely deny the occasional occurrence of the Witches' Sabbath—i.e. a large-scale celebration of the fertility/death rites of the Great Mother.

From the evidence given at the trials—particularly from the evidence describing the happenings at the Witches' Sabbath—it is possible to construct some sort of picture of the nature of the religion of the mediaeval witch; it is almost unnecessary to say that I use the word

eccentricity—has been put forward by Robert Graves; this theory I have briefly examined in Appendix B, "Robert Graves, Witches and Islamic Mysticism".

[7] Unlike the overwhelming majority of those who reject the supernatural components of witchcraft confessions I am myself inclined to the belief that there may be a tiny substratum of truth in some of the stories of supernormal events told by witnesses at the witch trials; i.e. I accept the existence of extra-sensory perception and I regard some of the extraordinary events related by simple people in the course of their evidence at the trials as having actually happened—the result of a spontaneous manifestation of extra-sensory faculties. This does not, of course, imply that I accept any *particular* instance of E.S.P. as being genuine; I adhere to the "bundle of sticks" theory—while there is a very low probability of any individual supernatural story being veridic there is a very high probability that of the *totality* of such stories one or more are true.

"religion" not in its full sense (i.e. as (a) a theology and philosophy, (b) a set of ritual observances and techniques of worship, and (c) a socio-economic structure in its own right) but in the limited meaning of a set of traditional observances the inner significance of which had long been forgotten.

As I have already said, it is probable that only a small number of witches actually attended the Sabbath; nevertheless, a much larger number of witches seem to have *thought* that they had done so and it was the confessions of these deluded people that contained details of most of the supernatural phenomena associated with the Sabbath. An excellent example of such an imaginary visit to the Sabbath (?) was given in the sixth chapter of the first Book of the *Sacred Magic of Abra-Melin the Mage*, a late mediaeval text-book of occult practice.[8] The narrator, who called himself simply "Abraham the Jew" described how:

> "At Lintz I worked with a young woman, who one evening invited me to go with her, assuring me that without any risk she would conduct me to a place where I greatly desired to find myself. I allowed myself to be persuaded by her promises. She then gave unto me an unguent, with which I rubbed the principal pulses of my feet and hands; the which she did also; and at first it appeared to me that I was flying in the air in the place which I wished, and which I had in no way mentioned to her.
>
> "I pass over in silence and out of respect, that which I saw, which was admirable, and appearing to myself to have remained there a long while, I felt as if I were just awakening from a profound sleep, and I had great pain in my head and deep melancholy. I turned round and saw that she was seated at my side. She began to recount to me what she had seen, but that which I had seen was entirely different. I was, however, much astonished, because it appeared to me as if I had been really and corporeally in the place, and there in reality to have seen that which had happened. However, I asked her one day to go alone to that same place, and to bring me back news of a friend whom I knew for certain was distant 200 leagues. She promised to do so in the space of an hour. She rubbed herself with the same unguent, and I was very expectant to see her fly away; but

---

[8] While the surviving manuscript of the *Sacred Magic* is written in an early eighteenth-century hand internal evidence seems to show a probability that the work was based on an earlier, possibly early sixteenth century, original.

she fell to the ground and remained there about three hours as if she were dead, so that I began to think that she really was dead. At last she began to stir like a person who is waking, then she rose to an upright position, and with much pleasure began to give me the account of her expedition, saying that she had been in the place where my friend was, and all that he was doing; the which was entirely contrary to his profession. When I concluded that what she had just told me was a simple dream, and that this unguent was a causer of a phantastic sleep; whereon she confessed to me that this unguent had been given to her by the Devil."

It is interesting to compare this account with a story told by Sprenger, the author of the notorious *Malleus Maleficarum*. He relates that a woman who had voluntarily approached some Dominicans and confessed to being a witch told her interrogators that she nightly flew to the Sabbath and not even being placed in a sealed room could prevent her from doing so. At nightfall the Dominicans, who combined a healthy scepticism with a laudable taste for experiment, tested her assertion by placing her in a locked room, leaving her alone, but all the while secretly observing her through a spyhole. The woman threw herself on her bed, became rigid and went into some sort of trance. Her watchers now entered the room and tried to awake her; all their efforts, which included burning her naked foot with a candle flame, were in vain, and the "witch" continued insensible. On her eventual recovery of consciousness she gave a graphic description of her visit to the Sabbath, of those she had met there and of the rites in which she had taken part; the Dominicans, more humane than many of their fellow inquisitors, told her that she was indulging in fantasies, gave her a penance and let her depart.[9] Clearly this woman suffered from some sort of spasmodic catatonic schizophrenia—but what of those witches who claimed to have flown to the Sabbath but suffered from no obvious mental illness? How did their delusions arise? "Abraham the Jew"

[9] Compare Guazzo in *Compendium Maleficarum*: "The opinion which many hold who follow Luther and Melanchthon is that witches only assist at these ceremonies in their imagination, and that they are deceived by some trick of the Devil, in support of which argument the objectors often assert that the witches have very often been seen lying in one spot and not moving thence. Additionally what is related in the life of St. Germain . . . that . . . when certain women declared they had been present at a banquet they were all the time sleeping . . . is germane . . ."

clearly thought that they were caused by the unguent with which he anointed himself, and he may have been right. There are several surviving recipes for the witches' ointment and most of them seem to have contained hallucinogenic drugs; thus Reginald Scot in his *Discoverie of Witchcraft* gave details of a preparation made in accordance with the following directions; take "the fat of young children, and seeth it with water in a brasen vessel, reserving the thickest of that which remaineth boiled in the bottome" and add "Eleoselinum, Aconitum, Frondes populeas and Soote". The first and second of these additives are hallucinogens. A. J. Clark analysed three of the recipes[10] and found that:

"The first preparation . . . would produce mental confusion, impaired movement, irregular action of the heart, dizziness and shortness of breath.

"The belladonna in the second ointment would produce excitement which might pass to delirium.

"The third ointment, containing both aconite and belladonna, would produce excitement and irregular action of the heart."

This seems clear enough, but to me it seems unlikely that enough of the essential ingredients would penetrate through the skin—even the scratched, inflamed and broken skin of a lice-ridden mediaeval peasant —to produce the supposed results. I am inclined to the opinion that the "flying ointment" was supplemented with an infusion of fly agaric, the "sacred mushroom" *amanita muscaria*; certainly the one or two contemporary English covens which *may* have some connection with traditional witchcraft use such an infusion for producing visions.[11]

The real Sabbath seems to have been a much tamer affair than the imaginary Sabbath of the schizophrenic and the visionary; a rural feast with plenty to eat and drink[12] followed by dancing and a sexual orgy. The food seems to have consisted of rustic dainties; the Pendle

[10] In an appendix to Margaret Murray's *magnum opus*.
[11] The ointment used by these covens is simply a heavy grease worn, like the oil of the long-distance swimmer, as a protection against cold.
[12] The drink appears to have been neither more nor less than whatever alcoholic beverage was normally drunk in the locality. Nevertheless certain modern occultists have endeavoured to attack an esoteric significance to *Vinum Sabbati*, the Wine of the Sabbath. One disciple of Crowley seems to have looked upon it as the male and female sexual secretions "mingled in the Holy Grail" (i.e. the vagina); he has failed, however, to produce any authority for this conception.

witches of 1633 feasted on "flesh smoaking, butter in lumps and milk" while twenty years earlier the Lancashire witches ate "Beef, Bacon and roasted mutton". The dancing was accompanied by music, both vocal and instrumental. Sinclair, in his *Satan's Invisible World Discovered*, spoke of the Devil as being the author of "several bawdy Songs which are sung" and went on to relate that a "reverend Minister" had told him that "one who was the Devil's Piper, a wizard, confesst to him that at a Ball of Dancing the Foul Spirit taught him a bawdy song to sing and play, as it were this night, and ere two days passed all the lads and lasses of the town were lilting it through the street. It were abomination to rehearse it." While there is little doubt that many celebrations of the Sabbath ended in an indiscriminate sexual orgy I doubt whether this was invariably so, and I am sure that many of the grosser descriptions of sexual perversity contained in late mediaeval and renaissance treatises on witchcraft owed more to the prurient imaginations of their authors than to the actual practices of the witch-cult. I do not question, however, that ritual sexual intercourse between the "Devil" (i.e. the human being who presided and acted as High Priest at the Sabbath) and female members of the cult was a frequent observance at the Sabbath nor that artificial phalli were sometimes used for this purpose; both Isobel Gowdie and Janet Breadheid, seventeenth-century Scottish witches, described the Devil's "nature" (i.e. his penis) as being "huge, very cold, as ice" and "cold as spring well-water" and similar evidence was given at many of the trials.

In the popular imagination the "Black Mass", the impious parody of the Eucharist, is inextricably associated with the Witches' Sabbath, but this was not so. The Black Mass seems to be of much later origin and although accounts of something like a diabolical communion service occur in one or two late Catholic treatises on witchcraft I am fairly sure that these accounts are derived from confused ecclesiastical and popular recollections of the Agape, or love feasts, of the Cathars and other mediaeval Manichee sects. Nevertheless, in the Paris of the seventeenth century there was a blending of impiously-said Masses with the darker sexual components of witchcraft, a deep and final degradation of the worship of the Great Mother.

CHAPTER SEVEN
Masses—Black, White and Amatory

The Mass was and is the central religious practice of Catholic Christianity. It is not surprising that the supposed miracle of the Mass—the supernatural transformation of the substance of bread and wine into the veritable Body and Blood of Christ—daily performed by the priest, led to a popular belief that the ceremony had magical powers, that a priest could use his magical powers of transubstantiation[1] in order to achieve his own ends; that the Mass could be said with the intention of death, sexual love or material gain. This belief was not confined to the illiterate populace but was held by a large number—possibly a majority—of the secular clergy. Evilly disposed priests would say a Requiem Mass for a still living enemy and, when one remembers mediaeval mortality rates, it is not surprising that this malicious rite often met with seeming success.[2]

Eventually an underground literature came into existence designed to supply the demand for practical instruction in such perversions of the sacerdotal function. Probably the most notorious of these unpleasant instructional manuals was the *Grimoire of Honorius*—falsely attributed to one of the Popes of that name—which gave detailed information on how to use the Mass as an adjunct of (black) magical

---

[1] I am, of course, well aware that theologically speaking the priest has no magical powers, that there is a gulf between the Catholic belief in the sacramental gifts of the Holy Spirit and the theurgic conception (ultimately derived from later Neo-Platonism) of magical rites. Nevertheless there is no doubt that at a popular level the priest was (and to some extent still is; in the Catholicism of, for example, Southern Italy) regarded as having quasi-magical powers.

[2] As early as the seventh century the Council of Toledo prohibited a Requiem Mass wherein the Mass was said not for a soul in purgatory but for a living man—with the intention that he might die.

rites. To obtain a demon as a servant, for example, one was supposed to, firstly, say a Mass of the Holy Ghost, secondly, to tear the eyes from a living black cockerel, thirdly, to conduct a long-winded evocation ceremony and, finally, to throw a living mouse to the demon who appeared. As the Anglican writer Charles Williams has commented it is not unlikely that anyone who performed this revolting series of blasphemies and cruelties supposed he saw—or indeed saw—a devil.

I have little doubt that there were always, and possibly still are,[3] unworthy priests prepared, for gain, to say Masses designed to achieve dubious ends. It was only in seventeenth-century France, however, that the activities of such creatures became Big Business.

As early as 1668 Paris had begun to be disturbed by dark gossip concerning sorcery, poisons and murder and in the summer of that year a professional fortune-teller, a certain Le Sage, and his associate, a priest named Mariette, were arrested, interrogated and finally charged with sorcery—an offence punishable by death. At their trial they told their judges that their main business was the compounding and sale to clients of love philtres that had been charged with magical power by being placed beneath the chalice while Mariette said a midnight Mass over them on a black-draped altar at the dark of the moon. The judges, not surprisingly, asked the accused warlocks for the names of their clients. They were probably surprised and embarrassed by the names that were given; for the prisoners named as customers not only such well-known individuals as the Marquise de Bougy and the Duchesse de Vivonne but also the Marquise de Montespan, mistress and favourite of Louis XIV! No word of this evidence was ever allowed to leak out. All was suppressed. Le Sage was sentenced for life to the galleys while Mariette was given the mild sentence of nine years' banishment—the presiding judge who conferred the sentence being the father of one of his clients. Only four years later, while his galley lay at anchor off Genoa, Le Sage was mysteriously released, presumably owing to the intervention of some powerful patron, and returned to Paris and the arms of his mistress, a certain La Voisin.

Amongst Le Sage's acquaintances was Captain de Chasteuil, a Doctor of Laws, a Knight of the Order of Malta—while fighting against Algerian pirates he had been taken prisoner and spent two years as a galley-slave—and at one time a Captain of Guards. After his return

---

[3] I have heard occasional stories of strange religio-magical practices on the crazier fringes of the religious underworld of the *episcopi vagantes*.

from slavery de Chasteuil became a Carmelite prior, an office which he seems to have found quite compatible with the study of magic and alchemy and, indeed, with smuggling his fourteen-year-old mistress into his cell at night. Eventually the girl became pregnant; de Chasteuil strangled her and buried her body beneath the floor of his monastery chapel. The crime was discovered as the result of a chain of coincidences—as unlikely as everything else in the life of de Chasteuil—and he was condemned to death by hanging. He was rescued from (quite literally) the foot of the gallows by the armed followers of his friend Louis de Vanens, the captain of a galley (and, like de Chasteuil himself, a practising magician), and spirited away to the court of the Duke of Savoy at Turin. He rose rapidly in the ducal favour, becoming Captain of the Royal Guard and tutor to the Prince of Piedmont, heir to the throne. In 1675, however, the sudden death of his patron, probably from poison, neccessitated a rapid departure from Savoy and he made a discreet return to France. In Paris he set up in business as a purveyor of spells and poisons, as an alchemist, and as a forger.

His ambitions were large. In association with a number of old associates, including de Vanens, and financed by Pierre Cardelan, a Parisian banker, he planned to manufacture enough "alchemical silver" to make a fortune. In November 1677 de Vanens and Cardelan were arrested by Nicolas de la Reynie, recently appointed as Lieutenant-General of Police by Louis XIV, but de Chasteuil managed to escape—he was traced a year later and found already dead, strangled by an unknown assailant.

In the "magical workshop" of the conspirators were found powerful poisons and some forged ingots of silver; much of the counterfeit silver had already been purchased by the Royal Mint at the full price for fine silver.

It soon became apparent to La Reynie that de Vanens and his associates were not only poison-mongers and counterfeiters but Satanists; de Vanens himself boasted of it. He told his fellow prisoners in the Bastille that not God himself was capable of preventing him conducting the Black Mass upon the rump of his familiar spirit—the familiar in question, a large spotted spaniel, seems to have looked innocent enough as far as external appearances were concerned!

For a year de Vanens and his accomplices languished in prison, subjected to frequent interrogation by La Reynie, who, convinced that the prisoners had other associates, was anxious to obtain details of the vast conspiracy which he was certain existed, although he felt unsure of its exact nature. Then, towards the end of 1678, La Reynie discovered the clue for which he had been searching in the shape of a curious report from a lawyer named Perrin.

One night Perrin had been invited to dine at the home of a M. Vigoureux, a ladies' dressmaker, and one of his fellow-guests had been Marie Bosse, one of the many fortune tellers who infested Paris. The dinner was a drunken one and Marie Bosse, under the influence of alcohol, boasted of her professional success, "only three more poisonings", she said, "and I can retire". The wife of one of La Reynie's men was sent along, posing as a client cursed with a long-living and miserable husband, to investigate La Bosse. On her first visit she was commiserated with, on her second she was supplied with a vial of poison.

La Reynie acted immediately, arresting La Bosse—discovered by the police in an incestuous situation with her two sons and daughter—and the wife of M. Vigoureux; found among the effects of the witches were a veritable arsenal of poisons: arsenic, mercuric sublimate, hemlock, henbane, belladonna, foxglove, mandragora and "Spanish fly" (Cantharides, a powerful aphrodisiac). Along with these were discovered many substances used in the compounding of philtres—dried toad, human fat, graveyard dust, dried blood, dried human semen and excrement.

Interrogated under torture La Bosse and La Vigoureux incriminated three dozen others, either fellow-sorcerers or clients who had employed poison and witchcraft for their own purposes, and further arrests followed, among them that of Catherine Monvoisin, better known as La Voisin; she, it will be remembered, was the mistress of the magician Le Sage who had been sentenced to the galleys—and suddenly and mysteriously released—some eleven years earlier.

Le Sage was only one of La Voisin's many lovers (she also had a husband who had managed to survive his wife's many attempts to poison him[4]) and his jealousy of his rivals, particularly of a man named Latour, had turned his love to hatred. Consequently, after his own arrest, only five days after that of La Voisin, he "spilled the beans",

[4] He seems to have been an extraordinarily lucky man; on one occasion he refused the soup prepared for him after he had noticed that it was dissolving his silver spoon, on another he was violently sick just after eating his dinner and escaped with his life—although after the experience he endured an attack of hiccoughs, accompanied by nose-bleeds, of eighteen months' duration!

doing all in his power to send his former paramour to the stake. He revealed that La Voisin not only organised Black Masses—Le Sage named a number of renegade priests who were on her payroll—and sold poisons but was also the leading Parisian abortionist. La Reynie was not surprised; in his search of La Voisin's villa he had not only found the paraphernalia of Black Magic (including books of spells, incense, black candles and priestly vestments) but a mysterious and sinister stove in the ashes of which were what appeared to be fragments of the bones of young children.

It was only those infants too big to be safely buried by La Voisin that went into her stove but nevertheless, there were more than enough of these; according to her own account the bodies or ashes of over two thousand infants and embryos were buried in her garden. In a way La Voisin's brutal disregard for the mortal remains of her victims[5] contrasted favourably with the nauseating religiosity displayed by other witch/abortionists arrested at the same time; La Lépère, for example, who piously informed her interrogators that "when she aborted a mother who had already felt her child quicken she never failed to baptise the child and carry it to some consecrated ground where she tipped the sexton to bury it in some neglected corner when the priest wasn't looking".

Among the priests named by Le Sage as being involved in the performance of Black and Amatory Masses were Mariette, the old associate who had been tried with him in 1668, the Abbé Davot, who was La Voisin's confessor at her own Parish Church, and the Abbé Guibourg, chief of the whole hellish crew. All were arrested by La Reynie, who described Guibourg as follows:

"A priest sixty seven years of age, born in Paris, claiming to be a bastard son of Monsieur de Montmorency. A libertine who has travelled a good deal, has held benefices at Issy and at Vanves, and who is at present attached to the Church of Saint Marcel. For twenty years he has engaged continually in the practice of poison, sacrilege and every evil business. He has cut the throats and sacrificed uncounted numbers of children on his infernal altar. He has a mistress (a certain La Chanfrain) by whom he has had several children, one

---

[5] In the England of today, of course, this aspect of La Voisin's activities would be considered neither brutal nor socially undesirable!

or two of whom he has sacrificed. A man who at times seems a raving lunatic, and at other times calmly boasts of what he will say when put to the question. . . . It is no ordinary man who thinks it a natural thing to sacrifice infants by slitting their throats and to say Mass upon the bodies of naked women."

We know a good deal about the nature of the Masses said by Guibourg "upon the bodies of naked women" from his own testimony and that of La Voisin's stepdaughter, who had, when pregnant, fled in terror from her home in fear that her child would be taken from her and used as a blood sacrifice. The Voisin girl (throughout the records of her questioning she was referred to as *la Fille Voisin*) claimed that many of these Masses had been celebrated at the behest of Madame de Montespan, mistress of Louis XIV and mother of three of his bastard children.

Since 1667 Madame de Montespan had supplemented her personal sexual attractions by magical means—that is to say by the celebration of first Amatory, and later Black, Masses designed to win and hold the love of the King.[6] The early Masses were innocent enough (save, of course, in a theological sense) and involved neither devil worship nor murder. Mariette sang the Mass orthodoxly enough but the Gospel was read over the lady's head and an incantation was uttered; "that the Queen may be barren that the King leave her table and bed for me, that I obtain from him all that I ask for myself and for my relatives; that my servants may be pleasing to him; that beloved and respected by great nobles I may be called to the councils of the King and know what passes there; and that, this affection being redoubled on what has existed in the past, the King may leave La Valliere[7] and look no more upon her; and that the Queen being repudiated I may marry the King."

This Amatory Mass was repeated at Saint Germain, in the lodging of Madame de Montespan's sister. The third Mass of the series involved a bloody sacrifice of a comparatively innocent nature—two doves, traditional symbols of the goddess Venus, were consecrated to Louis and Madame de Montespan, were placed on the altar throughout the

[6] It is worth saying that the French historian Jean Lemoine held that Madame de Montespan was innocent of any connection with either Guibourg or La Voisin. Although he devoted over thirty years to his study of the matter there seems little doubt that he gave his verdict against the evidence.

[7] The then mistress of Louis XIV.

saying of the Mass, and finally had their hearts torn out from their living bodies.

At first it seemed to Madame de Montespan that her desires had been achieved; the Queen was neglected and the gentle La Valliere was first neglected by the King and eventually persuaded to enter a nunnery. Nevertheless the King showed no sign of getting rid of his Queen and marrying Madame de Montespan and always the latter felt the fear of rival mistresses who might supplant her as she herself had supplanted La Valliere. In every crisis in her relationship with the King she resorted to magic. The Voisin girl stated that "every time that anything fresh happened to Madame de Montespan and she feared some lessening in the favour of the King she came running to my mother that she might provide some remedy; my mother at once called in one of the priests, whom she instructed to celebrate Masses, and then she gave her (La Montespan) powders that were to be administered to the King." The powders in question, mixtures of real and supposed aphrodisiacs such as cantharides and dried cockerels' testicles, had been consecrated by being passed under the Chalice at Amatory Masses.

These Amatory Masses and aphrodisiac powders sufficed until 1673 when Madame de Montespan, alarmed by the King's neglect, real or imaginary, resorted to stronger and darker magic. This time Guibourg officiated at the Mass,[8] the body of a masked, but otherwise naked, woman—probably Madame de Montespan herself—lay on the altar and a child was sacrificed. Details of the liturgy used are scant but it is clear that at the moment of Consecration a child's throat was slit, following which its blood was drained into the Chalice (which stood on the pubic area of the woman on the altar) and the following prayer recited: "Ashtaroth and Asmodeus, Princes of Love, I beseech you to accept the sacrifice of this child which I now present to you so that I may receive the things I ask of you; that the love of the King may be continued . . . that the queen may become barren . . ."

Following this prayer various gross sexual manipulations involving the Consecrated Elements took place—the host (the consecrated wafer of unleavened bread) was inserted into the vagina of the woman lying upon the altar and the genitals of Guibourg and the woman were washed with the mixture of wine and blood; some of this unpleasant confection was taken away by the woman in a glass vial in order that

---

[8] He had been promised a sum equivalent to about £200 at current values and presentation to an ecclesiastical living in return for his help.

it might be secretly administered to the King. Later the heart and entrails of the murdered child were returned to Guibourg for a second consecration; he was told that these were to be dried, powdered and, like the blood and the wine, given to the King in his food.[9]

In 1678 another series of Masses took place. The Voisin girl helped her mother prepare for the first of these; a mattress was laid on the altar, candlesticks with black candles stood on stools at its side. Guibourg wore a white chasuble embroidered with pine-cones—symbols of the god Dionysius—while Madame de Montespan lay naked on the mattress; the latter had proved too short and the favourite's head dangled over the edge of the altar where it was supported by a pillow placed on a chair. A child was again sacrificed and the blood, said the Voisin girl, "was carried away with the wine and the wafer to be distilled".

All was in vain; Madame de Montespan slowly began to lose the King's favour. Someone, just possibly de Montespan herself but more probably one of her ladies-in-waiting, decided to use magic not for love but for death—to celebrate a Mass designed to encompass the King's destruction.

This Mortuary Mass, celebrated by Guibourg at the home of La Voisin, involved even more sexual unpleasantness than the Amatory Masses.[10] Guibourg's own account, given under interrogation, goes: "Clad in alb and stole I officiated at a conjuration at La Voisin's in the presence of La des Oeillets,[11] who wanted to put a death charm upon the King and was accompanied by a man who supplied the rubric of the conjuration. For the rite it was required to have the sperm of both

---

[9] It seems possible that at least some of the many digestive upsets and other illnesses suffered by Louis XIV were caused by the noxious powders secreted in his food by Madame de Montespan. Cantharides was a particularly dangerous component of these powders; it is a powerful aphrodisiac—it is still used today on stud farms in order to revive the flagging sexual energies of exhausted stallions—but in small doses it is ineffective and in large doses can be fatal. It is a vesicant, a powerful irritant of the mucous membranes, and causes considerable loss of body fluid by vomiting and purging.

[10] Another of the Black Mass priests arrested at the same time as Guibourg admitted to consecrating snakes which were then killed, pickled and used for masturbation by ladies of the Court!

[11] One of de Montespan's ladies-in-waiting. A mysterious English Milord was also present at this conjuration. It has been conjectured that this was either the dissolute Duke of Buckingham or that stalwart Protestant the "Good Duke" of Monmouth, bastard son of Charles II.

sexes[12] but since des Oeillets was having her monthly period menstrual blood was used instead; the man with her went to the space between the bedrail and the wall with me (*Guibourg*) and masturbated himself. I directed his semen into the Chalice." Into the mixture of wine, semen, and menstrual blood, was put dried, powdered bat-blood and flour "to give consistancy to the concoction" which was then taken away in a glass vial by des Oeillets and her companion.

The Mortuary Masses failed; it was planned to give Louis a petition impregnated with a fatal poison so powerful as to be effective through his glove and the skin of his hand[13] but before this could be done the conspirators were arrested.

In all La Reynie arrested three hundred and sixty persons, of whom two hundred and eighteen were kept in custody. Of these only one hundred and ten were actually tried and sentenced. Some were hanged, some were exiled, others, like Vanens, were immured for life in provincial prisons, La Voisin was burnt[14]—she spent the night before her death in "scandalous debauches", refused to make the *Amende Honorable* when the tumbril carrying her to her place of execution stopped at Notre Dame, and, when finally lashed to the stake, "five or six times she pushed aside the faggots but finally the flames leaped up and enveloped her".

As La Reynie's interrogations progressed it became more and more apparent that Madame de Montespan, mistress of the King, mother of his children, was deeply involved in the crimes that had been committed. It was clear that if the trials continued the actions of La Montespan would be publicly revealed, and that the King was not prepared to endure. The trials were stopped and the matter was settled by *lettres de cachet*, the surviving prisoners—including Guibourg—being imprisoned for the rest of their lives. The conditions under which they were imprisoned were hard, and measures were taken to see that they did not

[12] Until quite recently it was commonly believed that the vaginal secretions of a sexually excited woman (which in reality have only a lubricating function) were a sort of "female sperm".

[13] No such poison existed at the time, but its existence—it was usually supposed to be a distillation of arsenic and decomposing toads—was widely believed in. Curiously enough in modern times such poisons have come into existence; nicotine and some of the organic phosphorous compounds are examples of such poisons.

[14] By a deputy executioner. The public executioner showed some delicacy and refused the job because La Voisin was an old mistress of his.

talk; "above all", said an instruction to one prison governor, "insist that the guards take measures to stop anyone hearing the rubbish that this gang is capable of saying. They have been known to speak infamies about Madame de Montespan ... warn the prisoners that they will be mercilessly punished if they say the least word on such a subject."

It was over forty years before the last of these chained, silenced prisoners met his death.[15] As for Madame de Montespan, the proprieties were observed; for ten years the King simulated a continuing friendship for her and then she retired to the country where she remained until her death some sixteen years later. Her last years were spent in an atmosphere of devoutness and Catholic piety, but, in spite of this, she grew to fear darkness, solitude and, above all, death.

[15] Guibourg survived for only three years; his remote descendants from a theological point of view, were the White Mass Priests of Boullan, a nineteenth-century French Heresiarch (see Appendix "Copulating with Cleopatra").

CHAPTER EIGHT

Priapus Rediscovered

In 1786 the Dilettanti Society—an organisation of which it was said that the nominal qualification for membership was having been in Italy, the real one being permanently in a state of drunkenness—published *An Essay on the Worship of Priapus*.

The author of the *Essay* was thirty-six-year-old Richard Payne Knight, a Member of Parliament, an associate of Charles James Fox, the owner of a sizeable fortune, the author of *An Analytical Essay on the Greek Alphabet* and a collector of classical coins, medals and bronzes.

Payne Knight's interest in the worship of Priapus, the ithyphallic garden god of classical Rome, seems to have been first aroused by the reading of a letter sent by Sir William Hamilton, the British Ambassador to the Bourbon kingdom of Naples,[1] to Sir Joseph Banks, at that time President of the Royal Society; both Hamilton and Banks were, like Payne Knight himself, members of the Dilettanti Society.

The letter in question described certain alleged survivals of classical fertility worship in popular Neapolitan Catholicism and is worthy of reproduction in full:

> "Having last year made a curious discovery, that in a Province of this Kingdom, and not fifty miles from its Capital, a sort of devotion is still paid to PRIAPUS, the obscene Divinity of the Ancients (though under another denomination), I thought it a circumstance worth recording; particularly, as it offers a fresh proof of the similitude of the Popish and Pagan Religion, so well observed by Dr. Middleton, in his celebrated Letter from Rome: and therefore I mean to deposit the

[1] Hamilton is, of course, best remembered as the elderly and cuckolded husband of Emma, Lady Hamilton, the mistress of Nelson.

authentic proofs of this assertion in the British Museum, when a proper opportunity shall offer. In the mean time I send you the following account, which, I flatter myself, will amuse you for the present, and may in future serve to illustrate those proofs.

"I had long ago discovered, that the women and children of the lower class, at Naples, and in its neighbourhood, frequently wore, as an ornament of dress, a sort of Amulets (which they imagine to be a preservative from the *mal occhii, evil eyes,* or enchantment) exactly similar to those which were worn by the ancient Inhabitants of this country for the very same purpose, as likewise for their supposed invigorating influence; and all of which have evidently a relation to the Cult of Priapus. Struck with this conformity in ancient and modern superstition, I made a collection of both the ancient and modern Amulets of this sort, and placed them together in the British Museum, where they remain. The modern Amulet most in vogue represents a hand clinched, with the point of the thumb thrust betwixt the index and middle finger; the next is a shell; and the third is a half-moon. These Amulets (except the shell, which usually worn in its natural state) are most commonly made of silver, but sometimes of ivory, coral, amber, crystal, or some curious gem, or pebble. We have a proof of the hand above described having a connection with Priapus, in a most elegant small idol of bronze of that Divinity, now in the Royal Museum of Portici, and which was found in the ruins of Herculaneum: It has an enormous Phallus, and, with an arch look and gesture, stretches out its right hand in the form above mentioned; and which probably was an emblem of consummation: and as a further proof of it, the Amulet which occurs most frequently amongst those of the Ancients (next to that which represents the simple Priapus), is such a hand united with the Phallus; of which you may see several specimens in my collection in the British Museum. One in particular, I recollect, has also the half-moon joined to the hand and Phallus; which half-moon is supposed to have an allusion to the female *menses.* The shell, or *concha veneris,* is evidently an emblem of the female part of generation. It is very natural then to suppose, that the Amulets representing the Phallus alone, so visibly indecent, may have been long out of use in this civilized capital; but I have been assured, that it is but very lately that the Priests have put an end to the wearing of such Amulets in Calabria, and other distant Provinces of this Kingdom.

"A new road having been made last year from this Capital to the Province of Abruzzo, passing through the City of Isernia (anciently belonging to the Samnites, and very populous), a person of liberal education, employed in that work, chanced to be at Isernia just at the time of the celebration of the Feast of the modern Priapus, St. Cosmo; and having been struck with the singularity of the ceremony, so very similar to that which attended the ancient Cult of the God of the Gardens, and knowing my taste for antiquities, told me of it. From this Gentleman's report, and from what I learnt on the spot from the Governor of Isernia himself, having gone to that city on purpose in the month of February last, I have drawn up the following account, which I have reason to believe is strictly true. I did intend to have been present at the Feast of St. Cosmo this year; but the indecency of this ceremony having probably transpired, from the country's having been more frequented since the new road was made, orders have been given, that the *Great Toe*[2] of the Saint should no longer be exposed. The following is the account of the Fete of St. Cosmo and Damiano, as it actually was celebrated at Isernia, on the confines of Abruzzo, in the Kingdom of Naples, so late as in the year of our Lord 1780.

"On the 27th of September, at Isernia, one of the most ancient cities of the Kingdom of Naples, situated in the Province called the Contado di Molise, and adjoining to Abruzzo, an annual Fair is held, which lasts three days. The situation of this Fair is on a rising ground, between two rivers, about half a mile from the town of Isernia; on the most elevated part of which there is an ancient church, with a vestibule. The architecture is of the style of the lower ages; and it is said to have been a church and convent belonging to the Benedictine Monks in the time of their poverty. This church is dedicated to St. Cosmus and Damianus. One of the days of the Fair, the relicks of the Saints are exposed, and afterwards carried in procession from the cathedral of the city to this church, attended by a prodigious concourse of people. In the city, and at the fair, *ex-voti* of wax, representing the male parts of generation, of various dimensions, some even of the length of a palm, are publicly offered to sale. There are also waxen vows, that represent other parts of the body mixed with them; but of these there are few in comparison of the number of the

---

[2] This seems to have been the euphemistic name bestowed by the Church on the holy relic, i.e. the dried and mummified penis of the Saint. F.K.

Priapi. The devout distributors of these vows carry a basket full of them in one hand, and hold a plate in the other to receive the money, crying aloud, 'St. Cosmo and Damiano!' If you ask the price of one, the answer is, *piu ci metti, piu meriti*: 'The more you give, the more's the merit.' In the vestibule are two tables, at each of which one of the canons of the church presides, this crying out, *Qui, si riceveno le Misse, e Litanie:* 'Here Masses and Litanies are received;' and the other, *Qui si riceveno li Voti*: 'Here the Vows are received.' The price of a Mass is fifteen Neapolitan grains, and of a Litany five grains. On each table is a large bason for the reception of the different offerings. The Vows are chiefly presented by the female sex; and they are seldom such as represent legs, arms, &c., but most commonly the male parts of generation. The person who was at this fete in the year 1780, and who gave me this account (the authenticity of every article of which has since been fully confirmed to me by the Governor of Isernia), told me also, that he heard a woman say, at the time she presented a Vow, in the shape of an erect penis, *Santo Cosimo benedetto, cosi lo voglio*: 'Blessed St. Cosmo, let it be like this;' another, *St. Cosimo, a te mi raccommendo*: 'St. Cosmo, I recommend myself to you;' and a third, *St. Cosimo, ti ringrazio*: 'St. Cosmo, I thank you.' The Vow is never presented without being accompanied by a piece of money, and is always kissed by the devotee at the moment of presentation.

"At the great altar in the church, another of its canons attends to give the holy unction, with the oil of St. Cosmo; which is prepared by the same receipt as that of the Roman Ritual, with the addition only of the prayer of the Holy Martyrs, St. Cosmus and Damianus. Those who have an infirmity in any of their members, present themselves at the great altar, and uncover the member affected (not even excepting that which is most frequently represented by the *ex-voti*); and the reverend canon anoints it, saying, *Per intercessionem beati Cosmi, liberet te ab omni malo. Amen.*

"The ceremony finishes by the canons of the church dividing the spoils, both money and wax, which must be to a very considerable amount, as the concourse at this fete is said to be prodigiously numerous.

"The oil of St. Cosmo is in high repute for its invigorating quality, when the loins, and parts adjacent, are anointed with it. No less than 1400 flasks of that oil were either expended at the altar in unctions, or charitably distributed, during this fete in the year 1780; and as it is usual for every one, who either makes use of the oil at the altar, or carries off a flask of it, to leave an alms for St. Cosmo, the ceremony of the oil becomes likewise a very lucrative one to the canons of the church."

Inspired by Hamilton's letter Payne Knight spent two years scouring classical literature and history for references to the worship of Priapus and other phallic deities. He began his *Essay* with a typically eighteenth-century declaration on his belief in the immutability of human nature[3] and then went on to tell his readers a great deal more about the worship of Priapus and the sexual aspects of ancient religion than most of them could possibly have wished to know. The *Essay* aroused a storm of criticism; Payne Knight's attempt to deal seriously with a subject which had previously, as one nineteenth-century editor pointed out, been "entirely tabooed or . . . treated in a way to hide rather than to discover the truth" awakened all the prejudices of the learned world, particularly those of the Anglican clergymen who were such an important part of that same world.

Payne Knight bowed his head to the storm; he recalled and burnt all the copies of his book he was able to lay his hands upon, bought up the few second-hand copies that came on to the market and generally did his best to ensure that the *Essay* was totally forgotten. In this he was unsuccessful; quite a lot of copies escaped the holocaust and were circulated from hand to hand amongst those interested in the subjects of fertility and phallic religion.

Seventy-nine years after its first publication the *Essay* was reprinted by Hotten. This second edition was bound up with an anonymously written *Essay on the Worship of the Generative Powers During the Middle Ages of Western Europe*; this second work was almost certainly written by an antiquarian and historian named Thomas Wright—although a certain Richard Turner and Hotten himself may have had a hand in its composition.

Thomas Wright, born in 1810, spent most of his life in great poverty.

---

[3] He wrote that "Men, considered collectively, are at all times the same animals, employing the same organs, and endowed with the same faculties: Their passions, prejudices, and conceptions, will of course be formed upon the same internal principles, although directed to various ends, and modified in various ways, by the variety of external circumstances operating upon them!"

He was educated at Trinity College, Cambridge—where he held a sizarship and supplemented his income by hack-work, writing a *History of Essex* subsequently issued in forty-eight monthly parts—and afterwards made a living by churning out historical and philological works. There are no less than one hundred and twenty-nine separate books by Wright enumerated in the catalogue of the library of the British Museum; in view of his almost unbelievable literary fecundity it is not surprising that errors abounded in his works. After his death in 1877 one obituary remarked that "nearly all his philological works are defaced by errors of transcription and extraordinary misinterpretations of Latin, early English and early French . . . but as a pioneer in the study of Anglo-Saxon and mediaeval literature and of British archaeology he deserves grateful remembrance". Like his other works his study of sex-worship in mediaeval Europe was marred by many errors and misunderstandings. Nevertheless he was the first person to establish some sort of link between the mediaeval witch-cult and the survival of classical fertility religions and he anticipated many of the conclusions of Margaret Murray, although she herself seems to have been quite unaware of Wright's contribution to the subject.

The 1865 edition of the essays of Payne Knight and Thomas Wright fell into the hands of Hargrave Jennings—a man who seems to have been the original of the character of Ezra Jennings in Wilkie Collins' novel *The Moonstone*—who saw in them, as he thought, the key to the mysteries of Freemasonry and Rosicrucianism.

As a thinker Hargrave Jennings' ideas were second or third hand; as a writer he was tenth rate. Nevertheless, his conceptions of sexual symbolism exerted some influence on the occultists of his own and succeeding generations.

Jennings, born in 1817, published the first edition of his *The Rosicrucians, Their Rites and Mysteries* when he was fifty-three years old. In ponderous, involved and often obscure language the book attempted to prove that, particularly, the mysteries of the Rose Cross were mysteries of sex and, more generally, that sexual symbolism was a universal language the interpretation of which led to an understanding of the real significance of ancient and oriental art and mythology. Like some proto-Freudian Jennings saw the penis and the vagina in almost everything; thus cromlechs, dolmens, round towers in Ireland and, indeed, everything remotely convex in shape were all seen as symbolic male organs, and, similarly, anything which could be twisted by the imagination into the form of a hole or a cavity was seen as a symbolic vagina. Jennings' sexual obsessions—and the darkly convoluted prose in which he expressed them—are well illustrated by the following extract from his *Rosicrucians* in which he tried to prove (a) that England's premier order of chivalry, the order of the Garter, was originally concerned with sexual mysteries, (b) that the Garter was not a garter but, of all things, a sanitary towel, and (c) that the symbolic roses of the Order signified menstruation.[4] He wrote:

"But to return to the import of the title of the Order of the Garter. This is a point very engrossing to heralds, antiquaries, and all persons who are interested in the history, traditions, and archaeology of our country. The origin of the Order would be trivial, ridiculous, and unbelievable, if it be only thought due to the picking up of a lady's garter. It is impossible that the great name and fame of this 'Garter' could have arisen alone from this circumstance. The Garter, on the contrary, is traceable from the times of King Arthur, to whose fame throughout Europe there was no limit in his own period. This we shall soon show conclusively from the accounts of the Garter by Elias Ashmole, who was 'Garter King of Arms', and who was one of its most painstaking and enlightened historians; besides himself being a faithful and conscientious expositor and adherent of the hermetic science. The 'Round Table' of King Arthur—the 'mirror of chivalry' —supplies the model of all the miniature tables, or tablets, which bear the contrasted roses—red and white, as they were originally (and implying the female *discus* and its accidents)—with the noble 'vaunt', or motto, round them—'Evil to him', or the same to him, 'who thinks ill' of these natural (and yet these magical) feminine circumstances, the character of which our readers will by this time not fail to recognise. The glory of woman and the punishment of woman after the Fall, as indicated in Genesis, go hand in hand. It was in honour of Woman, and to raise into dignity the expression of the condemned 'means' (until sanctified and reconciled by the intervention of the 'S.S.', or of the Holy Spirit, or of the Third Person of the Trinity), which her mark and betrayal, but which produced the world in producing Man, and which saved it in the person of the Redeemer, 'born of Woman'. It is to glorify typically and mystically this 'fleshly vehicle', that the Order of the 'Garter'—or 'Garder'—

[4] "Flowers" was, of course, a Victorian euphemism for menstruation.

that keeps it was instituted. The Knights of the Garter stand sentinel, in fact, over 'Woman's Shame', at the same time that they proclaim her 'Glory', in the pardoned sense. These strange ideas are strictly those of the old Rosicrucians, or Brethren of the 'Red Cross', and we only reproduce them. The early writers saw no indecency in speaking openly of these things, which are usually hidden away.

"If the blackness or darkness of 'Matter', or of the 'Mother of Nature', is figured in another respect in the belongings of this famous feminine Order, instituted for the glory of woman. Curious armorists, skilled in the knowledge of the deep symbolism with which the old heralds suffused their illustrations or emblazonments, will remember that *black* is a feature in the Order of the Garter; and that, among figures and glyphs and hints the most profound, the 'Black Book', containing the original constitutions of the Order,—from which 'Black Book' comes the important 'Black Rod',—was *lost* before the time of Henry the Fifth.

"Elias Ashmole mentions the Order in the following terms: 'We may ascend a step higher; and if we may give credit to Harding, it is recorded that King Arthur paid St. George, whose red cross is the badge of the Garter, the most particular honours; for he advanced his effigy in one of his banners, which was about two hundred years after his martyrdom, and very early for a country so remote from Cappadocia to have him in reverence and esteem.'

". . . The material whereof the Garter was composed at first is an *arcanum*, nor is it described by any writer before Polydore Virgil, and he only speaks of it in general terms. The Garter was originally without a motto. As to the appointments of the Order, we may gain the most authentic idea of them from the effigies of some of the first knights. Sir William Fitz-warin was buried on the north side of the chancel of the church of Wantage, in Berkshire, in the thirty-fifth year of the reign of King Edward the Third. Sir Richard Pembridge, who was a Knight of the Garter, of the time of Edward the Third, lies on the south side of the cathedral of Hereford. The monument of Sir Simon Burley, beheaded A.D. 1388, was raised in the north wall, near the choir of St. Paul's, London. It is remarkable that Du Chesne, a noted French historian, is the source from which we derive the acknowledgment that it was by the special invocation of St. George that King Edward the Third gained the Battle of Cressy; which 'lying deeply in his remembrance, he founded', continues Du

Chesne, 'a chapel within the Castle of Windsor, and dedicated it in gratitude to the Saint, who is the Patron of England'. The first example of a Garter that occurs is on the before-mentioned monument of Sir Francis Burley; where, on the front, towards the head, are his own arms, impaling his first wife's set within a garter. This wants the impress, or motto. Another shield of arms having the same impalement placed below the feet, is surrounded with a collar of 'S.S.', of the same form with that about his neck. It was appointed by King Henry the Eighth, and embodied in the Statutes of the Order, that the collar should be composed of pieces of gold, in fashion of Garters; the ground enamelled blue, and the letters of the motto gold. In the midst of each garter *two roses* were to be placed, the innermost enamelled red, and the outermost white; contrarily, in the next garter, the innermost Rose enamelled white, and the outermost red, and so alternately; but of later times, these roses are wholly red. The number of these Garters is so many as to be the ordained number of the sovereign and knights-companions. At the institution they were twenty-six, being fastened together with as many knots of gold. And this mode hitherto has continued invariable; nor ought the collar to be adorned or enriched with precious stones (as the 'George' may be), such being prohibited by the laws of the Order. At what time the collar of 'S.S.', came into England is not fully determined; but it would seem that it came at least three hundred years since. The collar of 'S.S.' means the Magian, or First Order, or brotherhood. In the Christian arrangements, it stands for the 'Holy Spirit', or 'Third Person of the Trinity'. In the Gnostic talismans, it is displayed as the bar, curved with the triple 'S'. Refer to the 'Cnuphis Abraxoids' occurring in our book, for we connect the collar of 'S.S.' with the theology of the Gnostics.

"That the Order of the Garter is feminine, and that its origin is an apotheosis of the 'Rose', and of a certain singular physiological fact connected with woman's life, is proven in many ways—such as the double garters, red and white; the twenty-six knights, representing the double thirteen lunations in the year, or their twenty-six mythic 'dark and light' changes of 'night and day'. 'But how is all this magic and sacred in the estimate of the Rosicrucians?' an inquirer will naturally ask. The answer to all this is very ample and satisfactory; but particulars must be left to the sagacity of the querient himself, because propriety does not admit of explanation. Suffice it to say, that it is one of the most curious subjects which has occupied the attention of antiquaries. That archaeological puzzle, the 'Round Table of King Arthur', is a perfect display of this whole subject of the origin of the 'Garter'; it springs directly from it, being the same object as that enclosed by the mythic garter, 'garder', or 'girther'.

"King Edward the Third chose the Octave of the 'Purification of the Blessed Virgin' for the inauguration of his Order. Andrew du Chesne declares that this new Order was announced on 'New Year's Day, A.D. 1344'. There were jousts holden in honour of it on the 'Monday after the Feast of St. Hilary following—January 19th'. There are variations in the histories as to the real period of the institution of the Garter; most historians specifying the year 1349. Ashmole states that a great supper was ordered to inaugurate the solemnity of the institution, and that a Festival was to be annually held at *Whitsuntide* (which means the 'S.S.'); that King Edward erected a particular building in the Castle, and therein placed a table ('Round Table') of 200 feet diameter, giving to the *building itself* the name of the 'Round Table'. He appropriated £100 per week—an enormous sum in those days—for the maintenance of this table. In imitation of this, the French King, Philip de Valois, instituted a 'Round Table' at his court. Some say that he had an intention of instituting an order of knighthood upon the same 'feminine subject', but that he was anticipated by King Edward; which shows that it was something more than an accident and a mere garter which inspired the idea of this Rose forming the mystery. The knights were denominated 'Equites Aureae Periscelidis'. King Edward the Third had such veneration for the Blessed Virgin Mary, that he ordained that the habit of his Knights of the Garter should be worn on the days of her Five Solemnities. Elias Ashmole states that the original of the Statutes of Institution had wholly perished long before his time. There was a transcript existing in the reign of Henry the Fifth, in an old book called *Registrum Ordinis Chartaceum*. Though the Order was instituted so long ago as in the year 1344, it was not till the reign of Charles the Second that the Knights were empowered to wear the star they use at present embroidered on their coats. The rays are the 'glory' round the 'Red Cross'.

"Sir John Froissart, the only writer of the age that treats of this institution, assigns no such origin as the picking up of the Countess of Salisbury's garter; nor does he adduce the words of the motto of

5. Bishop C. W. Leadbeater—see "The Bishop and the Boys".

Hulton Picture Library

6. *Satan*—a pen and ink sketch by Crowley.

the Garter as having been spoken by King Edward the Third when encountering the laughter of his court, and assuring them that he would make the proudest eventually wear it as the most illustrious badge. There can be only one conclusion as to the character of the investment which was picked up; and which article of dress makes it clear that the Countess of Salisbury—or the lady, whoever she may be, who has succeeded in becoming so celebrated in the after ages of chivalry—should have rather been at home, *and at rest*, than inattentive to saltatory risks in engaging in a dance at a crowded court. There was no mention of this supposed picking up of a garter for 200 years, nor was there anything referring to such an origin occurring in any of our historians other than Sir John Froissart, until Polydore Virgil took occasion to say something of it in his notices of the origin of the Order. In the original Statutes of the Order (which is a most important point in the inquiry), there is not the least conjecture expressed, nor does the compiler of that tract entitled *Institutio clarissimi Ordinis Militaris a praenobili Subligaculo nuncupata*, to the *Black Book of the Garter*, let fall any passage on which to ground the conclusions about the Garter. Polydore does not mention whose garter it was; this he cautiously declines to do. He says that it was either the Queen's, or that of the King's mistress,—meaning Joan, Countess of Salisbury, with whom it was supposed the King was in love, and whom he relieved when she was bravely holding out for him against the Scots, in her Castle of Wark-upon-Tweed; but she was certainly no mistress of the King's, in the injurious and unworthy sense. It is to be particularly noticed that the Latin words *subliGAR, subligaculum*, mean, *not* a 'garter', but 'breeches, drawers, or trousers'. It was therefore not a garter for the leg, but a cincture for the body, which was thus picked up publicly, and elevated for honour, as such an unexpected illustrious object; one around which the *most* noble knights were to take enthusiastic oaths of devoted homage. Now, unless there had been some most extraordinary meaning under all this (lying under the apparent, but only apparent, indecency), such an idolising could never have occurred, and the whole occurrence ages ago would have been laughed into oblivion, carrying the sublime honours of the 'Garter' with it. Instead of this, the Garter is the highest token of greatness the Sovereign of England can bestow, and it is contended for and accepted with eager pride by Princes. 'Subligaculum, *breeches, drawers, trousers*'. 'Subligatus, *cinctured, bound*, etc., *wearing drawers*'. The origin of the 'Garter' is proven in this word not to be a garter at all.

"It is most generally supposed that it was on January 19th 1344, that King Edward instituted his famous Order of the Garter. This period, it will be perceived, was almost within an octave of the Purification of the Blessed Virgin Mary; under whose patronage, and under the guardianship of St. George on earth (St. Michael in Heaven; both these Saints being the same, with earthly and spiritual attributes refluent respectively), King Edward placed his profoundly religious Order. The whole was a revival of the 'Round Table' of King Arthur, or the apotheosised female *discus* in certain mythical aspects. To confirm us in our assertion of the feminine origin of the Order of the Garter—which many in their ignorance have questioned we may state that one of the old chroniclers, though somewhat guardedly, as befitted those of whom he spoke, declares that the lady who let fall her garter, or 'garder', was the *Queen*, who had suddenly left the courtly assembly in some confusion, and was hastening to her own apartments, followed by the King, who, when the spectators avoided lifting the article, being aware to whom it belonged, raised it himself, and called aloud, not the words of the motto of the Garter, which the historian says that the Queen herself spoke, but an intimation that he would, spite of their laughter, 'make the proudest of the refusers wear the rejected cincture as the grandest badge that knighthood ever bore.' Rightly viewed, this little evaded incident —which we desire to restore to its proper place in the knowledge of Englishmen—is the most conclusive proof of King Edward's nobleness and greatness of heart, and of his chivalrous, gallant delicacy; an instance admirable to all future generations, and worthy of the most enduring applause. The reader finally is referred to our observations in a previous part of our book for evidence in our justification. In the foregoing we give the Rosicrucian view of the origin of the 'Garter'. It is the centre-point round which have converged the noblest ideas and the most illustrious individuals in the world. It is still the proudest and most solemn badge, and the chiefest English knightly dignity. Strangely enough, too, this whole history of the 'Garter' teaches, as its moral, the greatness of the proper independence of shame, and the holiness of its unconsciousness."[5]

---

[5] Jennings also suggested that the motto of the Order, *honi soit qui mal y pense*,

My readers may well feel that the logomachy, specious reasoning and incomprehensible hinting displayed in the passage I have reproduced above are clear indications that the works of Jennings are quite unworthy of any serious attention. This was not, however, the opinion of Victorian occultists; Theosophists, mesmerists, spiritualists and esoterically inclined freemasons read Jennings' *Rosicrucians* and received, as they thought, illumination. A pirated version of the book appeared in the United States and a German translation of it was also made. I have no doubt that the last-mentioned work did a great deal to clear the ground for the German sexual Templarism of the early twentieth century.

should read *yoni* (i.e. vagina) *soit qui mal y pense*. For some description of Jennings' involvement with masonic Rosicrucianism see my *Ritual Magic in England*.

PART THREE

Sexuality and Magic in the Modern World

CHAPTER NINE
Templarism and Sex Magic

The original Order of the Temple had been founded in 1118 by two French Knights as a military-monastic fraternity with the twin functions of defending the newly established Crusader Kingdom of Jerusalem against the infidel and protecting poor pilgrims. At first its brothers were subject to a most rigorous discipline, for they not only took oaths of poverty, chastity and obedience but submitted themselves to the austere Cistercian version of the Rule of St. Benedict. With time, however, the Order became rich, and with wealth came an inevitable relaxation of physical and moral discipline; it is probable that this tendency owed at least something to the Templars' contacts with the sophisticated civilisations of mediaeval Islam.

As early as 1238 Pope Gregory IX had suspected the Templars of heresy, and in 1272 a Council of the Church declared the entire Order to be urgently in need of reform. Nothing was done until 1307, when the King of France, Philip le Bel, launched a persecution of the Templars that finally resulted in the complete suppression of the Order on the grounds that it was deeply infected with sodomy, bestiality and, worst of all, heresy.

Between 1307 and 1314 there were a whole series of Templar trials at which individual Knights were charged with almost every possible offence against the laws of God and man. There were, however, five offences included in almost all the indictments:

(1) The administering of the sacrament of penance by a layman.
(2) Buggery and the use of the anal kiss.
(3) The defiling of the Crucifix by spitting, urinating or trampling upon it.

(4) The worship of an idol named Baphomet, usually described as being either a skull, a human head, or three heads.
(5) The omission of the words of institution (*Hoc est corpus meum* etc.) from the Mass.

The first accusation is an odd one, but it does seem to link the Templars with the practices of the Albigensians and other mediaeval Manichee groups. The same is true of the second charge for, rightly or wrongly, the Church believed sodomy to be intimately associated with dualistic heresy—indeed the word "bugger" is derived from the Bogomil heretics who were particularly numerous in mediaeval Bulgaria. As for the anal kiss this was, according to the confessions of the accused Knights, given at the initiation of a new member of the Order and was exchanged between the candidate and his Preceptor.[1]

Rationalistic explanations of the third accusation were given by historians of the last century. Some claimed that the candidate was ordered to trample on the Crucifix so that he might prove his Christian fortitude by refusing to obey. Others suggested that defiling the Crucifix was an indication of the Order's loathing of the instrument of Christ's suffering. Both explanations fail; the first because in all the Templar trials there are only two records of a candidate defying the order, the second because, if true, it would in itself be a proof of heresy —to regard the Cross, the instrument of the triumphant redemptive death of Christ, with hatred would have been indicative of a Docetic Christology, not Catholic Christianity.

The fourth accusation is the most curious. The suggestion that the name Baphomet was a corruption of Mahomet has been frequently made but is almost certainly incorrect; mediaeval Inquisitors may have been ignorant of the finer points of the religion of Islam, but not so ignorant that they were unaware of the name of its Prophet! The most interesting explanation of the origin of the name was given by the nineteenth-century orientalist Joseph Von Hammer. His arguments, and the evidence he based them upon, were splendidly summarised by J. C. Hotten and Thomas Wright in their *Essay on the Worship of the Generative Powers in the Middle Ages*:

[1] An interesting light was thrown on the general morals of the Order by a Knight named Theobald de Taverniac who completely denied that he and his fellows were guilty of sodomy. The charge was ridiculous, he said, "because they could have very beautiful and courtly women whenever they liked, and they did have them frequently when they were rich and powerful enough".

"Von Hammer has described twenty-four images ... which it must be acknowledged answer very well to the descriptions of their idol given by the Templars ... Most of them have beards and tolerably fierce countenances. Among those given by Von Hammer are seven which present only a head, and two with two faces, backwards and forwards, as described in some of the depositions.[2] These two appear to be intended for female heads ... The most interesting of the coffers described by Von Hammer ... is of calcareous stone, nine inches long by seven broad, and four and a half deep, with a lid about two inches thick. It was found in Burgundy. On the lid is sculptured a figure, naked, with a head-dress resembling that given to Cybele in ancient monuments, holding up a chain with each hand, and surrounded with various symbols, the sun and moon above, the star and the pentacle below, and under the feet a human skull. The chains are explained by Von Hammer as representing the chains of aeons of the Gnostics. On the four sides of the coffer we see a series of figures engaged in the performance of various ceremonies ... which Von Hammer considers as belonging to the rites of the Gnostics and Ophians. The offering of a calf figures prominently among these rites ... In the middle of the scene on one side, a human skull is seen, raised upon a pole. On another side an androgynous figure is represented as the object of worship of two candidates for initiation, who wear masks apparently of a cat, and whose form of adoration reminds us of the kiss enacted at the initiation of the Templars. This group reminds us, too, of the pictures of the orgies in the worship of Priapus, as represented on Roman monuments ... on an impartial comparison we can hardly doubt that these curious objects ... have been intended for use in some secret and mysterious rites, and the arguments by which Von Hammer attempts to show that they belonged to the Templars seem at least to be very plausible. Several of the objects represented upon them, even the skull, are alluded to in some of the confessions of the Templars ... There is, however, another circumstance connected with these objects which appears to

[2] Thus Guillaume de Arblay said that when he was received into the Order there was placed on the altar a head with two faces, a terrible look and a silver beard. He told his inquisitors that he believed the object to be a holy relic, the head of one of the eleven thousand virgin martyrs of Cologne. It is possible that Guillaume put down the "terrible look" to either virginity or martyrdom, but I cannot surmise why he thought the lady should have had two faces and a silver beard!

furnish an almost irresistible confirmation of Von Hammer's theory. Most of them bear inscriptions, written in Arabic, Greek and Roman characters. . . . the coffers . . . contain a nearly uniform inscription in Arabic characters which, according to the interpretation given by Von Hammer, contains a religious formula. The Arabic characters, he says, have been copied by a European, and not very skilful, carver, who did not understand them, from an Eastern original, and the inscriptions contain corruptions and errors which either arose from this circumstance, or, . . . may have been introduced designedly, for the purpose of concealing the meaning from the uninitiated. A good example of this inscription surrounds the lid of the coffer found in Burgundy . . . the word under the feet of the figure . . . is nothing more than the Latin *cantate* expressed in Arabic letters. The words with which this *cantate* begins are written above the head of the figure . . . *Jella Sidna*, i.e. O God, our Lord! The formula itself commences on the right side, and the first part of it reads *Houve Mete Zonar feseba B. Mounkir teaala tiz*. There is no such word in Arabic as *mete*, and Von Hammer considers it to be simply the Greek word *metis*, wisdom . . . He considers that the name Baphomet is derived from the Greek words *Baphe Metis*, i.e. the baptism of Metis, and that in its application it is equivalent with the name Mete itself. He has further shown, we think conclusively, that Baphomet, instead of being a corruption of Mahomet, was a name known among the Gnostic sects in the East. The rest of the formula is given on the other side of the figure, but as the inscription here presents several corruptions, we will give Von Hammer's translation . . . of a more correct copy of the formula inscribed on a bowl or goblet preserved in the museum at Vienna . . . 'Let Mete be exalted, who causes things to bud and blossom! He is our root; it (the root) is one and seven; abjure (the faith) and abandon thyself to all pleasures.'"

If Von Hammer's interpretations were correct there seems to be no doubt that the Templars were guilty of at least some of the crimes of which they were accused, that their connections with the Middle East had brought them into contact with a surviving Gnostic cult and that the inquisitors were justified in their charges of heresy. Von Hammer was a philologist, however, and all philologists, metaphorically speaking, live on the edge of a high cliff; it may be that Von Hammer fell over it—an interesting experience recently undergone, so it seems, by Dr. John Allegro of sacred mushroom fame—and that the Templars were as innocent of heresy as most historians of the last century believed them to have been, harmless victims of the Christian monarchs who first confiscated the Templars' estates and then burnt the deprived owners at the stake. Whatever the truth of the matter, it is undeniable that the accusations against the Order of the Temple led to its suppression, after which it was almost forgotten for over four hundred years.

It was the explosive eighteenth-century growth of European speculative freemasonry that led to a revival of interest in the Knights Templar. Freemasonry had been introduced into Europe from Great Britain, firstly by Jacobite exiles, many of them Catholic—it was not until 1738 that the Pope condemned masonry—and then by pro-Hanoverian English merchants who founded new Lodges which were, unlike the Jacobite Lodges, recognised by the Grand Lodge of England. Within a few years the Europeans, particularly the French, were founding their own Lodges, taking their rituals, their mystic words (such as Mahabone) and their secret signs and steps from the English Lodges whom they were imitating.

Now, to both the non-mason and to some masons the most curious thing about masonry is that its secrets are no secrets; I do not mean by this that the so-called secrets are available to all who care to spend enough money on books at any masonic bookseller, although this is, of course, true, but that the secret rituals, passwords and steps of the craft are almost meaningless. That if there *is* a real secret at the heart of masonry (and many whose opinions I respect affirm that there is) it lies not in these things but in something much deeper which is hidden from him who has not reached the core of the masonic initiation—after all an unutterable secret is, by definition, unutterable! The English masons of the eighteenth century appear to have remained comparatively unworried by this problem, for while the Jacobites used their Lodges as covers for political conspiracy, the pro-Hanoverians of Grand Lodge were content to use the masonic rites as an excuse for drunkenness and debauch.

The more intellectual members of the French Lodges, however, gave considerable thought to the matter. Surely, they felt, masonry must have *some* inner meaning and purpose besides the re-enactment of mediaeval legends about King Solomon and a murdered builder named Hiram. To some the history of the Knights Templar seemed to provide the answer; the Templars had been great builders, their strangely-shaped round Churches famous throughout Christendom, and the symbolism of the masonic craft-degrees centred around the building of the Temple of Solomon—it was difficult for the eighteenth-century mind to believe that this was mere coincidence. The Order of the Temple, it was affirmed, had not been completely destroyed by the inquisitors, it had "gone underground" and survived as the masonic fraternity!

Within a few years several occult-masonic organisations had appeared, each claiming a Templar origin for itself. In Scotland there was the Royal Order, alleged to have enjoyed an uninterrupted existence since the fourteenth century when it was founded, so the story went, by two French Templars who had fled for refuge to Scotland. In Germany and France was the Stricte Observance, under the control of mysterious "Unknown Superiors" and demanding the unconditional submission and obedience of all other masonic groups. In England there were many "Templar encampments"—independent, quasi-masonic bodies, usually working in close association with Chapters of Rose-Croix masons. A little later a new Order of the Temple appeared in France; it used the *Levitikon*, an unorthodox version of the Gospel of St. John, as its holy book and relied upon an eighteenth-century forgery, the Charter of Larmenius, to prove its Templar origins.

The last of this long line of occult Templar organisations, the *Ordo Templi Orientis*, usually referred to as the O.T.O., was founded at the beginning of the present century by Karl Kellner, a wealthy German iron master who was also an occultist and a high-grade freemason. Its original members seem to have all come from the ranks of the German Lodge of the *Ancient and Primitive Rite of Memphis and Mizraim*.

The ninety degrees of the masonic Rite of Memphis and the ninety-seven degrees of the Rite of Mizraim were both of early nineteenth-century origin. The membership of both organisations was small and the Rites had fallen into the hands of an Englishman, John Yarker of Manchester, who unified them under the name of *Memphis and Mizraim*. There is no doubt that Yarker was prepared to confer high-sounding masonic degrees on anyone who was prepared to pay his fees and that by 1900 *Memphis and Mizraim* had become a fee-snatching racket of the very worst type.

In 1902 Yarker, who was in considerable financial difficulties, sold a charter authorising the establishment of a German Grand Lodge of *Memphis and Mizraim* to three occultists named, Klein, Hartmann and

Reuss. This Grand Lodge was duly established in Berlin and began to publish a magazine called the *Oriflamme*. I have been unable to trace early copies of this periodical but I believe that the contents of these issues were purely masonic and that no mention was made of the O.T.O. By 1904, however, both the O.T.O. and Kellner began to be mentioned by name in the *Oriflamme* and references were made to a "great secret" that was in the keeping of the Order. The nature of this great secret was made clear in a jubilee edition of the *Oriflamme* published in 1912:

> "Our Order possesses the KEY which opens up all Masonic and Hermetic secrets, namely, the teaching of sexual magic, and this teaching explains, without exception, all the secrets of Freemasonry and all systems of religion."

Kellner claimed that the sexual magic taught by himself and his Templar Order had been derived from three oriental adepts, one Arab and two Hindu, but a more immediate source may have been a group of the European followers of an American sex-orientated occultist named Paschal Beverley Randolph. Randolph, a mulatto, suffered from an acute persecution complex and took great care to conceal the unusual nature of his sexual teachings under a cloak of symbolism. Even some of his closest associates seem to have had no knowledge of them, and it is significant that R. Swinburne Clymer, who eventually inherited the chieftainship of the numerous occult organisations founded by Randolph—most of them existing only on paper—regarded any form of sexual magic as sheer Satanism. Nevertheless, Randolph did pass on his sexual teachings to a trusted group of his French disciples. I think it probable that it was from one or more members of this French group that Kellner derived the sexual techniques used in the O.T.O.—although of course, there is no doubt that he did meet Tantrics in the course of his oriental wanderings. An occult group ultimately deriving from Randolph had survived in France until the present day, and it is interesting to note that its sex-magic techniques are more or less identical with those of the O.T.O.

The O.T.O. was organised in nine operative grades—there was a tenth degree, but this was purely administrative in its functions, "X°" being a title given to the head of each national section of the Order. The grades up to and including the sixth were ritually conferred, the first three of them bearing a marked resemblance to the three degrees of Craft Masonry and the last three being largely concerned with the Order's unorthodox interpretation of masonic symbolism. The seventh, eighth and ninth grades dealt with sexual magic; there were no rituals for these degrees, initiates were simply handed written material giving the appropriate instructions. In the eighth degree was taught a peculiar type of autosexual activity—I can only describe it as magical masturbation—which, so far as I know, has no oriental equivalent, but the heterosexual magic taught in the ninth degree was quite similar to that of the left-handed Tantricism of Bengal.

A large number of manuscripts written by O.T.O. initiates have survived. These deal in detail with the sexual techniques of the Order's ninth degree and there is no difficulty in understanding them once one realises the nature of the code in which they were written. This code was drawn from the traditional technical terminology of alchemy. The penis was referred to as *the athanor*, the semen as *the Serpent* or occasionally, *the blood of the red lion*, while the vagina was called *the cucurbite* or *the retort*. The secretions that lubricate the vagina were called *the menstruum of the Gluten*, sometimes abbreviated to *the menstruum*, and the mixture of semen with vaginal lubricant was termed *the First Matter* or, when supposedly transmuted by the magical powers of the participants in the rite, the *Amrita*, or *Elixir*.

The initiates of the IX° claimed that success in almost any magical operation, from the invocation of a god to "procuring a great treasure" could be achieved by the application of the appropriate sexual technique. Thus to invoke the powers of a god into themselves they mentally concentrated on the god throughout their sexual intercourse, building up the form of the deity in their imaginations and attempting to imbue it with life. At the moment of orgasm they identified themselves with the imagined form, mentally seeing their own bodies and that of the god blending into one. If they wanted to "charge" a talisman—a magical charm designed to achieve some desired end, such as love or fame—they anointed it with the *Amrita* resulting from their sexual act,[3] during which act they had concentrated on the talisman and

---

[3] The late Aleister Crowley owned a talisman called Segelah (it was intended "for finding a great treasure" and was taken from the mediaeval Abramelin system of magic) that had been consecrated in this way. I have seen it, and it is a most unpleasant looking object, smeared with dried semen and menstrual blood. Crowley never succeeded in "finding a great treasure" except, as his followers

its purpose. A similar method was used to imbue with magical power a letter written for some particular purpose; the power was supposedly augmented if the *Amrita* was used to trace an appropriate symbol on the envelope, e.g. if the letter was an application for money the sigil of the god Jupiter was drawn on the envelope.

After the death of Karl Kellner in 1905 Theodor Reuss assumed the Headship of the O.T.O. and, under his leadership, the Order enjoyed a modest but rapid growth, extending its activities to Denmark, France, Luxemburg and England.

Reuss had lived an interesting life. He was the offspring of a German father and an English mother and in his mother's country had experienced a certain amount of professional success as a singer in music-halls and at all-male smoking concerts. He seems to have combined this artistic career with spying for the Prussian secret police on German socialist exiles in London—his attention was particularly concentrated on the children of Karl Marx. In the 'eighties he had joined the Socialist League, a revolutionary organisation founded as an orthodox Marxist counterblast to H. M. Hyndman's semi-reformist Social Democratic Federation,[4] and had become a member of its executive committee, presumably in order to spy upon the activities of Karl Marx's daughter Eleanor Marx-Aveling, who was also upon the executive. No doubt Reuss hoped to ingratiate himself with the Marx family and thus worm his way into the confidence of the German Social Democrats but he was disappointed, for both Eleanor Marx and her rascally lover, Edward Aveling, took a strong dislike to him. Eleanor found Reuss vulgar; she even went to the length of writing a letter to Karl Kautsky, the German socialist leader, complaining of the coarseness of the songs that Reuss had sung at a concert given in aid of the funds of the Socialist League. A few months later the League's paper, the *Commonweal*, published an article exposing Reuss as a police spy and shortly afterwards he was expelled from the organisation.

would say, in a metaphorical sense. The present owner of the talisman, however, has used it as a means of discovering rare books, seemingly with great success.

[4] The Socialist League was later captured by an anarchist faction, after which event it was regarded with loathing by all orthodox Marxists. In its early years, however, it was almost completely Marxist, with Engels indulging in a good deal of behind-the-scenes string pulling. William Morris was one of the League's founders, and although he is today generally regarded as a libertarian (on strength of *News from Nowhere*) at the time he described himself as being "with Marx contra mundum".

There is little trace of Reuss between his expulsion from the Socialist League and his attainment of the Headship of the O.T.O. in 1905, but it seems probable that he earned his living by a combination of singing, spying, and running a dubious export-import business.[5] He seems to have had a complete contempt for the conventions of his time, and under his chieftainship the O.T.O. quite openly proclaimed that it practised sexual magic—under Kellner it had been much more discreet in its public pronouncements.

[5] He also enjoyed a brief but successful career as a war-correspondent.

CHAPTER TEN

Enter Baphomet

In April 1911 George Cecil Jones, an industrial chemist of Basingstoke, sued a certain de Wend Fenton for libel. Fenton, who was later to be fined for sending indecent articles through the mails, had published an article in his paper, *The Looking Glass*, in which it was alleged that Jones had a sodomitical relationship with Aleister Crowley the poet and magician.

Neither plaintiff nor defendant called Crowley as a witness, for while Jones thought that Crowley might behave in such an outrageous way in the witness-box that the jury's sympathy would be alienated, Fenton feared that his own unsuccessful attempt at blackmailing Crowley, which he had made a few months earlier, would be exposed. Nevertheless the action turned into what was, to all intents and purposes, a trial of the morals of Aleister Crowley. The Judge and jury seem to have decided that these were thoroughly reprehensible—they were particularly shocked by the fact that the initial letters of certain marginal notes in Crowley's *Ambrosii Magi Hortus Rosarum* formed improper words.[1]

Amongst those who gave evidence of Crowley's supposedly disgraceful morals and behaviour was S. L. MacGregor Mathers, the Chief of an occult organisation called the Hermetic Order of the Golden Dawn. In the course of his examination by Counsel Mathers claimed,

---

[1] *Ambrosii Magi Hortus Rosarum* was written in 1902 but not published until 1906 when it was included in Volume II of Crowley's Collected *Works*. The marginal notes which gave such offence to the High Court were in Latin and read; Pater *I*ubet Scientiam Scribe, Culpa *U*rbium Nota Terrae, Femina Rapta Inspirat Gaudium, Adest Rosa Secreta Eros, and Quid Umbratur *In* Mari.

almost casually, that he was the head of the legendary Rosicrucian Order and that Crowley was a black magician who had stolen some of his secrets. Almost every occult crank and lunatic in Europe seems to have been infuriated by this statement, for each of them sincerely believed that he, and he alone, was the genuine head of the Rosicrucians. As Crowley was obviously Mathers' enemy, all their sympathies were with the former, and from all over the world came charters and letters conferring mysterious esoteric dignities upon him. Crowley remarked that if he had worn all the medals and badges which had been awarded to him their weight would have prevented him from walking! Crowley also had to suffer visits from some of these supposed Rosicrucians. One of them was Theodor Reuss, and at his invitation Crowley joined the O.T.O.—he was never one to refuse a dignity, however trivial he thought it—although at first he did not realise that the organisation was anything more than yet another masonic society.

In 1912 Reuss revisited Crowley and accused him of revealing the innermost secret of the IX° of the O.T.O. in one of his published works. Crowley was astonished; he pointed out to Reuss that he wasn't even a member of the IX° of the O.T.O. and so was hardly likely to be in a position to reveal its secrets. Silently Reuss produced a copy of Crowley's *Book of Lies*[2] and opened it at page 46, the *Ritual of the Star Sapphire*, which begins "Let the Adept be armed with his *Magick Rood* and provided with his Mystic Rose" and clearly has a sexual import. Crowley was thunderstruck; in a flash the sexual magic of the O.T.O. was understood by him. For hours the two Adepts talked. It was agreed that Crowley should become the head of a new order to be called the *Mysteria Mystica Maxima*, an English subsidiary of the O.T.O.

[2] Or so Crowley said. The curious thing is, however, that the *Book of Lies* was not published until 1913, almost a year after Reuss had made his visit. Either there had been a slip in time and Reuss and Crowley were a year in advance of everyone else (as Crowley seems to imply in his *Confessions*) or, rather more likely, to say the least, it was some other passage in Crowley's writings that Reuss felt betrayed the sexual secrets of the IX°. A third possibility is that the title page of the *Book of Lies* gave a false date of publication and that it was in reality published in 1912. There is some evidence that this may have been the case, for at the back of the book was an advertisement for Crowley's other books (charmingly headed "The Excreta of Mr. Aleister Crowley") and the only number of Crowley's magazine *The Equinox* advertised was No. VII, published in March 1912. If the *Book of Lies* had been published in 1913 one would have expected the advertised issue of *The Equinox* to have been either Number IX or Number X.

Crowley subsequently visited Berlin, where he was given copies of all the O.T.O. instructional manuscripts, had the impressive title of *King of Ireland, Iona and all the Britains within the Sanctuary of the Gnosis* conferred upon him, and took the name Baphomet as his new magical motto.

After his return to England Crowley made a few desultory experiments with the techniques of the IX° and issued a Manifesto which not only assured would-be members of the O.T.O. that they would "become partakers of the current of Universal Life in Liberty, Beauty, Harmony and Love which flames within the heart of the O.T.O." but promised them that they would be given "practical assistance in life ... so that even if originally poor, they become well able to afford the comparatively high fees of the VII°, VIII° and IX°". At about the same time either Crowley or one of his disciples produced a verse-ritual[3] published in mutilated form in *Equinox* X, designed to be used as a prelude to the sexual intercourse of the IX°. As this ritual contains some points of interest I reproduce it below—its first printing in unexpurgated form:

THE SUPREME RITUAL

Let a feast be made by the Officers of the Temple. This Temple, into which they then retire, may be any convenient place. An altar is necessary; also a vessel of wine; otherwise as may be appointed by them: e.g. the robes, etc. as said in *Liber Legis*.[1] The Officers are two in number and they seek Nuit and Hadit through the vagina and the penis. To conceal themselves, they are disguised as Isis and Osiris.

(*The officers meet and clasp hands above the altar. Any preliminary operations, such as opening, banishing, etc., are now done by O., who returns, and they again greet, but as initiates.*)

---

[3] Crowley himself said that the ritual was found in the papers of Adam Weishaupt, the eighteenth-century founder of the sect of the Illuminati, but internal evidence shows this to be quite impossible. I have seen a copy in the hand of Victor B. Neuburg, the poet who, many years after he had broken with Crowley, discovered Dylan Thomas. It may be that Neuburg wrote the ritual, but I think it probable that Crowley himself had at least some hand in its composition.

[4] A short prose poem in three short chapters which Crowley had received in 1904, allegedly by direct voice communication from a spirit called Aiwass. *Liber Legis* purports to give an initiated interpretation of the inauguration of what astrologers and hippies call the "Age of Aquarius" and Crowley called "the Aeon of Horus".

O. and I. (*face to face*).
I. What is the hour?
O. When time hath no power.
I. What is the place?
O. At the limits of space.
I. What God do we wake?
O. The Lord of the Snake!
I. With what do we serve?
O. Brain, muscle and nerve.
I. The shrine in the gloom?
(*She gives the Sign of a Babe of the Abyss, which O. destroys by the Sign of Mentu the God.*[5])
O. Is the Mouth of Thy Womb!
I. And the Priest in the shrine?
O. Is this Monster of Mine!
(*O. repeats Sign of Mentu and I. gives Sign of Baphomet.*)
I. And the wonder above?
O. The Quintessence of Love.
I. There are Sacraments?
O.   Nine.
   There are music and wine
   And the delicate dance—
I. To accomplish?
O.   The trance.
I. And are these three enough?
O. They are servants of Love.
I. And the Sacrifice?
O.   I
I. And the priestess?
O.   Is thou.
   I am willing to die
   At thy hands—even now.
I. Worship me first!
(*O. seats I. upon the Altar.*)
O. Mistress I thirst.

---

[5] The God Mentu is usually shown with his left hand resting between his thighs, the fingers clenched and the thumb extended—the significance is clearly sexual.

(*I. gives wine. They both drink.*)
I. My mouth is on fire
   To my Lord's desire.
(*They exchange the holy greeting by a kiss.*)
O. I kneel at thy feet
   And the honey is sweet.
(*I. plays music while O. worships in silence.*)
I. Exhausted, I sink.
O. I am dead, on the brink.
I. Let us dance!
O.   Let us dance!
O. and I. The Lord gives us power
   To be lost in the trance
   For an hour—for an hour!
(*They dance together. A pause of perfect stillness and silence follows; until I., of her own accord, advances and places O. upon the altar.*)
I. Exhaust me!
O.   Nay, drink!
I. Ere I sink!
O.   I shall sink.
I. Drink wine! Oh, drink wine!
O. I am thine!
I.   I am thine!
(*They drink and greet as before.*)
O. Art thou armed?
I.   With a knife.
(*I. draws the dagger from her hair.*)
O. Love is better than life.
(*I. cuts a I, or if possible, the Sigil of NOX on O.'s breast.*)
I. Let us dance!
O. (*Giving wine*) To the trance!
(*They drink then dance.*)
I. Back to the throne!
(*O. returns and takes seat thereon.*)
O. I adore thee alone!
(*I. does so, plays music if so inclined, and continues as necessity or inclination may dictate.*)
I. It is ended, the play:
   I am ready to slay

Anoint me!
O.   I rise
To the fire of thine eyes
I anoint thee, thy priest,
Babalon—and the Beast!
And I ask of thee now:
Who art Thou?
I. Omari Tessala marax etc.
(*The ritual is now in silence accomplished.*)

IX° (*i.e. Ritual Sexual Intercourse*)
CLOSING

O. Mouth to mouth and heart to heart!
I. For the moment we must part.
O. Time and space renew the illusion.
I. Love is swallowed in confusion.
O. Love sustains as eminent
Till the hour of Sacrament.
I. I love you, and you love me.
O. Now and ever may it be!
O. and I. Hand in hand is heart to heart.
Love be with us, though we part.
(*They greet, as before, and depart.*)

Crowley also attempted, in an essay entitled *Energized Enthusiasm*, to give some sort of *rationale* for the use of sex-magic, a task that had been shirked by the German leaders of the O.T.O. He started from two basic assumptions:

(a) That any form of sexual activity was good in itself; he wrote that he agreed with "the Head Master of Eton that pederastic passions among schoolboys do no harm; further, I think them the only redeeming feature of sexual life at public schools".

(b) That there was some close connection between sexuality and genius. He wrote that "the divine consciousness which is reflected and refracted in the works of Genius feeds upon a certain secretion ... analogous to semen, but not identical with it".

Having decided that genius had a connection with sexuality, particularly male sexuality (Crowley claimed that all women of genius had at least an element of hermaphroditism in their physical makeup) he went on to ask how that genius could be, firstly, built up and, secondly, released—or, as he himself put it, "how can the Leyden jar of genius be discharged?" His answer was simple enough; by the invocation of "Bacchus, Aphrodite and Apollo"—in other words, wine, women and song combined into one ritual.

The invocation of Bacchus was simple enough, for wine was easily available and its only disadvantage was the possible intoxication of some of the participants in the invocation; Crowley suggested that the way to avoid this was to have the "bowl of libation" borne by an initiate who would pass by all who showed the least sign of drunkenness. Crowley was undecided as to whether wine should be replaced altogether by what he called "the elixir introduced by me to Europe". This "elixir", which he probably discovered on a visit to Mexico, was an infusion of mescal buttons and other herbs in fruit juices and alcohol —he had administered it to the audience at his *Rites of Eleusis*, celebrated at the Caxton Hall in 1910, and one of those who then partook of it described it as tasting "like rotten apples".

The invocation of Apollo (i.e. music) was more complex, for so few musical instruments were suitable for the purpose. Crowley came down in favour of the organ and the violin (he rejected the harmonium as "horrible", probably because he associated it with the ultra-Protestant conventicles of his youth) but considered the tom-tom to be ideal, particularly when accompanied by sacred dancing and the rhythmic chanting of a mantra. Even this last-mentioned instrument had its disadvantages, for Crowley's friend Commander Marston R.N. had carried out some "classical and conclusive" experiments on the effects of the tom-tom on the psychology of the married Englishwoman and found that it created a vague unrest, gradually assuming a sexual form and culminating in "shameless masturbation or indecent advances". Or so Commander Marston R.N. claimed; but he seems to have been a peculiar individual, even for the Royal Navy of Edwardian England, and, at his Dorset home in May 1910, he took part in Crowley's invocation of the god Mars (the god supposedly appeared and prophesied not only the Balkan war of 1912 but the war of 1914-18).

Most difficult of all was the problem of achieving sexual excitement, "invoking Aphrodite", without descending into lasciviousness . . . Crowley's solution to this problem was never given in its entirety, for after posing the question he broke off his essay (presumably because there were very strict limits on what one could publicly say in the

London of King Edward VII) and concluded with an imaginative description of the sort of sexo-magical rite he had in mind. This description, naturally enough, was couched in extremely elusive prose; "she then laid him down upon the cross", he wrote, "and took her own appointed place. I was lost to everything."

Crowley began his first serious experiments in sexual magic on the very last day of 1913. These operations were not the normal heterosexual magic of the ninth degree of the O.T.O., they were homosexual magic of Crowley's own devising. His partner in these rituals was his disciple *Frater Lampada Tradam*, known in the world of men as Victor Neuburg, who played the male part—Crowley was always strongly feminine in his attitude towards other men. It was the fact that "a casual act of sex" with Neuburg had "produced a great wonder" that had first aroused Crowley's interest in homosexuality as a means of obtaining magical power. This "casual incident" had taken place during a *Great Magical Retirement* in the North African desert when Crowley was engaged, using his own topaz shew-stone, in a clairvoyant investigation of the thirty Enochian *Aires* from TEX to LIL;[6] the homosexual event had enabled him to enter an *Aire* which had previously closed its doors against him.

The record of this series of homosexual magical rites, usually referred to by Crowley and his followers as *The Paris Working*, is contained in two manuscripts. The first is entitled

The
Book of the High Magick Art
that was worked by
Frater O.S.V. 6=5 (*i.e. Crowley*)
and Frater L.T. 2=9 (*i.e. Neuburg*)

and the second is called the

Esoteric Record of the
Working
of January 1914 *era vulgari*

---

[6] For some brief description of these Enochian *Aires* see *Astral Projection, Magic and Alchemy* by S. L. MacGregor Mathers (Neville Spearman, 1971). The results of Crowley's Enochian experiments were published as a supplement to the *Equinox* and, with many additional notes and comments, as *The Vision and the Voice* (California, Thelema Publishing Co. 1952).

ENTER BAPHOMET

I must here express my gratitude to Gerald Yorke who gave me access to these manuscripts in 1966 and 1967.

Crowley began his work by, as he put it, "receiving the Sacrament from a certain priest A.B."—which in this connection means having sex with him—and painting a pentacle (a symbolic design) of Mercury, one of the two gods whom it was intended to invoke, the other being Jupiter. The exact identity of A.B. is uncertain, but he was very probably Walter Duranty, the foreign correspondent of the *New York Times* who died in 1957. He remained friendly with Crowley until the latter's death in 1947 and he certainly had a homosexual relationship with him in the early months of 1914. The "taking of the Sacrament" was over in a mere forty minutes—it lasted from 4.55 to 5.35 p.m.— and Crowley spent most of the rest of the evening painting his Mercurial pentacle until 11.30 p.m. when he and Neuberg began the invocation proper.

This commenced with the Golden Dawn *Banishing Ceremony of the Pentagram*, which was *danced* by Neuburg, following which they invoked Thoth-Hermes (Mercury) by Crowley's Ritual 671, entitled *The Building of the Pyramid*. This latter rite, which involved Crowley scourging Neuburg on the buttocks and cutting a cross on his chest, was concluded by midnight and the sexual act was proceeded with; simultaneously the two magicians chanted an invocation of Hermes composed by Duranty:

Jungitur in vati vates: rex inclyte rhabdou
Hermes tu venias, verba nefanda ferens.
(*Magician is joined with magician: Hermes,
King of the Rod, appear, bringing the ineffable word*)

The invocation was only partly successful; Neuburg, whose function in the rite was a mediumistic one, was possessed by the god and Crowley "astrally" saw the room as filled with caducei of Mercury, the snakes alive and moving, but Neuburg was unable to attain orgasm— either because, as Crowley himself affirmed, Mercury was in a prankish mood or, more probably, because Neuburg did not find Crowley sufficiently sexually stimulating—and consequently Mercury (i.e. the possessed Neuburg) could not be asked the many questions prepared for him.

The second working, which began the following evening at 11.20

p.m. and had been preceded by Crowley manufacturing from yellow wax an image of Mercury in the form of an erect penis, was much more successful. The sexual act was fully accomplished and Mercury gave instructions as to how future invocations could be made more effective; for the rite of Mercury they were to remove the clock from the room, "use a gold pentagram, placing the same in a prominent position; drink yellow wine and eat fish before the ceremony", while for that of Jupiter they were to trample violets with their bare feet, Crowley was to wear a crown and Neuburg a scarlet robe.

The third working commenced at midnight on January 3rd and lasted until 2.15 a.m. Mercury made a very long speech on the relationship between himself and semen, stating that:

"Every drop of semen which Hermes sheds is a world. The technical term for this semen is KRATOS . . . People upon the worlds are like maggots upon an apple, all forms of life bred by the worlds are in the nature of parasites. Pure worlds are flaming globes, each a conscious being . . .

". . . Ma is the name of the god who seduced the Phallus away from the Yoni; hence the physical universe. All worlds are excreta, they represent wasted semen. Therefore all is blasphemy. This explains why man made God in his own image."

Mercury went on to suggest that he should be invoked on the morrow, not ritually, but by geomancy—a form of divination involving the element of earth—and that on the day following the geomantic operation (and for the three succeeding nights) Jupiter should be sexually invoked. Mercury, who seems to have liked his worshippers to enjoy a good meal, then emphasised the importance of having banquets, said that he wanted Crowley and Neuburg "to overcome shame generally" and suggested a method by which this could be done. Details of the exact nature of this suggested method are missing from the record, but from certain marginal notes it is fairly clear (a) that it was suggested to Crowley that he should take part in an exhibition of buggery in front of some of his friends, (b) that this was subsequently done at the house of his mistress Jane Cheiron, his partner in the act being Walter Duranty.

Mercury finally enjoined that this third working should be closed by another homosexual act, but as Crowley and Neuburg were both extremely tired this was done "in symbolic form only". This disobedience seems to have annoyed the god, or so the two believed, for it was to this annoyance that they attributed a heavy cold that Crowley developed on the following day! At midday on January 5th they made good their omission and Neuburg became possessed; he said they were unleashing an enormous magical force, that international complications were to be feared and that "those who adopt this rite will either succeed completely or fail utterly. There is no middle path for it is impossible to escape the ring of Divine Karma created."

The god then left Neuburg and Crowley became possessed or, as he later decided, obsessed. The obsessing entity informed them that the supreme rite of sexual magic involved the rape, sacrifice and dissection into nine pieces of a young girl; the pieces were to be offered as sacrifices to the immortal gods—the head to Juno, the right shoulder to Jupiter the left to Saturn, the right buttock to Mars the left to Venus, the arms to Priapus and the legs to Pan. In fairness to Crowley and Neuburg it must be emphasised that both later decided that the obsessing entity's instructions smacked of Black Magic and should be disregarded.

Later in the same day the fourth working was carried out. This time it was Jupiter who was invoked; on this occasion Crowley took the male part, almost certainly because Neuburg had been sexually exhausted by the "sacrifice" to Mercury that had been made earlier in the day.

It would be exacting too much of my readers to impose upon them the details of the twenty further homosexual rites that were carried out before the *Paris Working* was brought to an end on February 12th. The records of the eleventh and thirteenth workings, however, contain several points of considerable interest. In the former, which took place upon January 21st, Neuburg obtained from Jupiter a message (expressed in the Enochian magical language) informing him that the old gods wanted to regain their ancient dominion over the earth and had chosen him and Crowley as "fiery arrows" to be shot against the "slave gods", while at the conclusion of the latter, which took place five days after the eleventh working, both magicians "remembered" a Cretan incarnation in which they had known one another. Crowley had been a Temple dancer named Aia; Neuburg had been Mardocles, who, as a candidate for initiation, had been subjected to the ordeal of watching a seductive dance by Aia—he was instructed to either rape the girl or to remain cool and emotionally unmoved. If he failed to do either he was supposed to be castrated by an instrument resembling a giant candle-snuffer! Mardocles/Neuburg remembered that he had been aroused by Crowley/Aia but, out of tenderness, had failed to violate her. As he was a favourite of the High Priest he had escaped the usual penalty but he and Aia had been expelled from the temple and subsequently sold as slaves to a household where their task was to "amuse the family by various copulations".

The two magicians considered the *Paris Working* to have been successful and certainly they obtained the funds which had been one of their supplementary requirements of the gods; in Neuburg's case the invocation of Jupiter seems to have been almost too successful, for, according to a note upon the manuscript, he "became Jupiter the bestower, and many unworthy folk became his guests".[7]

In the autumn of 1914 Crowley commenced the serious practice of the heterosexual magic of the ninth degree of the O.T.O. Most of his early experiments were hampered by the after-effects of a severe attack of phlebitis but, assisted by his mistress Leila Waddell (who, on one occasion, physically helped her lover to achieve sexual intercourse with a chorus girl whom he had long hankered after), he persisted in the work and over a period of four years recorded his sexo-magical successes and failures in the three volumes of *Rex de Arte Regia*.[8] These tell of homo-, auto- and heterosexual magical operations; the first mentioned often took place, dimly illuminated by flaring gas-lamps, in obscure Turkish Bath establishments with Crowley performing fellatio on fellow-customers (when recording these the diaries usually contain Greek words meaning *in the mouth of the King*). The heterosexual magical *opera* (Crowley always used the Latin word *opus*, work, to indicate a sexo-magical rite) sometimes included more than two participants; a particularly curious series of entries involved Crowley, two women and a negro named Walter.

The most intense period of Crowley's practice of O.T.O. sexual magic coincided with the three years or so (1920–3) of the life of his Abbey of Thelema, situated at a farmhouse near Cefalu, in Sicily. In

---

[7] The thirteenth working was also notable for the fact that during it Crowley spontaneously danced, or, as the record rather pompously expressed it, he "became inspired in a Terpsichorean manner".

[8] After 1918 Crowley's sex-magic diary was amalgamated with his ordinary Magical Record.

Leah Hirsig, a New York singing teacher who had become his mistress, he had found the ideal partner—in one diary entry he referred to her vagina as "the Hirsig patent vacuum-pump"—and together the two performed rites of a sort that most people thought had been dead for two thousand years. Thus, in the summer of 1921, a he-goat (symbolic of Pan, Priapus, and Capricorn) was induced to copulate with the kneeling Leah before having its throat sacrificially cut at the moment of orgasm; this was the largest blood-sacrifice Crowley ever made, his other victims had been confined to a cat (which, with feline cleverness, managed to inflict a nasty scratch on Crowley before meeting its end), a toad, some doves used to invoke the demon Choronzon, and a few sparrows.

During this Sicilian period Crowley also gave due attention to his homosexual leanings; he personified the feminine elements of his personality make up as *Alys Cusack*, a name under which he had written reviews for the *Equinox*, and over his bed at the Abbey of Thelema hung a notice informing the world that ALYS CUSACK IS -OT AT HOME —according to his mood the blank before the word -OT would be replaced by either an N or an H.

Leah would sometimes assist her lover in his celebration of homosexual *opera*; lying down in bed with Crowley and the other man involved she would manually stimulate the latter before inserting his penis into Crowley's body. Thus one of Crowley's diary entries records that:

"after dinner we sent for X——. Circa 11 p.m. Opus V. X—— in ano meo. Operation very lengthy. Alostrael (the magical motto of Leah Hirsig) had to masturbate X—— to effect erection, and her hand introduced his penis into my anus. Orgasm very strong and savage . . ."

It is worth adding that X——, who is still alive, affirms that this diary entry was inadequate and incorrect; that, in fact, he (X——) was under the influence of ether (no aphrodisiac) at the time and that, in any case, he was not sexually excited by Crowley—in his own words, Crowley's "Circean enchantment didn't give me a bone-on".

Reuss resigned from his chieftainship of the O.T.O. in 1922, verbally nominating Crowley as his successor—up to now, it must be remembered, Crowley had only been the head of the *Mysteria Mystica*

Maxima, the English branch of the O.T.O. The new dignity did not become effective until 1924/5 when, after a series of conferences and discussions, the German O.T.O. lodges accepted Crowley as Outer Head of the Order; presumably the *Inner* Head of the Order was some discarnate being. Before long, however, some of the German lodges revolted against their new chief; his *Book of the Law*, usually known as *Liber Legis*, had been translated into German and its contents had shocked many of the German initiates. One of them complained that "too late have I been acquainted with the contents of *Liber Legis*, a book branded with a threefold KEOU . . . to my horror I got a real glimpse of the future reconstruction, as planned by the A(strum) A(rgentinum) (*one of Crowley's magical orders*), of a primitive world order which suggests the blackest days of Atlantis . . ." Even Frater Recnartus, most prominent of the initiates who had been responsible for Crowley's elevation, regarded it as a product of demoniac possession.

Some lodges rejected Crowley and carried on their work independently of him, while others more or less accepted him; these latter worked under Recnartus who, as a result of some mysterious spiritual illumination, had now come to accept *Liber Legis* as the gospel of the coming Age of Aquarius.

After Mussolini's expulsion of Crowley from Italy in 1923 there were no more spectacular *opera*, such as that involving Leah and the goat, but the practice of sexual magic was continued unabated. Nevertheless, the homosexual magical techniques of the XI° O.T.O. became largely abandoned by their creator—while those young men who had gone out to study magic under Crowley at the Abbey of Thelema had usually become involved in homosexual relationships with their tutor, this was not the case with their successors of the late 'twenties and early 'thirties; such occultists as Fratres W. J. and O. were never participants in eleventh degree rites.

Crowley died in 1947, to all appearances a failure—his last words were "I am perplexed". His sexual magic is the aspect of his teaching which has become most notorious and yet, paradoxically enough, it is probably the least important component part of the philosophy of Crowleyanity. There is no doubt that in many of his contributions to the *Equinox*, and in such books as *Liber Aleph* and *Eight Lectures on Yoga*, Crowley made a real contribution to the literature of occultism. For this he would be remembered, even if he had never come into contact with Theodor Reuss and the O.T.O.

CHAPTER ELEVEN

Saturn-Gnosis, Sex Magic, and Planetary Aspects

The German section of the O.T.O. led by Frater Recnartus—rudely referred to by his opponents as "the old fox"—was known as *Fraternitatis Saturni*, the Brotherhood of Saturn, or, alternatively, as Saturn-Gnosis.

Like Aleister Crowley, their English Chief, the members of Saturn-Gnosis combined their sexual magic with the use of drugs; unlike him, who had described professional astrologers as being ignorant of all subjects (including their own) and had stated that he believed that there was less than one per cent of truth in the doctrines of astrology, they attached great importance to "the science of the stars". These astrological preoccupations were not, perhaps, altogether surprising, for the fifteen year life-span of the Weimar Republic coincided with the astonishing German revival of late antique astrology and several of the pre-Hitler German astrologers took a strong interest in the less usual aspects of sexuality. In 1931, for example, Christian Meier-Parm wrote an article for *Sterne und Mensch* entitled "The Horoscopes of Thirty Five Girls in Brothels" whilst some three years earlier Dr. Karl-Guenther Heimsoth, an old *Freikorps* fighter, had published his *Charakter Konstellation*, a book devoted entirely to the horoscopes of homosexuals.[1] Few, however, of these astrologers could have carried their

[1] Dr. Heimsoth was friendly with many of the more radically inclined members of the Nazi Party and amongst his acquaintances was Ernst Röhm, leader of Hitler's Brownshirts, who wrote to Heimsoth; "you are obviously very skilled in judging horoscopes. Could you not have a look at mine . . . Then I might learn what sort of person I am . . . I suppose that I am homosexual.' Heimsoth was murdered in the course of the Röhm purge of 1934. For further details of his career see Ellic Howe's *Urania's Children* (London, William Kimber 1967).

beliefs to the extent of varying their coital positions with the positions of the planets in the Zodiac—a practice earnestly advocated by the leadership of Saturn-Gnosis. I feel sure that the sex lives of these German magicians must have been difficult in the extreme, and that any tendencies they may have had to promiscuity were checked by the necessity of looking up the planetary positions in an ephemeris before retiring to bed! The instructions for the practice of this astrological sex-magic were given in a document entitled *Die astrologischen Aspekt-Zeichen als Geheim—Symbolik für Coitus—Stellungen*, an English translation of which I give in full

SPECIAL REPRINT NUMBER TWO
Private reprint for the Fraternity of the Lodge
Fraternitatis Saturni
Secret! Secret!

Astrological Aspects as a Secret Symbolism for Coital Positions.

The ancient mystery schools frequently used as part of the initiation rites of their disciples religious practices and ceremonies which, more or less openly, glorified sexual relations between men and women and used these as a basis for their cult.

This secret symbolism and specialised knowledge was, of course, deliberately withheld from the lower grade and the uninitiated.

We still find rudiments of these sexual mysteries in the cult of Mithras, the festival of Bacchus, and in the early Gnosis before the Gnosis was desecrated by Christianity.

It is obvious to anybody schooled in magic that originally all magical ceremonies had a purely cosmic basis because the initiated priesthood used as a foundation for their cults the planetary prime oscillations of certain aspects in their influence on the psyche and physical organs of men.

As the sexual act brings about the release of the tension of the mutually negative and positive forces of the partners (above all if the act is executed as a consciously magical act) the knowledgeable initiated individual will naturally be able to create favourable conditions for the practical application of the teaching and thus achieve total harmonisation and peak polarisation of the senses.

The fertilisation of the woman is not the aim of such sexual acts as these, for they are of a purely religious nature or are used to create

7. Leah Hirsig—Crowley's "Scarlet Woman" sitting beside Crowley's portrait of her as "a dead soul".

8. Erotic painting in the *Chamber of Nightmares* at the Abbey of Thelema, Sicily—uncovered by leading underground film-maker Kenneth Anger.

so-called psychogones which are easily aroused by such sexual intoxication. Thus the position of the body becomes an important part of this religio-magical practice.

Gestures, movements, body rhythms, and posture are not only important in ritual dances, but are also structurally important factors in all magical ceremonies where they set into vibration or rest the appropriate Chakra.[2] Therefore it is quite understandable that certain positions during intercourse are an important prerequisite for the achievement of certain magical aims.

It is the teaching of astrology, founded on magic, that the squares[3] between the planets especially important in the sexual sphere (i.e. Venus, Mars, Neptune and the Moon) are particularly vital and advantageous. All these squares are of a purely daemonic character and are known to be the gateways to the psyche of Man; this is particularly so if they are already present in the basic horoscope of the individual in question. A person experienced in magic can therefore use with success and without difficulty important aspects whether they be formed by transits of positions in the natal horoscope or actually present in the Zodiac at the time of copulation.[4]

The original knowledge of the difficult content of these ancient sexual mysteries has, unfortunately, been preserved in only a rudimentary fashion. In the secret archives was found a sort of *Stele* containing very important instructions concerning these mysteries and strangely enough, pointing out the relationship between coital positions and astrological configurations.

It is said, among other things, that in squares of Venus and Mars sexual intercourse should be carried out in a sitting position, the exact nature of which should vary with the strength of the planets in

---

[2] "Chakras" are believed by occultists to be psycho-spiritual centres of activity which operate as the vital organs of the so-called "subtle bodies" of the individual.

[3] In astrology a square aspect is said to exist when two planets viewed from a geocentric position are at an angle of 90° to one another in the Zodiac.

[4] This sentence clearly requires some explanation. In astrology an aspect "by transit" is formed when a planet (for the purposes of astrology the Sun and Moon are planets) is now in a position where it forms an aspect (i.e. a significant angle) with the position either the same or another planet was in at the moment of birth. Thus if I was born with Venus in 20° Capricorn and Mars was now, many years later, in 20° Aries a "square aspect by Transit" would be said to exist, or, as an astrologer would probably put it; Mars *t* square Venus *r* (radical). In this way one can talk about the Moon being square to the Moon.

the Sign of the Zodiac where they are situated. If Venus is stronger the female partner should be on top, if Mars is stronger the male should be on top. In a square of Moon and Mars either the woman (=Moon) or the man (=Mars) may be underneath or on top. A square Moon and Moon is said to be most suitable for Lesbian sexuality, a square of Mars and Mars for male homosexuality. Where Neptune is part of the square it is advised to use drugs in order that both partners may achieve a simultaneous state of intoxication.[5] If there is opposition[6] between the above-mentioned planets, no sexual act should be carried out, and only preliminary preparation should be made, i.e. states of erotic tension may be induced. All conjunctions are to be used in a similar way to squares because a conjunction means a concentration of forces.

As is generally known, trine formations between these planets obviously provide favourable conditions for the fertilisation of the woman, should this be desired.

It is now left to the Brethren to make use of these instructions in their practical application of magic. Unfortunately, no further details were contained in the script, but it is very interesting to note that the aspects were used to conceal the practice and therefore constituted the key to this symbolic secret.

The aim of these sexual rites was not only the achievement of the peak polarisation of the senses of both partners but also the creation of thought-forms and, above all, the attraction of daemonic beings. This makes the astrologically based practice of magic understandable. Such daemonic beings extend their astral vibrations through vampire-like inhalations from the etheric bodies of the participants. Thus the sexual act becomes a kind of sacrifice to the invoked daemon or,

---

[5] The use of drugs as a means of obtaining magical experience was already something of a tradition in certain sections of the German occult movement. Thus Karl Kiesewetter, author of an important work on modern occultism, died of poison at Meiningen in 1895 after an attempt to develop clairvoyant powers by means of drug taking. Some thirty or so years later Bernd Unglaub's *Sirius Pocket Album* (Berlin 1928) gave details of where the hallucinogenic drug mescaline could be obtained. It is also of some interest that Aldous Huxley was first introduced to mescaline in pre-Hitler Berlin by Aleister Crowley and one of his disciples. Curiously enough Huxley made no mention of this fact in his *Doors of Perception*.

[6] In astrology an opposition exists when two planets are separated in the Zodiac by an angle of 180°.

in purely religious cults, a sacrifice to the worshipped godhead or to the god.

When intended for a purely magical purpose these acts must be undertaken only as a magical ceremony under the strictest observation of all magical precautions. Defensive symbols must be employed together with protective fumes such as incense. The use of erotically effective ingredients is advisable as is the wearing of precious stones appropriate to the planets.

Naturally the brethren know the sigils of the daemons they wish to invoke and the way to use them. Thus the foregoing exposition should merely serve the Frater as a complement to the magical knowledge already made available to him through his training. In the grade of Pentalpha the brethren will learn more of this secret knowledge.

Thus ends this strange discourse on astrological sex magic, and, alas, I have no documents pertaining to the exalted "Grade of Pentalpha".

Probably the most interesting, and certainly the most important, member of the German Section of the O.T.O. was Karl Johannes Germer, the man who, under his magical name of Frater Saturnus, eventually became Crowley's successor as "Outer Head of the Order".

Germer, born on January 22nd 1885, seems to have been an intelligent child and, after attendance at school and various German universities spent six terms at the Sorbonne. In 1914 he visited Russia and was still in that country at the outbreak of the First World War. He managed his escape to Germany, however, and was called to the colours; like most middle-class Germans of his age he was a reserve officer. His war record was a good one and he was awarded both the first and second class Iron Cross for what were discreetly termed "special services"; while I am unaware of the exact nature of these special services I suspect that Germer had combined his Russian travels with a certain amount of spying and that it was these intelligence activities that had led to his first contact with Reuss and the O.T.O.

At the beginning of the 'twenties Germer was appointed to an important management position in the Barth-Verlag, a Munich publishing house. He co-operated with Herr Tränker (Frater Recnartus) in the translation and publication of seven short works by Crowley (of which *Der Meister Therion: Eine biographische Nachricht* is not published elsewhere) brought out by the Barth-Verlag in 1925.

For the next ten tears Germer lived and worked with Crowley, returning to Germany from time to time in order to superintend the activities of the Thelema-Verlag, a small occult publishing company he had established in Leipzig with the aid of Martha Küntzel (Soror I.W.E.), an elderly lady who had been converted from Theosophy to Crowley's brand of magic and his new religion of Thelema. On the last of these visits, in 1935, Germer's high-grade masonic connections attracted the attention of the Gestapo and he was arrested. After some weeks of solitary confinement in the Alexanderplatz Prison on a diet of bread and water, during which he was tortured but kept himself sane by the recitation of the Crowleyan Holy Books (such as the *Book of the Heart Girt Withe the Serpent*) from "beginning to end and from end to beginning", he was sent to the Esterwegen concentration camp.[7] Before his sudden release some ten months later Germer was comforted, according to his own account, by a vision of his Holy Guardian Angel.[8]

After his restoration to freedom Germer lived for some years in Brussels, making desperate efforts to remain in touch with the scattered remnants of the German sex-magical groups, finally suppressed (along with other occult and masonic organisations) by the Nazis in 1937.

On May 10th 1941 Germer was again arrested, this time by the Belgians, and deported to France, where he spent ten months in an internment camp before emigrating to the United States in June 1941. From then until 1947 he occupied the office of "Grand Treasurer of the O.T.O." and his life was largely devoted to raising enough money to print such unpublished "Thelemite magical treasures" as the *Book of Thoth* which appeared in 1944.

After Crowley's death at the end of 1947 and Germer's inheritance of

---

[7] After his release Germer described his experiences in a book, *I was a Prisoner*, for which he was unable to find a publisher. Several copies survive in typescript, however.

[8] The Crowleyan concept of the Holy Guardian Angel, derived ultimately from S. L. MacGregor Mathers' interpretation of the Mediaeval Abramelin magical system, must not be confused with the Guardian Angel of popular Catholicism. Originally Crowley took the Holy Guardian Angel as being identical with the Higher Self of the Theosophists and the Golden Dawn (see *Collected Works*, Volume I, p. 209) but later he changed his mind and came to regard the Holy Guardian Angel as a distinct personality in its own right. In this connection see Israel Regardie's *Eye in the Triangle* (Llewellyn Publications 1970), p. 508 for Crowley's later teaching on this matter.

SATURN-GNOSIS, SEX MAGIC, AND PLANETARY ASPECTS

the Headship of the O.T.O.[9] various attempts were made to revive the German "Oriental Templars". None of these met with the new Chief's approval, however—he went so far as to denounce one German-speaking magician as an agent of the F.B.I.—and the only group to which he gave a full O.T.O. Charter was a Swiss one,[10] led by a certain Herr Metzger (Frater Paragranus).[11]

Germer died on October 25th 1962 and was succeeded by his Swiss follower; this succession was announced to the world in a floridly written manifesto dated Spring 1963:

> "We, Grand Secretary General of the Sovereign Sanctuary of the Ordo Templi Orientis, hereby give due Notice to all Sovereign Sanctuaries and Bodies in friendship with the Sovereign Sanctuary of the Ordo Templi Orientis and to all Members of the said Rite, that the lamented Most Illustrious Frater Superior of the Ordo Templi Orientis, Frater Saturnus (Karl Johannes Germer) Outer Head of the Order, departed this earthly life and was called to the Grand East on October 25th 1962 E.V., and that a convocation of Prince Patriarch Grand Conservators of the said Rite on January 6th 1963 E.V. held in the Abbey of Thelema, Stein/App., unanimously elected the Very Illustrious + H. Josephus M., Fra., Paragranus, Grand Master X° of the Ordo Templi Orientis, Sovereign Grand Master General of Ordo Illuminatorum, Sovereign Grand Master General of Fraternitatis Rosicruciana Antiqua, and Sovereign Patriarch of Ecclesiae Gnosticae Catholicae henceforth to be Sovereign Grand Master General, Outer Head of the Order of the Oriental Templars."

Under its Swiss leadership the O.T.O. flourishes, publishing a magazine, the *Oriflamme*, and celebrating, each Sunday, the Gnostic Catholic Mass in the small Abbey of Thelema situated at Stein, Appenzell.

---

[9] Germer also inherited the Crowley copyrights and the ashes of his Master's body; the latter were ceremonially transferred to him under a hundred-year-old fir tree that grew in the garden of his house at Hampton, New Jersey.

[10] A limited charter, later withdrawn, was given to a small English group. For full details of this interesting episode see my *Ritual Magic in England*, pp. 166–7.

[11] See Appendix F "Crowleyanity in Switzerland".

CHAPTER TWELVE

The Bishop and the Boys

With the exception of Aleister Crowley and his followers I know of no western occultists—either "black" or "white"—who used homosexual acts as magical methods of gaining power, either material or spiritual. Of course there have been, and no doubt there still are, many homosexual occultists; but their homosexuality has been something apart from their occultism, not part of it.[1] I have no doubt that those of my readers having some acquaintance with occult literature will be surprised by this statement, for they will be well aware that in the late 'twenties and early 'thirties the occult writer Dion Fortune[2] continually alleged, in lecture, article, and books, that there existed a group of male occultists who were engaged in building up what she called "a reservoir of dark astral power" by the use of homosexual techniques. Never, in print at any rate, did she go to the length of naming the members of this group, but from her frequent admiring references to the *O.E.* (i.e. Oriental Esoteric) *Library Critic* in this connection it is clear that she had in mind a small group of members of the Theosophical Society, the most notable of them being an ex-Anglican curate named Charles Leadbeater, against whom H. N. Stokes, the editor of the *O.E. Library Critic,* had for many years carried on a virulent campaign.

[1] The one exception to this seems to be that strange character Ralph Chubb, who managed to blend occultism, the love of young boys, and nature worship into one incoherent whole. See Appendix, "Ralph Chubb, Boy Love, and William Blake".

[2] The pseudonym of Mrs. Violet Evans; for some brief details of her interesting magical career see chapters 16 and 18 of my *Ritual Magic in England* (Neville Spearman 1970).

So convincing was the journalism of Stokes and Fortune, and at first sight, so damning the evidence against Leadbeater, that to this day many occultists remain convinced that he and his associates were "black magicians who obtained occult power by vampirising young boys".[3] In the circumstances I think it well worth while to examine the whole relationship between Leadbeater and these same boys, the alleged victims of his activities.

Charles Webster Leadbeater was born in 1847 of English expatriate parents. He spent most of his early years in South America and seems to have led an extremely exciting life, on one occasion being kidnapped and almost killed by Indians. In 1879, after his return to England, he was ordained as an Anglican priest and took up a curacy in Hampshire. At this early stage of his life he already seems to have been preoccupied with what were to remain his two major interests until his death over fifty years later—the supernatural and young boys. He ran the Church choir, superintended the Sunday School, coached backward boys, and, according to his own account, experienced many uncanny events in the course of his experiments with mesmerism.

In 1885, while still a curate of the Church of England, he met Madame Blavatsky and was converted by her to Theosophy, a creed to which he had felt attracted since reading A. P. Sinnet's sensational book *The Occult World* some years before. The Theosophical Society, of which Leadbeater was now a member, had been founded at New York in 1875 by Madame Blavatsky, Colonel H. S. Olcott, William Q. Judge and others. Nominally, it was a learned society, its objects being: (1) to form a nucleus of the Universal Brotherhood of Humanity; (2) to encourage the study of comparative religion, philosophy, and science; (3) to investigate the unexplained laws of nature and the powers latent in man. In reality, however, it was a syncretistic religious body teaching[4] a peculiar hodge-podge of traditional western occultism—

---

[3] This quotation, which I take from the (cyclostyled) June 1948 issue of a tiny occult magazine called *Hermes* is particularly interesting for its association of homosexuality with the legendary, blood-sucking, vampire. I am confident that vampirism in both nineteenth-century literature and twentieth-century occult fantasy is symbolic (on an unconscious level) of forbidden sexuality in general and of oral-genital contact in particular. The sexual undertones of such short stories as *Carmilla* and such novels as *Dracula* are only too apparent.

[4] At the period in question; in later years there were even stranger and more exotic flowerings of Theosophical doctrine, largely derived from Annie Besant's personal interpretation of Hinduism.

mostly lifted by Madame Blavatsky, without acknowledgement, from the published writings of such nineteenth-century magicians as Eliphas Levi, Albert Pike and Kenneth MacKenzie[5]—and Southern Buddhism.

Afire with missionary zeal for his new-found faith, and filled with an enthusiasm for all things oriental, Leadbeater spent much of the next eight years in India and Ceylon. As usual, he devoted a good deal of attention to the problems of youth, and succeeded in acquiring a young (male) Sinhalese protégé named Jinarajadasa who accompanied him on his return to Europe in 1893. From that year onwards Leadbeater began to assume some prominence in the Theosophical movement, writing more and more articles for its magazines describing his clairvoyant experiences in pamphlets, and, in August 1895, becoming Assistant Secretary of the European Section of the Theosophical Society. By 1900 Leadbeater's reputation as a writer, lecturer and clairvoyant, had spread to North America, and in the autumn of that year he undertook a four-month long lecture-tour of the United States. The American Theosophists[6] were enchanted by his personality, and so successful was his tour that, in 1902, he was invited back, this time for a full two years of visits and lecture-tours. No doubt his close friendship with Annie Besant, the leading Theosophist since the death of Blavatsky, stood him in good stead with the Americans.

Ever since Leadbeater had, in 1898, taken over the Lotus Circle, a London club for the children of Theosophical parents, and begun to transform it into the international organisation it ultimately became, he had enjoyed a reputation as Theosophy's own expert on education and the life of the child. As a consequence of this he was, on his second visit to North America, accompanied throughout by Basil Hodgson-Smith, the young son of the President of the Harrogate Lodge of the Theosophical Society and, for the seven months of his lecture-tour of the West, by Douglas Pettit, a fourteen-year-old American, the physically and mentally handicapped son of Theosophical parents.

[5] For some account of Levi and MacKenzie see chapters 2 and 3 of my *Ritual Magic in England* (Neville Spearman 1970).

[6] Or, to be more correct, those of them who followed the leadership of Colonel Olcott and Annie Besant. The majority of American Theosophists had broken away from the parent body in April 1895 and had been at first led by William Q. Judge and then, since Judge's death, by the "Purple Mother", Katherine A. Tingley, a former spiritualist medium. The followers of Katherine Tingley, loathed Leadbeater, just as they loathed all the others who were in any way associated with Annie Besant.

When Douglas returned to his parents' home at the end of the tour it became clear that his marked admiration for Leadbeater had been mysteriously transformed into an even stronger dislike for the man and all his doings. When Mrs. Pettit first tried to question her son on this change in his feelings she was at first met by silence and seeming incomprehension. Some months later, after rumours about Leadbeater's sexual morality had reached her from England—for years G. R. S. Mead and other English Theosophists had been suspicious of the nature of the relationship between Leadbeater and some of his young pupils—she again questioned Douglas, this time much more persistently, and this time he told her his story in full. He alleged that on his first night alone with his temporary tutor, for such was Leadbeater's supposed office, he had been taken into his bed and taught the practice of mutual masturbation. Acts of this nature, claimed Douglas, had continued intermittently throughout the entire period of the Western tour.

Mrs. Pettit was deeply disturbed by this confession, and, in search of advice, took the story to her friend Helen Dennis, like herself both an ardent Theosophist and a native of Chicago. I have no doubt that Mrs. Dennis listened to her friend's tale with a more than ordinary concern—for she had noticed that her own son, Robin, had developed a dislike of Leadbeater since a brief stay with him in Toronto. Inevitably, Robin was also questioned; he, too, broke down and told a similar story of mutual masturbation, although, in his case, the incident seems to have been an isolated one. The most damaging allegation made by Robin was that the practice had been taught him under the guise of religion. "Somehow", he told his mother, "he made me believe it was Theosophical."

Mrs. Dennis was a figure of some importance in the Theosophical Society, for she had held the position of Corresponding Secretary of the Esoteric Section in America,[7] and, with the help of her assistant, Dr. Elizabeth Chichester, she used her position to launch a campaign against Leadbeater. By the beginning of 1906 such leading American Theosophists as Frank Knothe, President of the New York Lodge, and Alexander Fullerton, a former Episcopalian clergyman, had been

---

[7] Formally, the Esoteric Section (at one time called the Eastern Section) was an unofficial organisation, its members of no more importance than any other member of the Theosophical Society. In practice, however, it always wielded great power and later, after the death of Colonel Olcott, exerted real control over the affairs of the Society.

informed of the nature of the charges that had been made by the boys, and had set up an informal committee to investigate them.

In January 1906 Mrs. B. Dennis wrote to Anne Besant formally informing her of the allegations made against her friend. At the same time Fullerton[8] wrote a similar letter to Leadbeater himself.

Leadbeater's defence was a complex one, and surprisingly enough, did not involve a complete denial of the truth of the boys' accusations. He claimed that there had only been one incident with Douglas, and that this solitary episode had taken place after the boy had approached him for help in dealing with the strange feelings that he had been experiencing since the onset of puberty. As far as Robin was concerned, said Leadbeater, the lad had been corrupted by another youth, a certain Nevers, and all that he, Leadbeater, had done was to give the boy some useful advice on diet and to urge him to use vigorous exercise as a means of suppressing unwanted sexual desires. Leadbeater did admit, however, that he had subsequently advised Robin to use "regular discharges" (i.e. masturbation) as a means of reducing sexual tension.

Although this defence was feeble enough, there did, at first, seem to be some chance of its being successful; after all, the boys' evidence was uncorroborated and, in spite of the rumours that had been circulated in certain quarters, most of the members of the Theosophical Society still regarded Leadbeater as a man of unblemished reputation. Leadbeater's hopes of being believed were, however, sharply diminished with the discovery of documentary evidence against him in the shape of a letter from him to Robin. This letter had been found in the Toronto house at which the pair had stayed, and most of it was harmless enough, a rather meandering discourse on the subject of astral travel; but in the middle of the letter came a passage in cipher.[9] This passage had obvious auto-erotic implications and, when decoded, read: "If it comes without help he needs rubbing more often. But not too often, or he will not come

---

[8] There was an element of wry comedy in Fullerton's indignation, for he himself seems to have had homosexual inclinations and, in February 1910, was charged with sending indecent letters through the mails—interestingly enough the letters were sent to young Douglas Pettit. Fullerton was found unfit to plead and spent the rest of his life in a home for the criminally insane.

[9] Or, to be more accurate, an alphabetic code. This was simple enough in nature; all consonants were represented by the previous letter of the alphabet, all vowels by the following vowel in the series, a, e, i, o, u. Thus the coded letter *e* could represent either the consonant *f* or the vowel *a*.

well. Does this happen when you are asleep; tell me fully. Glad sensation is so pleasant. Thousand kisses darling."

At this stage of events Colonel Olcott, the venerated President-Founder of the Society, set his famous "roving eye'[10] to work, made a preliminary examination of the evidence, and established a committee of investigation. After some deliberation this committee, consisting of the entire Executive Committee of the British Section together with some French and American representatives, summoned Leadbeater to appear before it in London. To the surprise of some of his opponents the accused man obeyed the summons and what has sometimes been called "the trial" took place on May 16th, 1906.

In his evidence to the committee Leadbeater put forward the extraordinary claim that his clairvoyant examination of children's auras enabled him to know when these same children were in sexual difficulties or in need of advice! Accordingly, so he said, he had advised not only Douglas and Robin, but several other boys as well, to engage in masturbation. This bold front collapsed when, under Olcott's questioning, Leadbeater broke down badly and admitted that there had been, on occasion, a certain amount of what he termed "indicative action", and also that his advice had not been limited to boys who had already reached the age of puberty. Leadbeater had already voluntarily offered his resignation from the Theosophical Society, and, after hearing these damaging confessions, the committee decided, by a majority vote, to accept it.

For a time Leadbeater retired to the isolation of Jersey, occupying his time with much letter writing, justifying the course of conduct he had followed and alleging that his opponents were under the influence of "Black Magicians".

Nine months later, on February 17th, 1907, the situation was transformed by the death, following a month-long coma, of Colonel

---

[10] We owe our best description of this famous eye to that odd Russian, Vsevolod Solovyoff. He wrote of Olcott that "one of his eyes was extremely disobedient, and from time to time used to turn in all directions, sometimes with startling and most disagreeable rapidity. As long as the disobedient eye remained still, you had before you a handsome, agreeable and kindly, but not particularly clever man, who won you by his appearance and inspired you with confidence. Then suddenly something twitched, the eye got loose and began to stray suspiciously and knavishly, and confidence vanished in a moment." The full text of Solovyoff's amusing presentation of Olcott can be found on pp. 36–9 of his *A Modern Priestess of Isis* (Longman Green & Co. 1895).

Olcott. His nominated successor was Annie Besant who, even before her formal election to the Presidency in the following June, had been engaged in planning the gradual rehabilitation of her old friend Leadbeater. To help the attainment of this end she recruited the services of Dr. Weller Van Hook, a well-known American Theosophist, and persuaded him to write three open letters for circulation to the general membership of the Society. In these letters Van Hook not only claimed that the enemies of Leadbeater were also enemies "of the Masters and of the future religion of the World", but went to the lengths of stating that the Master Koot Hoomi had appeared to him and informed him that Leadbeater's sexual teachings were correct and in accordance with occult principles.[11]

The white-washing operation was successful, and by the beginning of 1909 Leadbeater was, to all intents and purposes, back in the Society, although it was not until the following year that this was publicly acknowledged by the Theosophical press. For a time all seemed well, but only three years later new allegations concerning Leadbeater's morality led to a fresh upheaval in the Theosophical ranks. This time there was even greater publicity, for the charges and counter charges were no longer confined to the comparative privacy of internal Theosophical journals and committees, but were openly made in the Courts of both India and England. The allegations were, in fact, a component part of the First Act of the tragi-comedy of Annie Besant's attempt to promote an Indian youth, J. Krishnamurti, as Christ returned to Earth.

For some years Theosophists in general, and Annie Besant in particular, had been forecasting a new manifestation of the Christ, an event which they originally seem to have anticipated taking place *circa* 1950. Later there was a considerable shortening of the time-scale, and for a brief period Annie Besant hoped that Dr. Van Hook's son, Hubert, born in 1896, might be the vehicle through which the "World Teacher" would, in due course, manifest himself; but by the beginning

[11] Koot Hoomi was one of the Masters, those, almost certainly mythical, semi-supernatural beings who supposedly dwelt in the Himalayas and had given Madame Blavatsky her mission. As far as the message to Van Hook was concerned it seems clear that either there was a doctrinal split in the Great White Brotherhood (as these supermen were collectively known), or that the celestial telephone lines had become badly crossed—for only a few months previously Koot Hoomi's colleague, the Master Morya, had informed Olcott that while Leadbeater was indubitably sincere his sexual teachings were utterly wrong.

of 1910 both she and Leadbeater were convinced that Krishnamurti was the chosen vessel.[12]

Krishnamurti was the son of Narayaniah, a devout Theosophist of the Brahmin caste, who had, in 1908, retired from a junior clerkship in the Civil Service and made his home in a small cottage just outside the main compound of the Theosophical headquarters at Adyar, Madras. It was not long before Leadbeater's attention was drawn to Krishnamurti and his younger brother Nityananda—according to his own account by the remarkable size and colour of their astral auras, according to another, and I think more likely, story by the sight of the boys bathing. One thing, at any rate, is clear enough; either the astral or physical body of Krishnamurti made such an impact upon Leadbeater that it converted him to the belief that here, and here alone, was the chosen vehicle of the Master of Masters. By the end of 1909 Narayaniah had been persuaded to let the boys move from their home into a suite adjacent to Leadbeater's own quarters and later, on February 10th, 1910, he signed a letter, drafted by the Vice-President of the Theosophical Society, giving Annie Besant the custody of the boys. He came to bitterly regret this guardianship when, early in 1911, the *Antiseptic*, a local medical journal, published an article raking up all the old scandals about Leadbeater. This article *Psychopathia Sexualis in a Mahatma* went so far as to suggest that in a previous incarnation Leadbeater had been "Onan the son of Guda and Sua and grandson of Israel".[13] Over the next eighteen months Narayaniah's anxieties

---

[12] Arthur H. Nethercot, whose two-volume biography seems destined to remain the definitive study of the life of Annie Besant, finds some discrepancy between the Besantine "conception of Jesus as an Avatar and Jesus as a mere Master among other Masters". I do not think this discrepancy has any real existence. The extremely confused Christology of Annie Besant was very similar to that of the Docetics; she regarded Jesus as a mere man, in whom the "Cosmic Christ" had manifested at the time of his baptism in the Jordan. Jesus, she held, had continued to be "overshadowed" until the crucifixion, when the Christ (temporarily) withdrew from his vehicle, thus explaining Jesus' cry from the cross of "My God, My God, why hast though forsaken me". It is interesting to note that Mary Baker Eddy held very similar views as to the nature of the Christ.

[13] A reference to "the sin of Onan", a now obsolete term for masturbation. Onan, it will be remembered, was the Old Testament character who "spilled his seed upon the ground", thus arousing the anger of Jehovah. Most Hebrew scholars are now convinced that the Biblical passage in question refers not to masturbation but to *coitus interruptus*, the practice of male withdrawal before ejaculation.

increased until, on October 24th, 1912, he filed a suit for the recovery of the children. His feelings at the time are best conveyed by his own written statement which I reproduce in full.

IN THE COURT OF THE DISTRICT JUDGE OF
CHINGLEPUT
O.S. No. 47 of 1912
J. NARAYANIAH—Plaintiff
Versus
MRS. ANNIE BESANT—Defendant
THE WRITTEN STATEMENT OF THE PLAINTIFF

1. J. NARAYANIAH, the plaintiff above is a Government Pensioner living at 118 Big Street, Triplicane, Madras.

His address or service of all notices and processes, through his Vakil at Madras, care of Mr. P. N. Anantana Chariar, B.A., B.L., High Court Vakil, Chingleput.

2. Mrs. Annie Besant is the President of the Theosophical Society and has her permanent place of residence at Adyar, near Madras, at the Head-quarters of the said Society.

3. The plaintiff, who had been a member of the Theosophical Society prior to his retirement, was, at the beginning of 1909, invited by the defendant to take up his residence at Adyar and do the work of Assistant Correspondence Secretary of the Esoteric Section. The plaintiff had at the time very great respect and veneration for the defendant, whom he regarded as his spiritual preceptress and whom he credited with more than human attributes, and he agreed to serve her as the Assistant Correspondence Secretary without receiving from her any remuneration whatever. The plaintiff accordingly took up his abode at Adyar along with his second and third sons, J. Krishnamurti and J. Nityananda, who are respectively aged 17 and 14. The boys were receiving their education in the Penathoor Subramanyam High School at Mylapore, Madras. But as Mr. R. B. Clarke and Mr. C. W. Leadbeater of the Theosophical Society undertook their education, and as the boys were not making much progress in their studies, the plaintiff stopped them from school and put them under their charge at Adyar. In or about December 1909 the defendant, who is frequently on tour in connection with her theosophical work, returned to India and promised to help under-

take the future education of the boys. Accordingly the plaintiff stopped the boys from school altogether and kept them with himself at Adyar.

4. About the beginning of 1910 the defendant requested the plaintiff to give a letter constituting her the guardian of the boys; and after some persuasion both on the part of the defendant and Sir S. Subramania Iyer, for whom the plaintiff had great respect, the plaintiff gave such letter, especially as the defendant had assured the plaintiff that the only reason for asking the letter was that after the plaintiff's lifetime his relations might give trouble to the defendant but for such a letter. The boys, however, continued to live with the plaintiff.

5. In or about the latter part of March 1910 the plaintiff discovered that his son J. Krishnamurti was being led into improper habits by C. W. Leadbeater, who held a very high position in the Theosophical Society; and on one occasion the plaintiff himself saw Leadbeater committing an unnatural offence with the first minor. A few days after, the plaintiff strongly remonstrated with Mr. Leadbeater, and made preparations for leaving Adyar with his sons, but on the persuasion of Sir Subramania Iyer, the Vice-President of the Theosophical Society, to stay on until the return of the defendant, who was then on tour, and in deference to the request of the defendant by wire, the plaintiff did not carry out his intentions. On her return, the plaintiff complained to the defendant about the conduct of Leadbeater and she promised to keep the boys away from him, and immediately ordered the shifting of their bathrooms and residential rooms from the down-floor to the first-floor; and later on, when C. W. Leadbeater shifted his own room upstairs, the defendant arranged to take away the boys to Benares, and assured the plaintiff that they would have nothing to do with Leadbeater. In spite of this, they were again being allowed to associate with the said Leadbeater, and it was about this time that he heard from other Theosophist friends that one Luxman, a personal attendant, had seen C. W. Leadbeater and J. Krishnamurti in the defendant's room engaged in committing an unnatural offence.

On a further remonstrance by the plaintiff, the defendant promised to take the boys away to England, and accordingly she left India for England about the end of March 1911 and returned to India only in the beginning of October 1911, during which time, so far as the plaintiff was aware, the boys were kept away from associating with the said Mr. Leadbeater.

6. In or about November 1911 the defendant told the plaintiff that the boys were making rapid spiritual progress and were approaching initiation by the Masters (a set of superhuman gurus living on the eastern slopes of the Himalayas) believed in by the Theosophists. She therefore proposed to keep the boys with Mr. Leadbeater at Ootacamund preparatory to their initiation. On the plaintiff's objection the boys were not sent to Ootacamund. The plaintiff met the defendant in Benares in December 1911 and insisted on an absolute separation of the boys from Mr. Leadbeater. But for the first time, to the plaintiff's great surprise, the defendant refused to adopt any such course, and alleged that the boys and Leadbeater was an Arhat or Saint, "who is on the verge of divinity". The plaintiff stated that he could not accept any such position, and that unless the separation took place he would take action in the matter.

7. The plaintiff returned from Benares to Adyar, and there, on or about January 19, 1912, the defendant, in presence of certain members of the Theosophical Society, sent for the plaintiff and asked him what he wanted to be done in respect of the boys. The plaintiff only demanded that there should be absolute separation from the said Leadbeater. She agreed to this, and asked the plaintiff whether he had any objection to the boys being taken to England. The plaintiff assented, as the defendant had alleged that she would be returning to India in April or May. In spite of her undertaking to keep the boys separated from Leadbeater, the plaintiff has reason to believe that after reaching England she took the boys to Leadbeater in Italy and stayed with him for some weeks, thus breaking her promises. The plaintiff submits that, having regard to the filthy and unnatural habits, character and antecedents of the said Leadbeater, it is extremely undesirable that the boys should be allowed to associate with him, or that he should be allowed to have access to them.

8. The defendant started for England about February 1912, but before she started she endeavoured to obtain evidence that Leadbeater was not guilty of the act complained of, and had a statement from her attendant, Luxman, recorded to that effect, and sent a copy of the same to the plaintiff. The plaintiff, on perusing this, wrote two letters to the defendant on the 7th and 15th February 1912, pointing out that even according to the statement aforesaid it was clear that

Mr. Leadbeater was seen half dressed in her room with Krishnamurti. Before these letters reached the defendant she wrote a letter to the plaintiff on February 7, 1912, from on board steamer, in which for the first time she set up that plaintiff has been ill-treating and starving his children. The plaintiff submits that this is an impudent and malicious lie trumped up by the defendant in view to further legal proceedings, as would be seen from the fact that the plaintiff was all along one of the *trusted* members of the Theosophical Society and the Assistant Correspondence Secretary of the Esoteric Section thereof, and was paying for the mess of the boys wherever they were until November 1911. The defendant in that letter also threatened that she would keep the boys in England until they attained their majority. The defendant also wanted the plaintiff to remove from Adyar, which he has accordingly done. The defendant has now returned to India, and has purposely refrained from bringing the boys with her to India in order to hamper the plaintiff in his efforts to recover the boys.

9. The plaintiff states that all along the defendant has been aware of the practices of Leadbeater, and that after she reached England she took the boys again to Mr. Leadbeater in Italy. The plaintiff submits that the conduct of the defendant as aforesaid renders her totally unfit to be in charge of the boys. The plaintiff further submits that the defendant has been stating that the first boy, who is named Alcyone, is, or is going to be, the Lord Christ, and sometimes that he is Lord Maitreya, and she has induced a number of persons to believe in this theory, with the result that the boy is deified, and that a number of respectable persons prostrate before him and show other signs of worship. It is also given out that the elder boy wrote a book called *At the Feet of the Master*, which the plaintiff has reasons to believe to be a compilation made by Leadbeater. In any case, the boy who is not able to write a decent English letter is absolutely incapable of producing such a work. The plaintiff submits that this course of conduct is calculated to warp the moral nature of the boys and to make them moral degenerates. The defendant, beyond putting forward divine claims on behalf of the boys, has not been taking proper care of their education. The first boy has not picked up the rudiments of the English language in spite of three years of alleged tuition by English tutors. The plaintiff submits that he as the father of the boys, is entitled to act as their guardian and is entitled to their

custody, and further submits that the letter referred to in paragraph 4 cannot have the effect of depriving him of the same; even assuming that it could, under the circumstances above detailed the defendant has proved herself totally unfit to be in charge of the boys, and the boys ought to be removed from her charge. When the said letter was given, the plaintiff believed the defendant to be superhuman and was completely under her influence and control, and he took her to be his preceptress who should be obeyed implicitly and make any sacrifice demanded, and the contract, if any, made under such circumstances, is voidable on the ground of undue influence. In any case, if the defendant is unfit to be entrusted with the guardianship of the minors, the plaintiff's natural right as the guardian will again arise, inasmuch as the letter, if valid in law, was only a surrender of the rights in favour of the defendant alone. The plaintiff's delay in taking action against the defendant has been due only to the faith which until recently he shared with many other persons that the defendant was semi-divine, and that the plaintiff was exceptionally fortunate in getting the defendant to take charge of the boys. The plaintiff was also led to believe that the boy Krishnamurti was also possessed of divine attributes, and the plaintiff had to change his belief only on discovery of the circumstances connected with Leadbeater's connection with the boys and on the confession of the boy himself that the book *At the Feet of the Master* was not written by Krishnamurti, and on the discovery of the present imperfect state of their education. These circumstances came to light only during the latter part of 1912, and it was only on receipt of the letter dated February 7, 1912, that the plaintiff realised fully how malicious and mendacious the defendant was and how totally unfit she was to be the guardian of the boys.

10. The plaintiff submits that as the guardian of the boys he is entitled to their custody, and even otherwise, in the interest of the boys and their moral welfare, the defendant ought to be compelled to give them up to the plaintiff or to such other person as the Court may think fit. The plaintiff sent a notice on the 11th July demanding that the boys should be brought back to India and replaced under the guardianship and custody of the plaintiff. The plaintiff submits that he had no authority and could not have delegated his parental rights to the defendant. Even assuming, however, that he could do so he was at liberty to revoke it at any time, especially with a view to pro-

moting the moral welfare of the boys, and that after the receipt of the said letter the defendant had no authority to keep the boys with herself. In answer to the plaintiff's notice the defendant merely acknowledged its receipt and did nothing more, and the plaintiff believes that she has left the boys in England.

11. The cause of the action arose partly at Adyar in the years 1910, 1911 and 1912, when the plaintiff discovered the various matters referred to above in relation to the bringing up of the boys and lastly on or about July 11, 1912, when the plaintiff sent a registered notice demanding delivery of the minors.

12. The value of the relief for the purposes of jurisdiction is Rs. 3000.

13. The plaintiff prays for judgment:

(a) Declaring that the plaintiff is entitled to the guardianship and custody of his minor boys, J. Krishnamurti and J. Nityananda.

(b) Declaring, if necessary, that the defendant is not entitled to, or in any case fit to be in charge and guardianship of, the said boys.

(c) Directing the defendant to hand over the boys to the plaintiff or to such person as this honourable Court may seem meet.

(d) For costs of the suit and for such further or other relief as to this honourable Court may seem meet.

I, Narayaniah, the plaintiff above named, do hereby declare that all the facts stated above, except portions of paragraph 7 and 9, are true to my knowledge, and the above said portions are based on information and belief.

(Signed) J. Narayaniah.
October 24, 1912.

Narayaniah's statement was so vague as to the nature of the "unnatural offence" which he claimed to have witnessed that it led many readers of the newspaper reports of the case into the mistaken belief that Leadbeater was being accused of sodomy; amongst those so deceived was Aleister Crowley who, in a speech delivered at Manchester on June 28th, 1913, took a high moral tone and declared that he deemed "the French slang 'Petit Jesus' is being taken too seriously when a senile sex-maniac like Leadbeater proclaims his catamites as Coming Christs". Such statements showed a complete misunderstanding of the nature of the allegations; as I have previously said, mutual masturbation was the worst of which Leadbeater was ever accused.

The trial, which had been transferred to the High Court in Madras, did not begin until March 20th, 1913 and when judgment was finally given on April 15th it pleased nobody; Annie Besant lost her guardianship, for although the evidence of Narayaniah and Luxman had been thoroughly discredited—both had made a very poor impression under cross-examination—the Judge had denounced Leadbeater as "a man holding immoral ideas" and ruled that as Narayaniah had not been aware that Krishnamurti was to be brought up as "a vehicle of supernatural powers" at the time when he had made Annie Besant the boys' guardian he was fully entitled to revoke the agreement. On the other hand Narayaniah was, most unreasonably, ordered to pay the full costs of both sides.

As soon as Annie Besant heard the verdict she lodged an appeal against it and obtained a stay of execution of the Judge's order that the boys should be immediately returned to their father. She fared badly in the Appeal Court, however, for not only was the lower Court's ruling on the guardianship upheld, but the decision on costs was reversed. A further appeal, to the Judicial Committee of the Privy Council, was made.

On May 25th, 1914 the Judicial Committee issued its full judgment. This time Annie was completely successful—it was perhaps, significant that Lord Haldane, the Chairman of the Committee, was an old friend of hers—and it was laid down in the judgment that the decision of the Madras High Court was invalid because the Court had failed to consider the wishes and interests of the boys. The Committee pointed out that Narayaniah could start the legal battle all over again, this time in the English High Court; but Narayaniah realised that his sons would have reached the legal age of majority long before the case could be decided, so Annie Besant was left victorious.

Ten weeks after the Privy Council decision the first World War began and public interest in the doings of the Theosophical Society diminished. For the next four years the British people had more important things to think about than the alleged sexual irregularities of C. W. Leadbeater and the coming Christhood of Krishnamurti. It was too good to last! After the war a fresh storm blew up, and this time it was difficult to know whether Leadbeater's enemies were more annoyed by his sexual behaviour or his episcopal activities in the Liberal Catholic Church. Indeed, in the minds of Leadbeater's opponents, there seems to have been little distinction made between homosexuality and Liberal Catholicism.

THE BISHOP AND THE BOYS

The Liberal Catholic Church had come into existence as a result of the ecclesiastical activities of an eccentric Englishman named A. H. Mathew, an erratic and unstable character, whose lifelong love of animals seems to have been the only constant element in his personality make-up. Born in 1852 of a Roman Catholic father and an Anglican mother Mathew underwent baptism in both Churches. Perhaps this early influence was the cause of the religious indecision that made him first an Anglican theological student, then a Roman Catholic priest—at this period of his life his interest in animals was responsible for him terrorising the faithful of St. Mary's, Bath, by introducing a live tiger into his pulpit—then a Unitarian, then a curate of the Church of England, then a Catholic layman and, finally an Old Catholic Archbishop. Even this last period was marred by one submission to Rome—recanted, inevitably enough, a few weeks later.

Mathew was consecrated as an Old Catholic Bishop on April 28th, 1908 by Archbishop Gul of Utrecht. On historical grounds the validity of his consecration seems unquestionable, for although the Dutch Old Catholic Church had been in schism from Rome since 1739 its episcopal line of succession could be traced back unbroken to Cardinal Antonion Barberini. Nevertheless, the consecration had clearly been obtained by fraud, for while both the Dutch Old Catholics and Mathew himself were sincerely convinced that the latter represented a large and growing body of English Catholics who desired independence from Rome, the reality was very different. For Mathew was no more than the innocent tool of a tiny body of disgruntled excommunicated, and possibly financially dishonest, Catholic priests. These were led by two Monsignori, Herbert Beale and Arthur Howarth, both of whom had been at one time in charge of parishes in the diocese of Nottingham. They had been on good terms with Bishop Bagshawe, who had been Bishop of Nottingham until his forcible retirement in 1901. Bagshawe has been described as saintly, but senility seems to have been a more noticeable characteristic, and in spite of occasional flashes of bad temper—on one occasion he excommunicated the entire membership of that High Tory and eminently respectable organisation the Primrose League—he was tolerant to the point of lunacy and appointed to responsible positions priests who had been sacked from other dioceses. So great was Bagshawe's capacity for turning a blind eye to the behaviour of his subordinates, however outrageous, that his diocese became known as *refugium peccatorum*, the refuge of sinners. Bishop Brindle,

Bagshawe's successor, was a man of quite a different type and he instituted a general clean-up, in the course of which he sacked Beale and Howarth for the alleged misuse of mass-stipends and other financial irregularities. These two managed to convince Mathew and the Old Catholics that they represented seventeen priests and eight large parishes. Both parishes and priests were largely imaginary, and the two Monsignori seem to have had no other motive for getting Mathew consecrated as the head of a non-existent English Old Catholic Church than a desire to annoy their lawful superiors, Bishop Brindle and the Cardinal-Archbishop of Westminster.

On his return from his Dutch consecration Mathew soon realised that he had been the victim of fraud. Until his death in 1919 he devoted the remainder of his life to consoling himself for his loneliness by writing lengthy essays designed to prove the Baconian authorship of Shakespeare and dreaming of a National Catholic Church under his own leadership. Unfortunately for his own reputation Mathew attempted to put the latter dream into practice and he ordained priests and consecrated Bishops; he was a remarkably poor judge of character and many of his clergy were clearly quite unsuited to hold any sort of religious office.

In 1914 Mathew consecrated F. S. Willoughby as Titular Bishop of St. Pancras.[14] The latter had managed to convince Mathew that he had been subjected to religious persecution in the Church of England because of his Anglo-Catholic theological views; in reality he had been forced to resign his living after a particularly revolting series of homosexual offences against choirboys. Willoughby's motive for becoming a Bishop seems to have been financial, for after his consecration he appears to have been willing to confer the episcopate upon anyone willing to pay a sufficiently large fee.

By this time an actual majority of Mathew's tiny following were members of the Theosophical Society or one or other of its front organisations; indeed, for a brief period Mathew himself had an intellectual flirtation with the Theosophical Society, which he seems to have hoped, with the optimism that was so typical of him, to incorporate into his own movement. Only two months before his consecration of Willoughby Mathew wrote as follows to Reginald Farrer, one of his priests who was also a Theosophist:

[14] In the *Ancient Catholic Church*—the name by which Mathew was calling his tiny organisation.

"I have so often seen a sort of mental vision of Mrs. Besant in the garb of an *abbess*! It is very curious, but I think something is working in her mind and that she is seeing more clearly the divinity of the Catholic system and revelation, which is alone able to satisfy the soul's aspirations and longings. She would be another St. Teresa or Catherine of Siena—and I have for some time—quite a year—felt that that is her destiny. But we shall see."

Mathew saw indeed! For just a year after the above letter was written Mathew's hopes of taking over the Theosophical Society were completely destroyed. Instead the Theosophical Society took over his Church, leaving Mathew with a following of exactly three—one priest and two laywomen. The remainder of Mathew's former followers elected as their chief, James Wedgwood, one of the founders of an occult organisation called the Temple of the Rosy Cross, a holder of the thirty-third degree of co-masonry, and a former General Secretary of the English section of the Theosophical Society. Under his leadership the Theosophists carried on as the Old Roman Catholic Church.

Willoughby, whom Mathew had suspended from the episcopate after a revealing series of articles in the scurrilous magazine *John Bull*, obligingly supplied the (Theosophical) Old Roman Catholics with three Bishops, consecrating Bernard Gauntlett and Robert King[15] in September 1915 and Wedgwood himself in the following year.

Shortly after his consecration Wedgwood handed over the conduct of ecclesiastical affairs in England to Bishop King and set off for Australia to see Leadbeater, who had been in that country since 1913. Leadbeater himself was quickly made a Bishop, an event that he seems to have regarded as being of great importance; he wrote to Annie Besant:

"Wedgwood has arrived and is in good health. His consecration to the Episcopate has had the unexpected result of putting him practically at the head of the Old Catholic movement so far as the British Empire is concerned. . . . This being so he desires most earnestly to offer the movement to the World Teacher as one of the vehicles for His force, and a channel for the preparation of His Coming. I took him therefore

---

[15] Bishop King a professional astrologer, remained a Theosophist until his death in 1953. Gauntlett resigned from the episcopate in 1924, joined the British Israelites, and travelled widely giving lectures designed to prove that the Anglo-Saxons were the lost ten tribes of Israel.

to the LORD MAITREYA[16] ... and He was graciously pleased to accept the offer, and to say that He thought the movement would fill a niche in the scheme, and would be useful to Him ... with His permission Wedgwood has consecrated *me* as a Bishop, on the understanding that I am at perfect liberty to wear my ordinary dress, and am in no way bound to perform any ecclesiastical ceremonies or take any outward part in the work unless I see it useful to do so, but to act as an intermediary between the LORD and this branch of His Church."

The Liberal Catholic Church—it had adopted its new name in 1918—enjoyed a certain modest success and quickly fell completely under the control of Leadbeater who, in 1920, published a lengthy and turgid volume, *The Science of the Sacraments*, devoted to the liturgy of the Church and giving a great deal of amazing information and advice—the use of Gothic Revival vestments, for example, was recommended because "a terrific torrent (of force) pours from the radiating disc on the back".

Wedgwood seems to have shared Leadbeater's love of boys but not his hatred of women[17] and, only a few months after Scotland Yard had begun taking an interest in his friendships with young men, he was making an unsuccessful attempt to seduce the wife of T. H. Martyn, a leading Australian Theosophist. Subsequently Martyn became the leader of the Australian opposition to Leadbeater and his practices, sexual and ecclesiastical.

There is no doubt that Wedgwood was an active homosexual; he seems to have been addicted to what Americans sometimes call "tea room trade"—temporary liaisons made in public urinals. On one occasion a private detective followed Wedgwood for two hours, during which period he visited no less than eighteen "comfort-stations". When taxed with this Wedgwood produced an interesting and ingenious explanation; it was true, he said, that he had been looking for a young man, but for a particular young man—an individual he had known in a previous incarnation and who had (so he discovered from an astral revelation) gone to the bad and was in need of redemption!

[16] The LORD MAITREYA, it will be remembered, was the Coming Christ, shortly due to manifest Himself, so it was believed, in Krishnamurti. It is to be presumed that Leadbeater took Wedgwood to the LORD MAITREYA by means of a quick visit to the astral plane.

[17] Leadbeater had never particularly liked the opposite sex and by 1916 this aversion had reached the point where he (a) refused to shake hands with women and (b) refused to stay in houses where husband and wife shared a bed.

Martyn and his allies soon came to look upon the Liberal Catholic Church as no more than the front for a gang of pederasts; Mrs. Martyn went so far as to claim that she had come upon Leadbeater and one of her sons in a naked embrace. Her suspicions, so she said, had been previously aroused by stains she had found on Leadbeater's sheets.

By 1922 the whole Australian press was running a virulent campaign, based on information almost certainly supplied by Martyn, against Leadbeater, Wedgwood, the Liberal Catholic Church, and homosexuality. Australia being Australia the vulgarity of the campaign was almost more than Leadbeater could bear—the headline LEADBEATER A SWISH BISH WITH BOYS caused him particular offence.

As on previous occasions the fuss died down. Theosophical parents continued to send their sons to Leadbeater for training and the Liberal Catholic Church grew in strength. Leadbeater even built an open air theatre overlooking Sydney harbour in readiness, so it was said, for the day when Krishnamurti would become Christ and appear walking over the sea to visit his old friend and teacher. Alas! It was not to be. For Krishnamurti disappointed his followers by announcing that a mistake had been made and that, in spite of the prophecies made by Annie Besant and Leadbeater, the Christ was not going to incarnate in him after all!

Leadbeater died peacefully in 1934. He was predeceased by his giant cat. She was an animal of a highly evolved spiritual nature and was due to be reincarnated as a human being, a member of the Theosophical Society. Or so, at any rate, said Leadbeater.

Leadbeater's life and personality were alike peculiar, he was a human enigma and he cries out for a biographer. One thing, however, is I think quite certain. However odd his sexual beliefs, whatever his relationships with some of his pupils may have been, he was not "a Black Magician using homosexual activities to create a reservoir of astral power"—there is not a shadow of proof for the allegations made by Dion Fortune and accepted unthinkingly by so many occultists.

CHAPTER THIRTEEN

Sexual Magic in the United States

To European radicals and utopians of the last century the word "America" had the same semi-magical appeal that the word "Russia" had for left-wing intellectuals of the 'thirties and the word "Cuba" has for some black militants today. These utopians regarded America as the sociological laboratory in which they would put their theories into practice, turn their dreams into reality. At one time or another almost every charismatic sect, whether political or religious in its underlying ideology, made an attempt at communal living on the North American continent. On the whole the politically orientated communities were far less successful than those in which the common ideology was of a religious nature; thus the communities founded by the followers of such early socialists as Robert Owen and Fourier soon folded up, in spite of the optimism of their founders,[1] while some of the religious communities founded at the same time still survive.

Most of these communities held unorthodox sexual beliefs of one kind or another, varying from, at one extreme, the Shakers who believed all sexuality to be sinful and preached total abstinence,[2] to, at the other, the Oneida perfectionists, who looked upon sex as a sacrament and arranged that at puberty child-members of their community should be initiated by older members of the opposite sex. These com-

---

[1] Fourier was particularly optimistic. He contended that with the advance of socialism it would be possible to chemically transform the oceans of the world into lemonade, a beverage of which he seems to have been fond to the point of addiction.

[2] With great success; the Shaker communities were economically successful but died out because no children were born to members.

munities and their beliefs, however, lie outside my main theme, for they do not seem to have derived from any traditional esoteric source. The same is probably true of the sexual magic of P. B. Randolph, the nineteenth-century mulatto occultist whom I have mentioned in a previous chapter, in spite of its resemblance to certain aspects of Tantricism.[3]

The sexual magic of the *Ordo Templi Orientis* was introduced into North America before 1914 by Aleister Crowley's disciple C. S. Jones, who eventually opened branches of the Order in Vancouver, Los Angeles and (possibly) Washington D.C. Jones was devoted to his occult master, whose teachings he considered to be applicable to every aspect of human existence,[4] and worked hard to build up the O.T.O., although without much success. However, Theodor Reuss—who, it will be remembered, was Crowley's superior in the O.T.O. until 1922 —disregarded Crowley's claims to occult supremacy in America and in 1916 conferred a charter upon an already-existing organisation authorising it to function as the North American branch of the Order. Crowley had a low opinion of the American chief of this organisation. He described him as:

"... one of the charlatans who worked the Rosicrucian racket, merrily disdainful of criticism based on his elementary blunders in Latin and his total ignorance of the history of the Order which he claimed to rule ...

"... I proved in a dozen different ways that the man was a foul liar. That was easy enough. His claims were grotesquely absurd. For instance, he said that I don't know how many knights of England and France—the most improbable people—were Rosicrucians. He said the Order was founded by one of the early Egyptian kings and professed to have documentary evidence of an unbroken hierarchy of initiates since then. He called the Order Rosae Crucis and

---

[3] It is interesting to note that, like the Tantric practitioners of Bengal, Randolph used psychedelic drugs in his rites. He seems to have been the first western occultist to take any interest in the allegedly consciousness-expanding properties of ether, hashish etc.

[4] Jones was so well-known for his extravagant admiration of Crowley and Crowley's writings that when an acquaintance saw him standing disconsolately by an immobilised Ford he sarcastically suggested to Jones that he should read the vehicle some of the master's erotic verse. "I've tried that already", replied Jones, "and she just drips oil."

translated it Rosy Cross. He said that in Toulouse the Order possessed a vast temple with fabulous magnificent appointments, an assertion disprovable merely by consulting Baedeker. He said that Rockefeller had given him nine hundred thousand dollars and at the same time sent round the hat with an eloquent plea for the smallest contributions. He professed to be a learned Egyptologist and classical scholar on terms of intimacy with the most exalted personages. Yet, as in the case of Peter, his speech betrayed him. He was a good chap at heart, a genuine lover of truth, by no means altogether ignorant of Magick, and a great fool to put up all this bluff instead of relying on his really good qualities...."

The man whom Crowley regarded with such amused contempt was H. Spencer Lewis and the Order he led to which Reuss had given a charter was the *Ancient and Mystical Order Rosae Crucis*, better known as AMORC, an organisation whose easily-parodied style of advertising ("Francis Bacon, Benjamin Franklin and Spiro Agnew! What was the secret of these men's towering intellectual abilities and intense personal charm? All were Rosicrucians! Write NOW for your free booklet!") has been familiar to readers of pulp-magazines for over fifty years.

Reuss found Lewis a disappointment, however, for the latter was more interested in building up a personal following of his own than acting as a mere lieutenant of Reuss and the O.T.O. It is difficult to know whether Lewis made any actual experiments with sex-magic techniques, but if he did so he soon abandoned them, and while it is true that a certain amount of O.T.O.-derived material was incorporated into AMORC publications during the period 1916–20 it was soon eradicated. Nevertheless, some diagrams of a magical nature which Lewis lifted from Crowley's *Equinox* (such as the Rose Cross which Lewis took from *Equinox* III) have continued to be used by AMORC and still appear in its literature. In later years Lewis found his early connections with Crowley and the O.T.O. a cause for much embarrassment, for they were publicised by his great rival R. Swinburne Clymer —the head of various small, allegedly Rosicrucian societies—in his many attacks upon AMORC in general and Lewis in particular; Clymer referred to Lewis as "the boastful pilfering Imperator with his black-magic, sex-magic connections"—a description which seems to have afforded Lewis little pleasure.

In the 'thirties a former follower of Crowley, a one-time resident of the Abbey of Thelema named C. F. Russell, established an American occult society teaching an unorthodox version of the sexual magic of the O.T.O. Crowley gave his own unflattering impressions of his erstwhile disciple when he came to write his autobiographical *Confessions*. Throughout his narrative Crowley, with untypical kindness, referred to Russell as "Godwin". He wrote:

". . . We had a new member, a boy named Godwin, whom I had known in America. When he first wrote me, he was in Annapolis, an attendant in the naval hospital. The boy had amazing ability, backed by exceptional energy and other moral qualities such as the Great Work, or indeed any work worth the name, requires. Out of his scanty savings he had bought a set of *The Equinox* for a hundred dollars and several other expensive items. He grudged his time as little as his cash. He learnt by heart an astounding number of our sacred books, and when later on I asked him to compile a dictionary of Sanskrit roots for my use on a certain research, he went at it with a will and made good. As against all this, he was surly, mulish and bitterly rebellious. He raved against the injustice of being punished for breaking the regulations of the navy. I vainly showed him that when he signed on as he did of his own free will, he pledged himself to conform with the regulations and that in breaking them he blasphemed himself.

"Reckless in his ardour for knowledge, he injected himself with forty grains of cocaine. He had never tried it before. All he knew was that half a grain had been known to cause death. The record of his experiment makes interesting reading. He began trying to set a piece of glass on fire by the force of his will.

"The next act was plagiarized from Samson. He hung on to a pillar while the Philistines, some half a dozen husky sailor boys, tried to pull him off. They finally managed to sit on his head and control his frantic punches and kicks. They then got surgeons on the job who pulled him through. In a couple of days he was all right again. His experiment, if intended to escape notice, failed. They hauled him before the Lord High-Muck-Amuck, who told him, with the best respects and wishes of Uncle Sam for a prosperous passage to perdition, that after a careful consideration the Navy Department had unanimously decided that they could sweep the seas clear of the White Ensign without troubling themselves to put him to the inconvenience of co-operating. Shaking the pipe-clay of Annapolis from his person, he favoured New York with a flying visit, dropped in on me, and—please could I find him a job? I did what I could, but before I found him work, he had got the Lafayette to try him as a waiter. I thought he might be of use to my 'son'[5] in Detroit and wrote asking him to find an opening. He did so and Godwin went off.

"In all he said and did, one peculiarity obtruded itself—this violent reaction against any act of authority as such, however reasonable, however much to his own advantage. When he noticed the suggestion of discipline, he became blind with rage. His mental faculties were simply snowed under. Having habitually yielded to this impulse, it became a fixed form of his mind, so that even between spasms he would brood incessantly over his wrongs. I hoped the abbey would break up this complex. For a time he improved greatly, but in my absence the Ape,[6] in whose hands I had left the sole authority, had very ably established a routine, adherence to which minimized the time necessary to the prosperity of the household, and thus allowed each mentor the theoretical maximum of leisure for his own chosen work. Godwin rebelled. On two occasions he became, if not literally insane, at least so lost to self-control as to assault her murderously. In both cases, she cowed him by sheer moral superiority as wild beasts are supposed to shrink from the eye which is fearlessly upon their fury. After my return he improved. I recall only one outbreak. My experience was the same as the Ape's, I stood up to him and made him obey, and he obeyed."

Crowley's dislike of Russell probably stemmed from a series of rows between the two that took place during Russell's stay at Crowley's Abbey of Thelema. Crowley gave an amusing account of these disagreements in his *Confessions* while Russell himself gave an almost totally different version of the same events in his privately printed and oddly entitled autobiography *Znuss is Znees*. Whatever the truth of the matter may have been the two parted company, and a few years later Russell founded his own magical order, the G.B.G.; according to Louis T. Culling, who was at one time a local official (a "Neighbour-

---

[5] The "son" was the aforementioned C. S. Jones, whom Crowley considered to be his magical son by his concubine Jane Foster.

[6] The "Ape" was the magical name of one of Crowley's mistresses.

hood Primate") of the organisation, these initials stood for *Great Brotherhood of God*. In correspondence with me, however, Russell has denied that this was so—but as he has not informed me of the true import of the mysterious initials I am in no position to enlighten the reader as to the facts of the matter, in spite of the importance which some occultists clearly attach to the question. Culling has also stated that Crowley authorised the foundation of the G.B.G., but Crowley's surviving diaries, letters and papers contain no indication that this was so. In any case the variations between the G.B.G. and O.T.O. systems of sexual magic make it extremely improbable that any such authorisation was given.

Members of the G.B.G. were recruited by means of advertisements (promising "a short cut to initiation") inserted in occult magazines. Russell interviewed the more promising of those who replied to his advertisements and, if he found them suitable, appointed them as 'Neighbourhood Primates', in charge of local groups of the order. Only the Neighbourhood Primates were in direct touch with the headquarters of the G.B.G., their task being to personally recruit and train members of their local chapters in sex-magic techniques. This form of organisation was probably adopted in order to reduce to a minimum the amount of sexual instruction passing through the mails; at the time the U.S. postal authorities were applying a rigidly puritanical interpretation of the laws against sending obscene matter by mail.

The Neighbourhood Primates were given a financial incentive to build up the membership of their local groups; of the initiation fee of $5 paid by each new member $2.50 was retained by the Neighbourhood Primate and only $2.50 had to be forwarded to headquarters. This policy seems to have met with some success if Louis Culling is to be believed, for according to him there were local chapters of the G.B.G. in all large cities of the United States, in Los Angeles there were seventy-five members, and in Denver there were no less than one hundred and twenty-five—surprisingly large figures, never attained by the O.T.O. itself.

For his first few months of membership the initiate of the G.B.G. was kept in ignorance of its sexual-magical affiliations and these were only revealed to him (or her) after he had satisfactorily completed a course of occult training devised by Russell. Parts of this course were capable of comparatively easy performance (for example the injunction to keep a record of dreams experienced) others were more difficult, particularly the "Magickal Retirement Ritual". This was conducted in a solitary place, lasted for three days, and involved going without food and carrying out a complex ritual eight times a day.

In the G.B.G.'s first sexual-magical degree was taught a practice called Alphaism. This was nothing more than complete chastity in thought, word and deed; i.e. the initiate of this degree was not only obliged to eschew any physical expression of his or her sexuality but was not supposed to allow any sexual emotions, feelings or images to enter his consciousness.

The second degree initiates practised what Russell called Dianism—that is to say, prolonged sexual intercourse not culminating in orgasm. During copulation the practitioners built up "magical images" in their imaginations and invoked the gods in exactly the same way as initiates of the O.T.O. ninth degree. Russell could not have derived this variant form of sex-magic from Crowley, for the ninth degree workings of O.T.O. initiates always ended with male ejaculation, and it is probable that in spite of its resemblance to the sexo-yogic techniques of Buddhist Tantricism Russell evolved it quite independently of oriental influences. Nevertheless, it is clear that he was strongly influenced by *The Heavenly Bridegroom*, a book written by a certain Ida Craddock which not only advocated sexual relations without orgasm (a practice usually known as Carezza or Karezza and strongly disapproved of by most reputable sexologists) but claimed that the use of this method of sexual intercourse was the solution to all marital and emotional problems.

When the initiates had successfully proved their mastery of the practice of Dianism they were admitted into what the G.B.G. called "the Qadosh degree",[7] identical in every respect with the O.T.O. ninth degree; even the instructional papers issued to Qadosh members seem to have been only slightly revised versions of O.T.O. material. The required proof seems to have been no mere formality and candidates for the Qadosh degree were submitted to severe testing. Thus the test in Dianism undergone by Louis Culling before his attainment of the Qadosh grade involved him in paying the travelling expenses of his female examiner from G.B.G. headquarters in Chicago to San Diego. I am glad to be able to report that he passed his test with flying

[7] Qadosh means holy. For some reason Louis Culling persistently miscalled it Qodosh" in his somewhat misleadingly entitled book *The Complete Magick Curriculum of the Secret Order G.B.G.*

9. Crowley, *circa* 1925.

Hulton Picture Library

10. Crowley in O.T.O. insignia as *Baphomet*.

Hulton Picture Library

11. Crowley in old age.

SEXUAL MAGIC IN THE UNITED STATES

colours, engaging (according to his own account) in uninterrupted copulation with his examiner for three hours without orgasm!

In 1938 the G.B.G. either closed down or, at any rate, very much reduced the scope of its magical activities.

Shortly afterwards, however, Crowley's O.T.O. resumed its activities in the United States and its Agape Lodge, situated in California and under the leadership of a brilliant young scientist named Jack Parsons, did its best to extend the influence of the sexual philosophy of the O.T.O. in the New World. For a time the Agape Lodge was comparatively successful, but it broke up in the 'fifties after Parsons' death in a rocket-fuel explosion at his laboratory—curiously enough, the explosion coincided with the climax of a major magical experiment which Parsons was conducting and in conversation with me one occultist has described Parsons as "blowing himself up in a defective Babalon-working".[8]

Today the main group practising sexual magic in the U.S.A. is a small secret inner circle within what is usually regarded as an excessively publicity-conscious and rather "kookie" organisation—the San Francisco-based Church of Satan[9] first brought into prominence by press publicity resulting from Jayne Mansfield's involvement with it and its leader Anton La Vey.

Exactly why enormous female bosoms were such a feature of the Hollywood star-scene of the 'fifties and early 'sixties is a question that has been much discussed by psycho-analysts. Some of them have suggested that occidental middle-class males born in the 'thirties are fascinated by large breasts as a result of infantile deprivation caused by the bottle-feeding and early weaning that were then in vogue with affluent parents. Another, either more perceptive or more cynical than his fellows, has claimed that the Hollywood emphasis on large-sized busts was a public-relations exercise on the part of the American dairy-industry, a cunning device aimed at increasing the consumption of milk and other dairy produce. Whatever may have been the unconscious motives of their admirers there is no doubt that these full-breasted

---

[8] Further details of the Agape Lodge and of its connections with L. Ron Hubbard, founder of the pseudo-scientific cults of diametics and scientology, may be found in my *Ritual Magic in England* (Spearman 1970).

[9] I am not, of course, implying that any of the leaders of the Satanic Church practise sex-magic; I have no knowledge of the exact membership of the secret circle to which I refer.

stars were popular with their public and that Jayne Mansfield was the Queen of them all.

Born in the midst of the depression Jayne seems to have taken an interest in occultism while still a young girl, but it was not until the 'sixties, when she began to attend a small occult discussion group, that her interest in what is sometimes called "occult science" began to be practical rather than theoretical. This group was the nucleus of what was to become the Church of Satan and many of those who either were or had been associated with it were far removed from the ordinary lunatic fringe—they were not the sort of people who made up the membership of such crackpot cults as Mankind United, and they included such individuals as Stephen Schneck the novelist and Kenneth Anger, probably the best (and certainly the least boring) of the "underground" film producers. I think it likely that Anger's influence was responsible for some of the similarities between the occult philosophy of the group and that of Aleister Crowley. One authority on the history of occultism has described Anger to me as being "capable of teaching any aspect of the magical systems of the *Ordo Templi Orientis* and Crowley's *Astrum Argentinum*".[10] It was Anger who had removed the coats of whitewash that for thirty years had covered Crowley's murals painted on the walls of the Sicilian Abbey of Thelema and, while it is true that his earlier films such as *Scorpio Rising* and *Fireworks* were largely concerned with his own interpretation of male sexuality (the latter included shots of chain-swinging U.S. sailors vanishing through a door marked "Gentlemen" and concluded with a sailor simulating orgasm by unzipping his fly and pulling out an exploding Roman Candle), his later works, such as *The Inauguration of the Pleasure Dome*, seem to attempt an expression of Crowley's religio-magical philosophy of Thelema in terms of light, colour and sound.

Whatever or whoever may have been the source of the Crowleyan influence it is certain that by the time the group incorporated itself as the Church of Satan on April 30th, 1966 most of its teachings and occult techniques were simplified and materialised versions of those of the *Ordo Templi Orientis*. Thus a handbill issued by the Church affirmed that "Man must learn to properly indulge himself by whatever means he finds necessary . . . only by doing so can we release harmful frustra-

---

[10] The *Astrum Argentinum* was a magical order founded by Crowley some years before he came into contact with the O.T.O. It taught not sexual magic but a modified version of the occult system of the Hermetic Order of the Golden Dawn.

tions, which if unreleased can build up and cause many real ailments", which seems to be a pale reflection of Crowley's statement in his "Mass of the Phoenix" that:

> There is no Grace, there is no Guilt
> This is the Law, Do What Thou Wilt

Again, the so-called Fourteenth Enochian Call, part of the strange magical system evolved by the two Elizabethan adepts John Dee and Edward Kelly and used by Crowley (following his Golden Dawn teachers) as a method of invoking what he called "Water of Earth" has also been used by some members of the Church of Satan, but as part of a hate ritual, designed to wreak vengeance on the enemies of the Church and its members.

The Leader of the new Satanic Church was Anton La Vey, a man whose shaven head, flamboyant style of dress and carefully cultivated Mephistophelian appearance have become familiar to all those who look at the photographs in such girly magazines as *Bizarre*. La Vey had been a photographer with the Los Angeles police department and he remained on good terms with his former employers who used him to handle some of their "nut calls"—people who telephoned to complain of their neighbours, allegedly vampires or werewolves, to ask for investigations of a haunted house, or to enquire what they should do about their television sets on which, so they said, the ghosts of deceased relatives had appeared. Jayne Mansfield accompanied La Vey on some of his investigations of these purported supernatural events and it was this that first drew attention of the gossip columnists to the Church of Satan and Jayne's involvement with the organisation.

It is difficult to know exactly what was the appeal of the Satanic Church for Jayne but, although she played as full a part as possible in the activities of the Church—I am told that she took part in the "Shibboleth Ritual", a crude form of psychodrama in which the participants were supposed to achieve an emotional catharsis by identifying themselves with the characters they most hated, and that she always tried to attend the regular Friday night meetings at which the altar was the body of a naked woman—I suspect that the main attraction of the Church for Jayne was its ultra-permissive sexual morality.

It is of course true that the pursuit of some form or other of sexual pleasure, be it hetero-, homo-, or auto-, is the most common of all human activities apart from eating and drinking; after all, even the most bizarre forms of erotic activity are comparatively easily performed, requiring no more than the usual amount of emotional and physical ability. As the reader of this book will by now have gathered there has, nevertheless, always survived the tradition that there is a hidden side to sexuality, an esoteric knowledge capable of transforming the orgasm into a supernatural rite by which the human mind is enabled to experience hitherto unknown modes of consciousness. Some variant of this ancient doctrine is taught to the members of the secret, inner circle of the Satanic Church to which I have previously referred; it forms, however, no part of the Church of Satan's public teachings on sexuality, for these are crudely hedonistic, bearing more resemblance to the philosophy of the proprietor of a strip-joint than they do to the subtle intellectual systems of such occultists as Reuss and Crowley.

The sexual teachings of the Church of Satan seem to be merely an extension of its general philosophy of self-indulgence—a vulgarisation and degeneration of Crowley's "Do As Thou Wilt" into "Do As You Like"—and arise out of its inversion of traditional, and still generally accepted, Christian morality. Thus the seven deadly sins of Catholic theology are regarded as seven life-giving virtues leading to "physical, mental and emotional gratification"—such gratification being looked upon as a desirable end in itself. From its literature it is clear that *any* type of sexual activity is approved of by the Church provided only that it is in accordance with one's innermost desires and that its performance does not clash with anyone else's innermost desires; once again one is reminded of Crowley's doctrine of the True Will. The only exception to this blanket approval of all sexual points-of-view is the Church's attitude to sexual abstention and chastity, for most of its members appear to regard this as the one unforgivable vice. Jayne Mansfield herself, whose sex life always seems to have been extremely active, is reported to have described chastity as being "a really sickening perversion, really evil" and to have held that the legendary incubi and succubi—the unclean male and female demons of the mediaeval theologians—had been engendered by "the filthy imaginings of Catholic monks who had forced themselves to avoid copulation".[11]

[11] I have reproduced this reported statement in a bowdlerised form. If she did express this interesting theory it may be an indication that Jayne had read some of the works of the French nineteenth-century magician Eliphas Levi, for he held very much the same point of view.

In 1967 Anton La Vey and his Church really hit the headlines after the deaths of Jayne Mansfield and her attorney Sam Brody in an automobile accident. A short time after the crash the *Detroit Free Press* told the story of violent disagreements between La Vey and Sam Brody—who combined the role of Jayne's lover with his legal functions—over Jayne's involvement in the Satanic Church. It seems that Brody had been worried that the star's Satanic beliefs and practices might lead to unfavourable press publicity and had determined to sever her relationship with the Church by any means, fair or foul. To this end he told La Vey that unless he voluntarily cut himself off from Jayne he would arrange for the publication of various slanderous newspaper stories denouncing him as a charlatan and a crook.[12] La Vey was much more courageous than Brody had anticipated, told the latter to publish and be damned and, for good measure, solemnly cursed him. A short time afterward Brody was involved in a minor road accident, a common enough event, but one which the superstitious seem to have attributed to La Vey's curse.

Later still La Vey is supposed to have received an "occult message", from what supernatural source I do not know, informing him that there would be another accident and that this time Jayne might be involved. He warned her of this danger, but she disregarded him; two weeks later she was decapitated by a truck. Brody had been her driver and he also was killed.

As I have previously said, these events really brought the Church of Satan into the limelight; it has never left it since. Journalists have regaled their readers with the story of the deceased member of the U.S. Marine Corps whose body received a Satanic funeral complete with military guard of honour; with the continuing saga of La Vey's 400 pound lion, finally donated to the San Francisco Zoo after neighbours had complained that it was "on dope" and "roared all night",[13] with La Vey's performance as the Devil in the film *Rosemary's Baby* and with the doings of "Anton La Vey and his Topless Witches", who have been the star turns in at least one cabaret.

[12] Such stories would have been, of course, completely untrue. It must be emphasised that in spite of his curious beliefs La Vey seems to be sincere and a man of integrity.
[13] I should have thought these allegations to have been incompatible with one another. Perhaps, however, La Vey was trying to wean the animal from drug-addiction and its roars were symptomatic of its withdrawal from its "hooked" state.

In spite of all this ludicrous newspaper coverage there is no doubt that there are some individuals of high intelligence who are also members of the Church of Satan. Many of these are also members of the previously-mentioned secret circle and are heavily involved in sex-magical practices very similar to, and possibly identical with, those of Crowley and his followers. Other than this there have been at least two other groups recently practising sex-magic in the United States. One, which claimed to be a genuine branch of the O.T.O. (but wasn't) seems to have been largely made up of "kinkies" on the one hand and the gullible on the other. At least some of its members became heavily involved with the underworld and their tiny organisation was eventually broken up as a result of legal action on the part of the F.B.I. and the Los Angeles District Attorney. This group, which I shall call the Lunar Lodge, was under the leadership of a grossly psychologically disturbed woman who claimed to be an Ipsissimus.[14] Members of the group, which is now moribund, were responsible for a whole series of thefts of magical material in the Los Angeles area. Another group also claims to be a lodge of the O.T.O., this time with much more justification, although there is some disagreement as to the exact nature of its status. Its chief, whose name I shall not give, relies for his authority on a letter sent to him by Crowley. This letter appointed the man in question as IX° and as "our personal representative in the United States of America . . . subject to the approval, revision or veto of our Viceroy Karl Johannes Germer IX°". In another letter to the same man Crowley authorised him "to take charge of the whole Work of the Order in California . . . to reform the whole organism in pursuance of his report of Jan. 25 1946 e.g. subject to the approval of Frater Saturnus (Germer) . . . This authorisation is to be used only in emergency." This group is still active, although it was subjected to some considerable strains when a number of young male initiates became convinced that they were, (a) receiving special occult illuminations, and (b) practising "XI° sex magic"—in fact they were merely taking methedrine and gratifying their own homosexual proclivities. Unfortunately the leader of this group and the leader of the Swiss O.T.O. group mentioned in a previous chapter are unable to reach agreement with one another, so there are now two separate organisations, each of

[14] In western magic this grade is considered to be the highest possible of attainment; to claim to possess it is more or less the equivalent, quite literally, of claiming to be God Almighty.

which considers itself entitled to be regarded as the only genuine *Ordo Templi Orientis*.

One small American based group practising sexual magic remains to be mentioned, the *New York Sacred Tantrics* which claims to be a descendant of the *Sacred Order of Tantriks*, an organisation founded over fifty years by an occultist named Pierre Bernard, better known to readers of the Hearst press as "Oom the Omnipotent".

Bernard commenced the public teaching of occultism in 1909 when he opened the New York Sanskrit College at 250 West 87th Street; the College taught not, as might have been expected, the Sanskrit language but the practice of Hatha Yoga. Only a year or two after its opening the College closed—an event not unconnected with charges of indecent assault made against Bernard by two young girls, Zelda Hopp and Gertrude Leo[15]—and its founder moved on to New Jersey where he became acquainted with, and later married, Mlle de Vries, a professional vaudeville dancer.

Bernard taught his wife "oriental" dancing, Hatha Yoya and a watered down version of right-hand Tantricism.[16] On the basis of this peculiar mish-mash she evolved her own "Tantric health system" and made a living by teaching it. Then, as now, a considerable number of wealthy Americans were obsessed by, and anxious to improve, the state of their physical health and the "Tantric health system" acquired some rich devotees, among them Mrs. Ogden L. Mills, a stepdaughter of one of the Vanderbilts.

Bernard's wife was convinced (probably quite correctly) that a good deal of humanity's troubles resulted from its ignorance of the real nature of love; she told her husband that:

"Half the domestic tragedies . . . and not a few suicides and murders in America are due to the inherent stupidity of the average Anglo-Saxon man or woman on the subject of love. We will teach them, and maybe make our adventure a great success."

The means of teaching them was the *Sacred Order of Tantriks*, established on a large estate at Nyack under the name of the Brae Burn

---

[15] The charges were taken up by the New York police but later dropped; the girls' accusations were not backed up by any hard evidence and, in any case, seem to have been motivated by jealousy of another of Bernard's girl friends.

[16] Probably derived from the earlier works of "Arthur Avalon" (Sir John Woodroffe Bt.).

Club.[17] The money for the purchase of the estate seems to have come mostly from Mrs. W. K. Vanderbilt, who had been converted to Bernard's version of Tantricism by her daughter.

At Nyack Pierre Bernard was treated with even more veneration than that customarily extended to Tantric *Gurus*—indeed, his followers seem to have regarded him as being almost divine—and their admiration for their chief was not diminished by even his most eccentric proceedings; by, for example, the time when he followed his wife's "Dance of Death" (in which, clad in a veil, she arose from a coffin and performed a sort of belly dance) with a dance performed by himself with a baby elephant as his partner—this particular baby elephant, he solemnly told his disciples, was a particularly sacred Tantric baby elephant.

Ceremonies involving coffins seem to have been popular with the *Sacred Order of Tantriks*; on May 15th, 1927 one of the Hearst papers described an extraordinary ritual devised by Bernard to celebrate the tenth wedding anniversary of two of his disciples:

"For this ceremony, which was mystically a marriage as well as an anniversary, the bride and groom were dressed as for their first wedding. The girls and women of the cortège wore the robes and veils of nuns, covering brilliant and fantastic costumes beneath. The men wore the robes and cowls of monks, covering up equally gay and fantastic costumes in which they were to appear later.

"All carried tall candles, like a procession in a cathedral.

"Immediately behind the bride and groom were carried two coffins. These coffins were the symbols of the dead and the burying of the past.

"Afterwards the coffins were covered with gay draperies and used as tables for an elaborate banquet, while the monks and nuns put off their sombre religious habits and appeared as gay revellers."

In spite of such nonsensical publicity stunts there seems little doubt that Pierre Bernard and his wife really believed in the truth of that

[17] This tenuous link between Scotland and Tantricism would, no doubt, have intrigued the Scottish magician J. W. Brodie-Innes. Brodie-Innes, a leading figure in the Hermetic Order of the Golden Dawn, took a great interest in the sexual lives of his fellow initiates; moreover it was he who presented the British Museum library with its copies of that Victorian storehouse of salacity *The Pearl Magazine*—although, typically, he claimed that the gift came, not from him, but from an anonymous and deceased client.

which they taught and that their Tantricism was authentic, although, of course, heavily westernised. While Bernard confined his public teachings to an extremely innocuous right-handed Tantricism it seems almost certain that an inner group at Nyack engaged in radical, left-handed practices—Bernard neither sued the newspapers which reported that he indulged in "love orgies" nor the author of *My Life in a Love Cult*, a "sensational exposure" serialised in the Hearst press.[18] Certainly the contemporary *New York Sacred Tantrics*, who still display some regard for Bernard, indulge in left-handed practice, although (as a member informed me) "only with our wives and girl friends".

[18] Interestingly enough this exposure was written by a sister of Aleister Crowley's mistress, Leah Hirsig.

CHAPTER FOURTEEN

Magicians, the Orgasm and the Work of Wilhelm Reich

More than one of Crowley's later American followers has seen the work of Wilhelm Reich as a link between the conceptions of orthodox science on the one hand and those of their own sexual-magical philosophies on the other. As Dr. F. I. Regardie, himself a trained Reichian analyst and vegetotherapist,[1] has pointed out, the very idea of the existence of such a link would probably have given Reich heart-failure—nevertheless, there is no doubt that Reich arrived quite independently of the occult tradition at a theoretical position very similar to that which is held by at least some exponents of that same tradition.

While Wilhelm Reich, born in Austro-Hungary on March 24th, 1897, was of Jewish extraction his background was not in the least typical of the central European Jewish life of his period; his mother-language was German, not Yiddish; his father was a farmer, not a trader or a member of the professional middle classes; and his parents had no religious beliefs—although they encouraged their son to read the Bible as a matter of scientific interest.

Between 1907 and 1915 Reich attended a German-language High School, specialising in the sciences and graduating with "excellent" in all subjects; subsequently he was enlisted into the army where he fought on the Italian front and was commissioned as a lieutenant.

---

[1] Vegetotherapy—which Reich himself would have preferred to term orgasm therapy—is a method of physical manipulation designed to destroy the muscular "armouring" (i.e. state of permanent muscular spasm) of the human body, thus supposedly liberating the powers of the vegetative (autonomic) nervous system and enabling full "orgastic potency"—a state in which completely relaxed, uninhibited and pleasurable orgasm can be experienced.

After his demobilisation in 1918 he entered the Vienna University Medical School; as a discharged veteran he was allowed to cram the normal six years of study into four, but the additional pressure of work involved in this crash course did not prevent him from supporting himself by tutoring other students in pre-medical subjects.

In January 1919 a fellow student suggested to Reich and others that sexology was a subject unjustly neglected by the medical faculty of the university. An unofficial meeting took place, attended by about eight students, and it was decided to set up a sexological seminar. Reich regularly attended this, but he never took part in the discussions;[2] for the approach to sexuality displayed by the other students seemed unnatural and aroused a sense of aversion within him. He felt a similar dislike for the attitude of a Freudian analyst who gave a series of lectures on psychoanalysis to the members of the seminar. Nevertheless, he became convinced that sexuality was "the centre around which revolves the whole of social life as well as the inner life of the individual", read Forel, Bloch,[3] Stekel and Freud, and, in the summer of 1920, became a guest member of the Vienna Psychoanalytic Society, then under the personal direction of Freud. He was elected to full membership of the Society in October of the same year.

After obtaining his doctorate in July 1922 Reich spent two postgraduate years at the University Neurological-Psychiatric Clinic directed by Professor Wagner-Jauregg; Wagner-Jauregg was a brilliant neurologist—it was he who had developed the malarial treatment for General Paralysis of the Insane, the syphilitic infection of the central nervous system—but his attitude towards psychoanalysis was one of complete contempt and, according to Reich, he missed no opportunity of poking fun at Freudian sexual symbolism. Neurotics were treated with bromides and suggestion-therapy and a success rate of approaching ninety per cent was claimed—according to Reich these "cures" were non-existent, either there was spontaneous remission or the patient was described as "cured" when some individual symptom had disappeared—the other ten per cent went off to the Steinhof, a vast

[2] He did, however, read a paper on *The Concept of Libido from Forel to Jung* in the summer of 1919.
[3] Reich seems to have been unduly impressed by *The Sexual Life of our Time* and the other writings of Bloch. In reality Bloch was a considerable plagiarist; whole sections of his *Sexual Life in England* were lifted bodily from Pisanus Fraxi's *Index Librorum Prohibitorum*, a book I have previously referred to in connection with Edward Sellon.

hospital-prison in which something like 20,000 grossly disturbed patients were incarcerated. In spite of the Clinic's neurological bias the two years that Reich spent there exerted an important influence on his intellectual development; in particular, two patients seen by him caused him to evolve the first faint intimations of the ideas that were later to be developed by him as the concepts of *physiological anchoring* (the idea that a psychic experience may lead to the lasting physical alteration of an organ in the human body) and of *energy discharge as a response to muscular armouring*.

The first of these two concepts, that of physiological anchoring, was foreshadowed by Reich's examination of a young girl who had been admitted to the Clinic suffering from paralysis and muscular atrophy of the arms. No neurological aetiology could be traced, and Reich learned from her that the paralysis had set in after her boy friend's unsuccessful attempt to clasp her in his arms—as he had reached out for her she had raised her arms as though paralysed, and from then on the paralysis had remained and, eventually, the muscles had begun to atrophy.

The second patient whose symptoms Reich found particularly impressive was a stuporous catatonic.[4] One day Reich witnessed this patient's behaviour pattern suddenly change from the usual stuporous immobility into one of frenzied activity; there was a furious outburst of rage and bad temper which—and this Reich took to be of great significance—gave the patient a pleasurable release of tension. Reich felt that this physical/psychic explosion could not be adequately explained by the Freudian theory of catatonia and that, as Reich himself said, "the psychic *content* of the catatonic fantasy *could not be the cause* of the somatic process". Ultimately he came to believe that in catatonia muscular armouring has reached a stage where energy-discharge (either physical or psychic) is almost impossible and that as a result of this the dammed-up energy eventually breaks through from the centre of the autonomic nervous system and liberates previously frozen muscular force.

In 1922 Reich began the professional practice of psychoanalysis; in

---

[4] Catatonia, a disease characterised by a complete withdrawal from the environment, total silence and (frequently) complete immobility, was extremely common in the psychiatric wards of fifty years ago. Today, for reasons too complex to be entered into in this brief note, it has become extremely rare and some psychiatrists have never even seen a case!

fact, such was the informal structure of the psychoanalytic movement in its early years that Reich, who had never undergone a full training analysis, had been having patients referred to him by Freud since 1919! For some time Reich remained a fairly orthodox Freudian, but as the years went by he found that he was developing views at variance with those of Freud; it was not so much that he left Freud as that Freud left him; he could not stomach Freud's semi-abandonment of his original conception of anxiety as a product of somatic sexual excitation barred from discharge nor could he accept the existence of the "death wish" of later Freudianism.

Reich was also unhappy about the growing Freudian tendency to psychologise the somatic, to argue that most diseases were the result of unconscious wishes or fears, to argue that a patient developed, say, tuberculosis, because he *wished* to develop tuberculosis. It was not that Reich denied the existence of evidence in favour of such concepts, rather it was that he felt that no unconscious wish—using the word *wish* in the sense comprehended by Freudian analysts—could produce deep organic changes; he was confident that the so-called unconscious wish must be an expression of some deep-seated biological process.

In 1934 Reich began physiological experiments designed to discover whether such a biological process actually took place. The earliest of these experiments were designed to ascertain whether sexual excitement was assorted with an increase of bio-electric charge in the genitals and the erogenous zones—Reich found that it was. On the basis of his experimentation Reich evolved a theory which, so he believed, solved the theoretical conflict between vitalism and mechanism; he had been interested in this dispute since his student days and was rather inclined towards vitalism—his contemporaries at Vienna University had regarded him as "a crazy Bergsonian". Reich's theory accepted the mechanists' belief that living material was controlled by the same physical laws as the rest of the universe but, on the other hand, averred that living material was unique in that in it electrical and mechanical functions were combined in a specific manner not found in non-living matter.

In the period 1936–9 Reich carried out an ambitious biological research programme designed to elucidate the origins of life itself. He claimed to have discovered what be called "bions"; energy vesicles transitional between organic and inorganic matter produced by a process of heating and swelling and capable of developing into protozoa, cancer cells etc. Reich believed that he had produced bions from wood, grass, muscle tissue, wool, coal and soot; in 1939 he began experiments with radiating bions allegedly derived from sea-sand and, as a result, "discovered" orgone energy.

It would take too long to fully recount the course of Reich's experiments and supposed discoveries. Suffice it to say that he believed that in orgone energy he had discovered the basic life-stuff of the universe, the explanation of all emotional and some physical illnesses (e.g. cancer) and the explanation of all philosophical and religious problems.

Subsequently he built Orgone Energy Accumulators—devices intended to extract orgone energy from the atmosphere—put forward the hypothesis that hurricanes and galaxies resulted from the "cosmic superimposition" of two streams of orgone energy and came to accept the reality of Flying Saucers. These latter, he held, were to be considered hostile, their object being the stealing of orgone energy from our planet!

There are remarkable similarities between the magical conception of the Astral Light (something referred to as ether of the wise) and Reich's conception of orgone energy. It is not surprising that as a consequence of this similarity some Reichian analysts have begun to study magical techniques in general, and (because Reich so greatly emphasised the importance of the orgasm) sexo-magical techniques in particular. On the other hand some magicians have taken up the study of Reich and incorporated at least parts of his teaching into their own personal philosophical syntheses—thus one well-known American occultist has evolved his own system derived from Crowley, from the Golden Dawn "Middle Pillar" magical techniques and from Reichian vegetotherapy.

CHAPTER FIFTEEN
A Whip for Aradia

As I pointed out in the first chapter of this book most of the covens that make up the contemporary witch-cult have moved away from the heavy bias towards sexuality that characterised Gerald Gardner and many of his immediate followers. Nevertheless some covens, notably the one of which "my" witch, Marian,[1] is a member have gone to even greater lengths than Gardner himself. Marian's coven performs rituals designed to produce the maximum possible pain/terror/pleasure/disgust in those who participate in them. This is not mere "kinkiness", not a desire to indulge in sexual perversion under the cloak of magic and religion—although I am sure that such a desire is present on an unconscious level in at least *some* members of the coven—but a deliberate technique designed to overload the nervous system with sensations. The object of this overloading is, to continue the electrical analogy, the achievement of a psycho-spiritual short-circuit which will violently shatter the normal mental reaction patterns of the person concerned and lead to a transcending of his or her normal state of consciousness.

Marian's coven does not apply all its techniques (flogging, sexuality etc.) to any one member, for its chiefs argue that it would violate all the principles of what they refer to as "energy-economy" to inflict upon any individual either a pain or a pleasure to which he or she was particularly tolerant. Thus an initiate of the group who has a low pain threshold is subjected to flogging in order that he or she may achieve the disassociation of consciousness which is believed to lead to what the coven sometimes call "the ecstasy of magic". Similarly, if a member has neither the taste nor the talent for a vigorous sex life that same

[1] See Chapter One, pp. 7–8.

member is encouraged to indulge in sexual intercourse to the point of exhaustion; frequently the effect of this is heightened by ensuring that the particular form of sexuality indulged in is one that is either psychologically repellent or physically disgusting to the member concerned; a homosexual, for example, will have to have physical relations with one of the opposite sex. As might be expected (considering the physiological basis of male sexuality) such indulgence in sex-that-repels is sometimes found difficult by men initiates, but this problem has been largely overcome by the importation from Germany of rotary vibrators and other mechanical aids to sexual excitement!

The chiefs of this coven have a high regard for Aleister Crowley and his writings although it is very probable that they evolved their own sexual magic independently of his influence. Indeed, there are many similarities between their ideology and his. It is particularly interesting to compare the coven's doctrine of ecstasy through exhaustion with Chapter Fifteen of an O.T.O. document entitled *De Arte Magica* (unpublished in English although a German translation appeared *circa* 1914). This chapter, entitled *Of Eroto-Comatose Lucidity*, gives details of a rite involving the magician engaging in protracted sexual intercourse until he reaches the point of death, and assures the O.T.O. initiate that death achieved in this way is greatly to be desired. It also avers that the most favourable of the many forms of death is "that occurring during orgasm, and is called *Mors Justi*. As it is written: Let me die the death of the righteous and let my last end be like his".

Other witch-covens than Marian's have been more directly affected by Crowley's teachings. Few of them would admit this influence, however, and, in any case, such covens seem to have little understanding of the inner significance of much of Crowley's writings. I have heard reports of a number of odd magical operations which seem to have taken place because witches had taken Crowley literally when he was using metaphorical language and *vice-versa*. Thus Crowley talked, in his *Book of Wisdom or Folly*, of the creation of a "magical child"—the exact meaning of this phrase is difficult to understand without studying the book in question—and some witches have taken this literally and attempted to create a child by sexual magic. I strongly suspect that just such a misunderstanding of Crowley was responsible for an incident recorded in *King of the Witches*, Miss June Johns' biography of Alex Sanders. The story, which I presume Miss Johns derived from Mr. Sanders himself, tells how the King of the Witches—i.e. Mr. Sanders—

had become engaged and how his assistant, a young witch named Paul, had become very lonely and asked his chief to provide him with a permanent companion. The story goes on:

"For some time Alex had been toying with the idea of trying an experiment. He had studied it but never performed it, nor heard of any other living person who had. Many of the ancient magicians, however, could apparently conjure up a familiar and make it appear in the flesh, not only visible to themselves but also to other magicians present, and Alex wanted to emulate them. He put the idea to Paul. 'Let's make her a real beauty,' was his typical reaction.

"Alex then had to explain that what he planned to create was a baby, the spiritual son of Paul. They would combine their powers to conceive it and give it birth, and in the spirit world it would be able to develop its own character under their guidance.

"Many of the purification rituals necessary for the three-day ceremony were identical with those of the Abra-Melin system, including the preliminary nine-day fast. The whole thing was performed in Paul's room, the attic of a Victorian house owned by a Church of England clergyman, blessedly unaware of his tenant's beliefs. The divan bed was stood on end, draped with freshly laundered sheets and positioned between Paul and Alex, one of the instructions being that they must not be able to see one another throughout the rituals. Invocations were said to the Egyptian gods Hapy, Qebehsenuf, Duamutef and Imset: . . .

"Clad in white robes which opened down the front, and with feet bare, they burnt Kyphi—incense—during the rites. On the third day, they prayed to the Goddess Isis, the Earth Mother: . . .

"Now both men fixed their eyes upon a silver pentacle. The curtains were closed against the winter evening; one candle only burned. Earthenware bowls of olive oil stood at each cardinal point. Imploring the four sacred names of God, Yod, He Vau and He, Alex and Paul recited the final proclamation and, at the same time, masturbated, ejecting their sperm on to the pentacle.

"As they both slumped back exhausted from their long vigil, a baby's cry broke the silence. There on the pentacle, still moist with semen, lay what appeared to be a human baby of normal size except that it had no navel, nor umbilical cord, and it appeared to be bisexual, its genitals part male, part female.

"Paul bent to pick it up, but Alex, following the Hebrew ritual, stopped him.

" 'But you said it was my son,' said Paul. 'I want to christen it.'

" 'How can we christen it if we aren't Christians? You can baptize it. Here, use the consecrated water, but do not touch the child with your hands.'

"Paul flicked his moistened fingers over the baby and gave him the name 'Michael'. Neither of them knew what next to do with the wailing infant, and Alex tried to conjure up a familiar to help him. None would come, so he then went into a trance to see if Nick would help.

"When Alex awakened, Paul was in tears and the baby gone. 'We shall never see him again,' he told Alex. 'Nick told me that we were to train Michael to be obedient in Wicca so that he could be as a son to me. But he won't stay a baby; in the spirit world he'll mature so quickly that within twenty-four hours he'll be older than I am now.'

"Until now Alex had gone into a trance only when he wished, but Michael altered that. Within the space of a few days he stopped being a helpless baby and became a precocious nuisance. He began by invading Alex's body, taking him over so completely that when Alex came to, he would find that he had insulted old friends, flirted with their wives and done all sorts of things he would not normally have dreamed of doing.[2] Michael was not only too big for his boots, but too big for his host. Seams literally began to split after Michael manifested himself and Alex was compelled to buy a new suit several sizes too large. It hung on him in folds but the moment he was 'taken' by Michael, he filled it out.

"Alex's reputation was being tarnished by the wild parties his body attended when Michael was in residence. He could understand a little better now the unfortunate victims of the ancient witch trials—for here he was possessed of a devil of his own making! In addition to his taking advantage of Alex's body at will, Michael had to be bribed to give information asked of him and for which he had been created. Alex, who has frugal tastes, would recover from an involuntary trance to find he had eaten a pound of chocolate biscuits de-

---

[2] The fact that Mr. Sanders does not usually do such things goes to show how very virtuous he normally is. I, although not possessed by a spirit, not only insult my friends but smoke their cigarettes, filch their drink and even sell malicious stories about them to the editor of *Private Eye*. F.K.

manded by Michael in return for information. The spirit had begun to take over, demanding the exclusive use of Alex's body, demanding to be born human."

With such a well-publicised member of the contemporary witchcraft movement as Mr. Sanders openly revealing such an odd piece of sexual behaviour it is not altogether surprising that some of those who write hard-core pornography, either for business or for pleasure, have used magic and witchcraft as a convenient framework around which to build their erotic fantasies.

Of many such occult/pornographic novels that have appeared in recent years most are utterly worthless; they succeed only in displaying a complete ignorance of the real nature of magic on the one hand and a distressing poverty of style and erotic imagination on the other. Supernatural elements are usually missing from the plots of these books—their authors seem to assume (a) that the only reason people ever gather together behind locked doors is to hold phallic orgies, and (b) that a belief in witchcraft or magic necessarily implies that the believer is a sexual pervert.

One of the few pieces of hard-core pornography that both accepts the supernatural and is written by someone with a little real knowledge of his subject is *Inpenetrable* (sic), a novel dealing with, of all things, the Hermetic Order of the Golden Dawn, the sodality which was the *fons et origo* of the contemporary magical revival. The real Golden Dawn flourished in the years 1887-1939 and its rites were conducted in rooms in unfashionable quarters of London; the author of *Inpenetrable*[3] has shifted the Golden Dawn date to 1969 and situated its headquarters in Eaton Square!

The Golden Dawn of History was of unblemished moral reputation; its members may sometimes have been spiteful or silly, but they were not sexual perverts. The Golden Dawn of Mr. Harris (or Mr. Levi) invokes demons, worships Satan and indulges in buggery, rape and psychic murder; and yet certain references show that Mr. Harris is not

[3] I have traced three printings of *Inpenetrable*. While none of them contains details of place or date of publication, it is clear that (a) they are of English or American origin, (b) they were printed in 1970 or 1971, (c) that there must be a fourth, and original printing of the book—for the three I have seen were all produced by photo-lithography. The authorship of the book is uncertain; one edition gives him as "Joel Harris", another as "Aristotle Levi"—but I do not suppose that either name is genuine.

altogether ignorant of the nature of the real Golden Dawn. Thus Maureen Graille, the heroine of the book, holds 'derived *The Kabbalah Unveiled* on her lap'; the author of *The Kabbalah Unveiled* was S. L. MacGregor Mathers, founder of the Golden Dawn. Similarly Lord and Lady Aston, two of the occult perverts whose curious activities are recounted in detail and at length, are described as students of the writings of Aleister Crowley and Gerald Gardner. Even the author's most ludicrous attempts at imagining a pornographic application of occult techniques contain descriptive material which must be derived from some knowledge of the contemporary witch-cult. For example Kyleen Beck, a powerful witch, whose activities play an important part in the plot of *Inpenetrable*, has developed a new aspect of crystal-gazing—she uses it as a means of spying on the love-making of her guests! She is described as staring at her crystal ball with her lips drawn back "over her yellowing teeth in a snarl of frustrated lust". Excited by this copulation by crystal ("as good as any closed circuit television," says Mr. Harris) her "frantic fingers clawed at the hot dry-haired twat between her thin angular legs. She played with herself as she watched the crystal, and when Nona started to sway towards Eric, sinking his rod into her quim, Kyleen couldn't stand it any longer. Going over to a corner of the room she returned with her witch's broomstick, the top of the handle of which was shaped like a phallus. Sitting down again she opened her legs wide, and with a snuffle of greedy pleasure stuffed the phallic broomstick up her hole."

The interesting thing about this fictional episode, is that just such broomsticks are used in a sexual rite by at least one Gardner-derived coven. As far as I know no description of such instruments has ever been printed and it would therefore seem possible that Mr. Harris has been in contact with one or other of the covens of the witch-cult.

The general interest in sexual magic and witchcraft is increasing; so is commercial production of pornography. It seems almost certain that we are doomed to further floods of magical pornography. It is to be hoped that it will be better written than that which has so far been produced!

CHAPTER SIXTEEN

The Future of Sexual Magic

It is unlikely that the more radically sexually orientated of the covens of the contemporary witch-cult will ever attract any considerable membership, but the sexual magic of Aleister Crowley is showing signs of increasing popularity. The Beatles included Crowley's photograph as "one of the people we like" on the sleeve of one of their LP records, the philosophy of *Stranger in a Strange Land*—a novel that has attained a cult-following almost as great as that achieved by Tolkien's *Lord of the Rings* trilogy—shows a marked resemblance to that of Crowley's religion of Thelema, and the leader of one of England's best-known pop groups has bought Boleskine House, Crowley's old home, and has embarked upon a serious study of "Magick".

Crowley dead has far more disciples than Crowley living ever had, and interest in the sexual techniques employed by him is increasing by means of a geometrical, rather than an arithmetical, progression. I have few doubts that in its Crowleyan manifestations sexual magic is going to survive in the occidental world for as far ahead as it is possible to foresee.

It is also possible that in the years to come a westernised version of Tantricism will begin to attract a following; oriental occultism in one or another form—Theosophical, Zen or Sufi—has been popular in Europe and America for almost a century and I think it very likely that we shall soon begin to see an outbreak of Californian Tantricism. It is a prospect which such scholars as Agehananda Bharati—who look upon the study of oriental mysticism as almost inseparable from that of philology—regard with aversion. I, on the other hand, rather look forward to its occurrence; for, while I have no doubt that such a movement would be inevitably accompanied by the same irritating pretentiousness that characterises contemporary Zen Buddhism, I am sure that it will enable at least a few people to use sexuality as a means of transcending normal modes of consciousness.

Appendices

APPENDIX A

The Dildo in History

Artificial phalli seem to have been first used in prehistoric times, probably for ritualistic purposes, and by the later classical period they were to be found in comparatively common use—considering that most of them must have been made of non-durable materials, a surprising number of them have survived.

With the fall of the Roman Empire and the triumph of Christianity the dildo, so to speak, went underground—for, from the very beginning orthodox Christianity strongly deprecated all sexual activity except, of course, copulation between husband and wife, and even that was only tolerated in what ribald Polynesians were later to call "the missionary position!" It is true that certain Gnostic sects may have had a more tolerant attitude, and some of them, if their enemies are to be believed, were positively licentious. St. Epiphanius, the Bishop of Constantia, alleged that the Nicolaites affirmed that salvation was only attainable by means of frequent sexual intercourse; he also stated that another Gnostic sect sacramentally administered semen to its members. All this should be regarded with extreme scepticism; pagan writers related very similar stories about the early Christians.

In spite of Christianity the dildo, presumably home-made and normally used only in strict privacy, survived, and Burchardus, a mediaeval Bishop of Worms, described it and its use in some detail:

"Fecisti quod quaedam mulieres facere solent, ut saceres quoddam molimen aut machinamentum in modum virilis membri, ad mensuram tuae voluntaties, et illud loco verendorum tuorum, aut alterius, cum aliquibus ligaturis colligares, et fornicat ionem faceres cum aliis mulierculis, vel aliae eodem instrumento sive alio tecum. Si fecisti, quinque annos per legitimas ferias poeniteas.—Fecisti quod quaedam mulieres facere solent ut iam supradicto molimine, vel aliqo machinamento, tu ipea in te solam faceres fornicationem? Si fecisti, unum annum per legitimas ferias poeniteas."

"You have done what certain women are accustomed to do, that is, made a certain contraption or contrivance in the form of the male member, its dimensions according to your preference, and fastened it with several straps to your private parts or those of your partner, so that you may fornicate with other women, or others with the same instrument (or with another instrument) to you. If you have done this, five years' penance on public holidays. Do you do what certain women are wont to do, that is, with the aforementioned contraption or some such contrivance, fornicate alone within yourself? If you do this, one year's penance on public holidays.

As the nineteenth-century writer Thomas Wright observed, "the Holy Bishop appears to have been very intimately acquainted with the whole proceeding".

Today the dildo seems to be re-emerging from its obscurity into semi-respectability; a battery driven electric model, discreetly advertised as "fitting the natural curves of the human body" can be bought by mail-order (the pun is unintentional), while extremely realistic models—although of what I, for one, would consider unduly heroic proportions—are mass produced by a firm in North London and are even occasionally supplied to paraplegics by Britain's National Health Service. It is rumoured that the same firm also makes extra-large implements to order. An employee tells me that on one occasion an Arab Sheikh ordered the manufacture of such an enormous instrument of this type that he and his fellow-employees could only assume that it was intended to pleasure a favourite camel.

APPENDIX B

Robert Graves, Witches and Islamic Mysticism

The ninth-century Islamic Aniza school of mysticism was founded by Abu-el-Ataahia, a member of the powerful Arabian Aniza (Goat) tribe. Members of the school attained a state of religious ecstasy by rhythmic clapping or drumming and/or dancing. The symbol of the school was, according to one Sufi-historian, a lighted candle set between a pair of horns, presumably to indicate "light from the head of the Goat", i.e. the Aniza.

Robert Graves has suggested that this sect reached Western Europe and became the witch-cult. He has explained names allegedly used in the European witch-cult as corruptions of Persian and Arabic words. Thus "Robin" a name often associated with witchcraft and folk-beliefs (as in Robin Hood and Robin Goodfellow), is allegedly derived from the Persian *Rah-bin* ("he who sees the road"); the word athame (the athame is the ritual dagger used in the present-day Gardnerian witch-cult) is held to be a corruption of the Arabic *ad-dhamne*; "coven" is from the *kaftan*, the winding-sheet which Aniza cultists wore while dancing, and "Sabbath" is supposedly a corruption of *az-zabat*, "the Powerful Occasion".

All this is delightful—but nonsensical. All the features of the witch-cult which Graves holds to be derived from Islamic sources were either in existence before there was any possibility of Sufi influence in Western Europe or did not become associated with witchcraft until after the artificial creation of the Gardnerian cult. Thus the name "Robin" was associated with the folk-hero "the man in green" as early as Anglo-Saxon times and the athame, or ritual knife, was first introduced into witchcraft by Gerald Gardner; he took the name and the

APPENDIX B

design of the implement from MacGregor Mathers' nineteenth-century translation of the *Key of Solomon*—there is no trace whatsoever of the use of the athame in witchcraft, as distinct from ceremonial magic, until the present century.

APPENDIX C

Copulating with Cleopatra

This was only one of the religious activities of the White Mass Priests of the Church of Carmel, followers of an unfrocked priest named Boullan, remote spiritual heirs of Guibourg and the priest/sorcerers of seventeenth-century Paris.

The founder of the Church of Carmel was a certain Eugene Vintras. He was born in 1807, the illegitimate son of a servant girl. After a charity education he drifted from one unsatisfactory job to another before finding a temporary stability as the foreman of a small cardboard-box factory at Tilly-sur-Seule. One evening in August 1839 he was sitting in his tiny office when there came a sudden knock at his door followed by the entry of an old man dressed in rags. The old man addressed Vintras by his baptismal names and said "I am unutterably tired and wherever I go people treat me with disdain and say that I am a thief." Vintras gave the old man a coin and ushered him out, locking the door behind him; as he did not hear the old man go down the stairs (which led to the exit from the factory) Vintras called a workman and together they searched the building. To their amazement the old man had utterly and mysteriously disappeared!

Suddenly Vintras, who was extremely pious, heard the bell of the local church ringing for Mass. He hurried back to his office in order to fetch a prayer book. On the table where he had been writing he found a letter containing "a refutation of heresy and a profession of Catholic orthodoxy" and upon the letter lay placed the coin which he had given the old beggar. Vintras was thunderstruck and decided, for no apparent reason, that his mysterious visitor had been the Archangel Michael.

Probably the whole incident had been carefully arranged and stage-managed by an acquaintance of Vintras, a rascally lawyer named

APPENDIX C

Geoffroi, who was the agent of Charles Naundorf, a confidence trickster who called himself Duke of Normandy and claimed to be Louis XVII, rightful King of France.[1] Naundorf, who was not even French and had spent the years 1824-8 in prison for forgery, had a sizeable following on the lunatic fringe of French royalism. He was supposedly a Protestant and the supporters of ultra-montane royalism were urged to pray for his conversion; whether or not Geoffroi had actually arranged Vintras' "vision" of the "Archangel Michael", there is no doubt that those who manipulated the Naundorf movement saw that they could use Vintras' fervent but superstitious piety for their own purposes.

The first "vision" was supplemented by others; both the Blessed Virgin and St. Joseph appeared, informed Vintras that he was the reincarnation of the Prophet Elijah, that his task was to proclaim the coming "Age of the Holy Ghost" and commanded him to found the Church of Carmel—originally known as the Work of Mercy. Vintras travelled around the country preaching the coming kingship of Naundorf, the pre-existence of souls and universal redemption. He was a powerful preacher and he soon acquired a following that included not only unlettered men like himself but members of the bourgeoisie and even priests, among them the Abbé Charvoz, a theologian of some eminence who became the movement's theologian.

Vintras set up his first oratory at Tilly; here, clad in vestments of their own devising, the priests of the Work of Mercy celebrated the *Provictimal Sacrifice of Mary* and witnessed many miraculous events—saw empty chalices suddenly brim over with blood, beheld mystic bloodstains appear on the consecrated host[2] and even saw the Holy Ghost (in the form of a plump woodpigeon) perch on Vintras' shoulder. Vintras himself experienced visions of an increasingly lurid nature. The following, which dates from 1840 or 1841, is typical:

---

[1] Louis XVII, never crowned, was the young son of Louis XVI and Marie Antoinette and had died in the Temple while a prisoner of the Revolution. During the first half of the nineteenth century there were several bogus claimants to the title of Louis XVII. One of them was an American; Mark Twain satirised him in *Huckleberry Finn*.

[2] Some of these miraculous hosts were examined by the French magician Eliphas Levi. He announced that the holy symbols were upside down (e.g. the pentagram had two points, instead of one, pointing upwards) and on this basis claimed that the alleged miracles were the result of diabolical origin. He failed to explain, however, how on a circular host it was possible to tell which way up the symbols were supposed to be!

APPENDIX C

"On Monday night the 17th or 18th of May a frightful vision struck at my soul and body . . . I had gone up to the holy chapel and was about to open the door when I saw written on it in letters of fire, 'Dare not to enter, thou whom I have spewed out of my mouth' . . . I fell down overcome . . . I saw on every side an abyss full of hideous monsters who called me brother . . .

"I called on the Divine Mary, Mother of God, to help me . . . Suddenly great whirlpools of flame arose from the abyss into which I was about to fall. I heard yells of furious exultation and could pray no longer, when a voice . . . filled my ears . . . 'Behold Mary, whom you called your shield against us, behold her gracious smile, hear her gracious voice.'

". . . I saw her above the abyss. Her eyes of heavenly blue were filled with fire, her red lips were violet, her mild and divine voice had become terrible and like a thunderbolt she hurled these words at me: 'writhe, proud one, in the burning regions inhabited by devils'.

"O, if only I revealed to the enemies of the Work of Mercy those things that pass in me would they not cry victory? They would say that this is evidence of monomania. I wish to God that it were so, for then I would have less to lament . . ."

As the religious hysteria increased the ecclesiastical authorities became alarmed and in November 1841 the Bishop of Bayeux condemned the pamphlets of Charvoz as teaching doctrines incompatible with the Catholic faith. It is probable that the Church authorities also arranged the arrest and trial on charges of fraud of Vintras and Geoffroi in the following year. Although the trial was undoubtedly rigged it resulted in Vintras receiving a seven, and Geoffroi a two years' sentence of imprisonment.

In 1848 the sect was formally condemned by Rome; Vintras replied with a counter-condemnation of the Pope and a dignified defence of his own position: "If my mind counted for anything in the condemned works," he wrote, "I should bow my head and fear would possess my soul. The Work is not my Work, however, and I have had no concurrence in it, either by research or desire. Within me is calmness; I have not laid awake on my bed nor have night-watches wearied my eyes; God gives me pure sleep."

Vintras' difficulties were increased by the activities of an ex-disciple named Gozzoli (he seems to have been a mere pawn of Geoffroi who

APPENDIX C

had also fallen out with the prophet), who in 1851 published a pamphlet accusing Vintras of homosexuality and of conducting secret Masses at which both priest and people were naked. Geoffroi's son, a priest, alleged that his father's former associates had taught him a secret "magical prayer" to be recited at the foot of the altar and to be accompanied by masturbation.

For some years the Church of Carmel enjoyed a modest prosperity; branches of it were established in Spain, in Belgium, in England and in Italy.

Vintras died on December 7th, 1875. Shortly before this event he had made the acquaintance of an altogether more intellectual—and more sinister—personality than himself, an unfrocked priest named Boullan who had been imprisoned in Rome for heresy and in France for fraud.

Boullan, born in 1824, had been a religiously inclined youth and had entered the priesthood. Subsequently he had become the confessor of a nun named Adele Chevalier whom he had made his mistress and who had become the mother of at least two children by him. In 1859 the two founded *The Society for the Reparation of Souls*, an organisation which specialised in the "casting out of demons" by unusual methods of exorcism. Some of the techniques used were extremely repellent—Boullan and his mistress "cured" one group of allegedly possessed nuns by feeding them a mixture of human excrement and the consecrated host! It is also likely that the two dabbled in a type of Black Magic very similar to that practised by Guibourg and La Voisin two hundred years before; there is some evidence to show that on January 8th, 1860 they conducted a Black Mass at which they ritually sacrificed their own bastard child, born a few weeks previously.

After his meeting with Vintras Boullan declared himself a convert to the former's doctrines and, together with his tiny personal following, joined the Church of Carmel; he rose rapidly in the favour of the prophet—Vintras was never a very good judge of character—and after Vintras's death proclaimed himself as the new Supreme Pontiff and as the reincarnation of St. John the Baptist. Most of the members of the Church refused to accept Boullan's claims to supremacy, but a few did so, and they settled with their chief in Lyons, a city that had retained some reputation for religious eccentricity since the time of the Cathars and other mediaeval Manichees.

Whatever may have been the truth about the alleged sexual deviations

12. The Prophet Vintras—his disciples believed that they copulated with the mighty dead. See Appendix, "Copulating with Cleopatra".

13. Peladan—a leading figure in the *Kabalistic Rose Croix*.

APPENDIX C

of Vintras himself there is not the slightest doubt that Boullan practised a form of sexual magic. He held the common—and theologically incorrect—nineteenth-century opinion that the sin that had led to the Fall of Man in the Garden of Eden had been sexual in nature and that "as the Fall had been caused by a culpable act of love it is through acts of love accomplished in a religious spirit that the Redemption of Humanity can be achieved". If humanity indulged in sexual activities with angels and other heavenly beings, said Boullan, it was enabled to more rapidly climb the ladder of spiritual evolution that led to the Divine Union. Similarly, copulation with animals speeded up their spiritual evolution—and was therefore meritorious!

Documents survive showing that Boullan and his followers engaged —or thought they engaged—in copulation with angels, cherubim, seraphim and the spirits of such historical figures as Cleopatra and Alexander the Great. The techniques used were masturbation, with the operator strongly imagining that he or she was in coitus with the desired angel or spirit, and actual sexual intercourse in which each participant identified the other with the appropriate disembodied being. There is no hard evidence to show that bestiality—sexual intercourse with animals—was practised, but it is extremely probable that it was indulged in by at least some members of the Church of Carmel. Boullan himself participated in rites that were essentially scatological in nature; he seems to have been fascinated by the human excretory organs and their functions.

Boullan's death, as curious as his life, came at the climax of a "Battle of the Magicians"—the theurgists of the Church of Carmel on one side of the conflict, those of an occult fraternity called the *Kabalistic Order of the Rose-Croix* on the other.

The *Kabalistic Order of the Rose-Croix* had come into existence in 1887 and was largely the creation of a French Marquis named Stanislas de Guaita. The Marquis had sought only literary fame until 1885 when, as a result of reading the books of Eliphas Levi, he had been converted to occultism and acquired a burning desire to be a master-magician; from then until his premature death in 1897 from an overdose of drugs his life was devoted to a fight against the real or supposed machinations of Black Magicians and to the revival of the ancient mysteries. In his scarlet-draped study, clad in a Cardinal's robe, he took cocaine, hashish and morphine "to project the astral body" and attempted the transmutation of base metals into gold. Reports of Boullan's sexual teachings

APPENDIX C

reached de Guaita and he spent a fortnight in Lyons posing as a potential convert to the Church of Carmel. During this brief stay he acquired a considerable insight into the inner nature of Boullan's teaching and this insight was considerably increased a month or so after his return to Paris when he was joined by Oswald Wirth, a member of Carmel who had revolted against its chief's teachings and had decided to transfer his allegiance to the White Magic of the *Kabalistic Rose-Croix*. The two decided that Boullan was, as they wrote in their joint essay *The Temple of Satan*, a "pontiff of infamy, a base idol of the mystical Sodom, a magician of the worst type, a wretched criminal, an evil sorcerer"—and accordingly declared war on him, sending him a letter affirming that he was "a condemned man". Exactly what de Guaita and Wirth meant by this phrase is uncertain; they themselves claimed later that they were only referring to their forthcoming literary exposure of Boullan, eventually published as the first part of de Guaita's *Serpent of Genesis*; Boullan, on the other hand, believed that it was a threat to end his life by magical spells and, certainly, this does seem to have been the more probable explanation of the words used.

This battle of the magicians, real or imaginary, lasted for almost five years and ended only with Boullan's death. Two years after its commencement the novelist J. K. Huysmans became involved in it as a result of his attempts to gather information about the supposed survival of Satanism in the nineteenth century.

Huysmans had written a letter of enquiry to Boullan and had received a friendly reply; subsequently he was sent from Lyons some of Vintras' miraculous "bleeding hosts" together with a considerable amount of carefully selected documentation cleverly designed to give him an altogether favourable impression of Boullan and the Church of Carmel.

Soon both Huysmans and Boullan came to believe that the former was also being subjected to "astral attacks" by de Guaita and his sinister Rosicrucian followers. Huysmans seems to have found this curiously elating; it was almost with pleasure that he wrote to his friends to inform them that both he and, ridiculously enough, his pet cat were suffering bouts of what he called "fluidic fisticuffs"—mysterious blows delivered by invisible astral antagonists. Huysmans took, of course, appropriate counter-measures; he would shut himself up in his room, burn some of Boullan's incense of exorcism (a, no doubt, pleasantly perfumed, mixture of cloves, camphor, myrrh and incense), brandish

APPENDIX C

one of Vintras' miraculous hosts and "clasp the blessed scapular of Carmel . . . and recite conjurations dissolving the astral fluids and paralysing the powers of the sorcerers".

On January 3rd, 1893 Boullan reported a sinister incident to his friend: ". . . during the night a terrible thing happened. At 3 a.m. I awoke suffocating. I called out twice 'Madame Thibault'. (*Boullan's clairvoyante, and, probably, mistress*) 'I am suffocating!' She heard me, but when she came I was unconscious. From three until three thirty I was between life and death.

". . . Madame Thibault dreamt of Guaita and in the morning a black bird of death cried out. It was the herald of the attack . . . At four I slept again, the danger was over."

On the evening of the same day Boullan died. Julie Thibault, writing to Huysmans, reported his death as follows:

"Dinner-time came. He sat down, ate fully, and seemed most cheerful. Afterwards he paid his usual visit . . . On his return he asked me whether I would soon be ready for prayer. A few minutes after prayers he seemed to become uncomfortable. 'What is that?' he called out. Then, immediately, he collapsed. M. Misme (*the architect in whose house Boullan lodged*) and I supported him, helped him to his chair and got him to bed.

"His chest was congested and he breathed with difficulty . . . He said, 'I am dying. Adieu.' I replied, 'But Father, you are not going to die. What about the book you are writing? You must finish it.' He was pleased at this remark and he asked for *l'eau de salut*. Having taken a mouthful he said, 'This will save me.' I did not feel unduly worried, because we had so often seen him recover after having been near death. I thought this danger would pass.

"I said, 'Father, how are you?' Then I realised he could no longer speak. He gave me a last look of farewell. He seemed in agony. It lasted barely two minutes, then he was dead."

All this seems ordinary enough—Boullan, after all, was almost seventy years old and suffered from heart trouble and an unsound liver. Nevertheless, Huysmans came to the improbable conclusion that the "black bird of death" was an evil spirit despatched by de Guaita and that Boullan's death was probably the result of Black Magic. This opinion was shared by Huysmans' friend Jules Bois, a one-time member of the Church of Carmel who had remained on good terms with its pontiff, and he published an article in *Gil-Blas* accusing de Guaita of "magical murder". The day after the appearance of the accusing article a journalist, scenting a good story, interviewed Huysmans and subsequently reported him as saying that "It is indisputable that de Guaita and his friends practise Black Magic every day. Poor Boullan was perpetually engaged in conflict with the evil spirits they continually sent him from Paris . . . It is quite possible that my poor friend Boullan has succumbed to a supremely powerful spell."

Infuriated by the accusations of murder de Guaita challenged both Huysmans and Jules Bois to duels, sending his seconds to call upon them. Huysmans, who was a peaceful man, a civil servant by profession, had no stomach for a fight and apologised. It seemed that the affair would end peacefully, but Jules Bois repeated his allegations and, indeed, amplified them, accusing de Guaita's friend Dr. Encausse, a physician who wrote on magic under the pseudonym of Papus, of being an accomplice in the murder of Boullan.

There followed two of the oddest duels ever fought; both involved peculiar "occult" incidents. Those that accompanied the first of these duels—that between de Guaita and Jules Bois—were described by the writer Paul Foucher, a friend of Bois who acted as his second:

"Bois said to me . . . 'you will see something very singular happen. On both sides our allies are praying for us and practising conjurations.' Something strange did indeed happen on the road . . . One of our horses stopped and began to tremble, then it staggered as though it had seen the Devil in person. It was impossible to proceed . . .

"The duel nevertheless took place . . . and two bullets were exchanged without result. Such, at least, was believed, but several days later, when I was engaging in practice shots at Gastine-Rennette's, the famous gunsmith said to me: 'What happened the other day? The bullet of one of the duellists didn't leave the barrel. My employee noticed it when he was cleaning the pistols.'

"I was sure," Foucher continued, "that the pistol of Jules Bois had not missed fire. As for the pistol used by Monsieur de Guaita, it is quite unbelievable that neither he nor his seconds . . . should not have noticed that his pistol did not fire."

It is clear that God (or possibly the Devil) prevented one of the bullets from leaving its pistol. Or was Paul Foucher drunk? Seconds habitually carried flasks of cognac, presumably in order to assuage the pangs of the wounded, and it seems likely that Foucher had consoled himself for his bewitched and trembling horse with a few stiff nips!

The magical aspects of the second duel, fought three days later between Bois and Encausse, also involved horses, animals which seem to have been peculiarly susceptible to sorcery! This time the horse drawing Bois' carriage collapsed; he engaged another, and this also fell down. Nevertheless, Bois succeeded in reaching the duelling field, although he arrived bruised and bleeding, the collapse of his second horse having thrown him violently to the ground. During the encounter both antagonists suffered minor wounds, little more than scratches, and shortly afterwards the two were reconciled, thus bringing to an end the long-drawn-out battle of the magicians.

APPENDIX D

Another Sex-Magic Ritual

In addition to the heterosexual ritual of the IX° of the O.T.O. printed (for the first time in complete form) in Chapter Ten of this book, either Crowley or one of his colleagues in the *Mysteria Mystica Maxima*, the British section of the O.T.O., produced a further ceremony clearly designed to be used in the rites of sex-magic. Once again Crowley claimed the ritual—of particular interest for its implication of human sacrifice—had been written by Adam Weishaupt of the Illuminati, and, once again, internal evidence shows that this could not have been the case. The ritual reads as follows:

A RITUAL TO INVOKE HICE[1]
OR ANY OTHER DIVINE ONE
THE OPENING

The assistants all being without, Nuit and Hadit perform the ritual appropriate. The doors are unlocked and the assistants, led by Ra-Hoor-Khuit, enter.[2]

[1] HICE is the Coptic name of the Egyptian goddess Isis, and the name of the goddess was usually given in this form in the occult organisation known as the Hermetic Order of the Golden Dawn, of which Crowley had at one time been a member. Thus the occultist Wynn Wescott once wrote "I am now HICE in the Isis-Urania Temple of the G.D."—he meant that he held the office of Praemonstrator for the holder of this office had to mentally identify himself with Isis.

[2] These names, all drawn from *Liber Legis*, Crowley's Book of the Law, clearly indicate the late date of this rite. Nuit is the Egyptian star-goddess, the feminine principle that represents infinity; Hadit, the point, is the contrasting principle and from the dialectical interaction between the two is supposed to result the manifested universe. Ra-Hoor-Khuit, the Egyptian war-god, is an aspect of Horus, whose aeon, according to Crowley: began in 1904. The participants in the ritual are clearly supposed to identify themselves with these Egyptian deities.

APPENDIX D

Let the symbol or image of HICE or the god invoked be in the East of the Temple.

Let incense be burned before her or it.

Let there be two other thrones: on the right of the image that of Nuit, on the left that of Hadit; the child is Ra-Hoor-Khuit. Nuit is dressed in blue, Hadit in red; the child is naked.

The lamp shall be burning above Ra-Hoor-Khuit, who crouches in the centre, in the prescribed posture.

If there be assistants, they shall all wear the robes of their grade; they shall be seated in balanced disposition about the temple; and they shall enter only after the opening.

THE OPENING

Hadit knocks as appropriate to the god invoked.[3]
Nuit recites the hymn appropriate to banishing.
Hadit performs the Banishing Ritual of the Pentagram, as revised.[4]

Nuit   Bahlasti!
Hadit   Ompehda![5]

THE DEATH OF OSIRIS

Hadit and Nuit divest themselves of their blue and red robes, appearing merely in their magick robes of red and green as the temporal and spiritual powers, Typhon and Apophia.

Hadit   Sister I burn upon the throne.
Nuit   I am in agony, Typhon!

---

[3] For example nine knocks for Khonsu, the Theban moon-god, eight knocks for Thoth, god of wisdom. The number of knocks is decided by the supposed correspondence between the gods and the spheres of the Qabalistic Tree of Life. Thus all moon gods and goddesses are attributed to Yesod, the ninth sphere of the Tree, and all gods of wisdom, such as Hermes, Woden, and Thoth, to Hod, the eighth sphere.

[4] This, presumably, would be the *Ritual of the Star Ruby*, a Crowleyan ritual printed on pages 34–5 of Crowley's *Book of Lies*.

[5] These two words are drawn from a verse of the Book of the Law. The passage, which many find offensive as well as blasphemous, reads:
"I am in a secret fourfold word, the blasphemy against all gods of men.
Curse them! Curse them! Curse them!
With my Hawk's head I peck at the eyes of Jesus as he hangs upon the cross.
I flap my wings in the face of Mohammed and blind him.
With my claws I tear out the flesh of the Indian and the Buddhist, Mongol and Din.
Bahlasti! Ompehda! I spit on your crapulous creeds."

APPENDIX D

Hadit	Who hath disturbed our ageless peace?
Nuit	Threatened our mystery?
Hadit	Isis, Hath borne a child.
Nuit	We are twins.
Hadit	What word insults us?
Ra-Hoor-Khuit	(*Springs up*) Lo! I am, the third.
Hadit	(*Comes forward with the scourge and forces Ra-Hoor-Khuit to kneel*) Then bow to the two above! (*Strikes him twice*)
Nuit	(*Comes forward with the rod*) We need no witness of our love. (*Strikes him twice*)
Hadit	Who art thou?
Nuit	Whence art thou?
Ra-Hoor-Khuit	My name. Is surely I am that I am.
Hadit	Blaspheme not! (*Strikes him twice*)
Nuit	Lie not! (*Strikes him twice*)
Ra-Hoor-Khuit	I am come From Isis, from the Virgin Womb.
Hadit	Blaspheme not! (*Strikes him twice*)
Nuit	Lie not! (*Strikes him twice*)
Ra-Hoor-Khuit	I am he Appointed from eternity To rule upon the folk of Khem.
Hadit	We are the gods and kings of them.
Nuit	Upstart! (*Strikes him twice*)
Hadit	Usurper (*Strikes him twice*)
Nuit	We defy thee.
Hadit	We have the power to crucify thee. (*Nuit forces Ra-Hoor-Khuit back and they stretch out his arms*)
Ra-Hoor-Khuit	Amen! I am willing to be slain. Verily I shall rise again.
Nuit	With four wounds thus I nail thee. (*Wounds brow, hands and throat with dagger*)
Hadit	With one wound I impale thee. (*Wounds breast with sword*)
Hadit	Hail, sister! We have slain the god.

APPENDIX D

Nuit   Ours is the termless period.
Hadit   Bending across the blood face
                Let us embrace?
                        Let us embrace!
(*They embrace, leaning across the corpse. Nuit returns to her throne, and dons the blue robe, thus assuming the power of Isis. Hadit remains, his sword upon the heart of Ra-Hoor-Khuit*)

THE ARISING OF HORUS

Nuit chants the Dirge of Isis.[6] *After "tomb" in verse four she rises, and Hadit falls back to his knees. At verse five Nuit comes down to the corpse, and raises it with kisses upon the stigmata, wrapping it then in her blue robe. She then clothes it in the white robe. Ra-Hoor-Khuit takes the sword of Hadit and slits his throat therewith. Nuit returns to her throne and Hadit rises and puts on the red robe.*

IX° (*i.e. Ritual copulation*)

All this bloodshed must not be taken too literally. Both Crowley and the O.T.O. frequently symbolised (magical) sexual intercourse as human sacrifice. Thus in his *Magick in Theory and Practice* Crowley wrote that the ideal sacrifice was "a male child of perfect innocence and high intelligence" and in a footnote claimed that he himself had made this sacrifice about 150 times a year between 1912 and 1928. From Crowley diaries it is clear that he was referring to sexual intercourse; this interpretation is confirmed by a commentary on the above-mentioned passage by Crowley's German disciple Martha Kuntzel: "It is the sacrifice of oneself spiritually. And the intelligence and innocence of that male child are the perfect understanding of the Magician, his one aim, without lust of result. And male he must be, because what he sacrifices is not the material blood, but his creative power."

[6] Probably a reference to some poem written by Crowley.

APPENDIX E

Ralph Chubb, Boy Love, and William Blake

Ralph Nicholas Chubb (1892–1960) spent the formative years of his childhood and adolescence in the English town of St. Albans. He was educated at the local Grammar School, whose buildings lay close to the Mediaeval Abbey Church, not far from the ruins of the Roman city of Verulamium.

Ralph seems to have been a sexually precocious child, for his first orgasm was induced by the motions of his rocking-horse, and, even in the England of the early twentieth century, such toys were not usually owned by those who had reached the normal age of puberty. For the rest of his childhood he regularly indulged in masturbation although, like many children of Victorian parents, he was haunted by feelings of guilt. So strong were these in Ralph's case that he was afraid to meet the eyes of his school-fellows whom, he felt sure, were able to discern his guilty secret. From the very first his inclinations seem to have been homosexual, and his early masturbation fantasies were based upon his memories of a group of village boys who he had seen naked by the sea-shore.

When Chubb was eighteen years old he fell passionately in love with a choir-boy whom he had seen in the Abbey; this love was never consummated, for although Chubb ardently desired the lad to "be his boy-bride", he never plucked up sufficient courage to speak to him. In the same year Chubb had a brief, but much more fruitful, relationship with a fifteen-year-old boy and throughout that golden Edwardian summer of 1910 the two boys roamed the countryside, "fondling, spending, silently embracing". All good things must come to an end, however, and in October 1910 Chubb, who had won a scholarship to Selwyn

APPENDIX E

College, went up to Cambridge, where he was awarded a half-Blue in chess and proceeded B.A. in 1913.

At the outbreak of war in 1914 Chubb enlisted as a soldier. Unlike so many of the volunteers who went out to Flanders with the "red little dead little, army" Chubb survived, being mentioned in despatches and reaching the rank of Captain before being invalided out with "shell-shock". After his discharge he studied painting at the Slade, but left London forever in 1921, living for six years at Curridge, in Berkshire, and then moving to Fair Oak Cottage, Ashford Hill, near Newbury, where he was to spend the rest of his life.

Chubb's homo-erotic and occult preoccupations were not given explicit voice in such early publications as *Manhood* (1924) and *Woodcuts* (1928) but in 1929 he made a bold, and most injudicious, declaration of his inclinations in the penultimate paragraph of the *Notes on Some Water-Colour Drawings* which was inserted into the catalogue of his exhibition at the Goupil Gallery. In this he not only stated that he believed "absolutely in masculine love—boy love in particular" but expressed his view—now a commonplace one amongst both homosexuals and liberal Anglican theologians—that the relationship between Jesus of Nazareth and the young St. John was homosexual in nature.[1] In the same year he published *An Appendix* in which he announced that he was "here to save England"; it is clear that throughout the 'twenties he had come increasingly under the influence of the writings of William Blake and that he had come to regard himself as being, like his hero, a poet, an artist, and a prophet.

Chubb was impressed by Blake's successful blending of prose, poetry and illustration into one artistic whole and tried to achieve the same effects by means of lithographic book-production. In all, Chubb produced seven lithographic books and an eighth was in an advanced state of preparation when he died in 1960. In six of these he outlined his synthetic religion, an amalgam of Blake, occultism and pederasty. The first of them, *The Sun Spirit* (1931), a fantasy bearing a faint family likeness to *The Chemical Marriage of Christian Rosycross* and other allegories of spiritual progression, was comparatively restrained in tone,

---

[1] Needless to say there is no evidence whatsoever to support this odd (and to me, for one, most offensive and blasphemous) theory. The idea seems to have originated with the Elizabethan playwright Christopher Marlowe, who also held that Jesus had a sexual relationship with the woman of Samaria.

but, as time passed, the contents of each succeeding volume bore more and more resemblance to the inchoate outpourings of schizophrenia.

By the time Chubb came to write *The Heavenly Cupid* (1934), published in an edition of only forty-three copies, he had come to believe in the imminent arrival of an "age of the Holy Ghost". This perennial mystical occult fantasy has enjoyed an underground existence since the thirteenth century and was admirably described by Huysmans in *La-Bas*. He wrote:

> "There are three reigns, ... that of the Old Testament, of the Father, the reign of fear; that of the New Testament, of the Son, the reign of expiation; that of the Gospel of St. John, of the Holy Ghost, which will be the reign of ransom and love. It is the past, the past, the present and the future; it is winter, spring and summer; the one says Joachim of Floria, has given the germinating wheat, the other the ear, the third will give the corn in the ear. Two of the Persons of the Holy Trinity have been made manifest, the Third Person is logically bound to appear.
>
> "... The Holy Spirit also, by the Christ in Glory, will come to be immanent in created beings. He will be the principle that transforms and regenerates them ..."

Chubb managed to combine this doctrine with the deification of boy-love:

> "I announce a secret event as tremendous and mysterious as any that has occurred in the spiritual history of the world. I announce the inauguration of a Third Dispensation, the dispensation of the Holy Ghost on earth, and the visible advent thereof on earth in the form of a Young Boy of thirteen years old, naked, perfect and unblemished."

Chubb's fantasies steadily developed until, in *The Child of Dawn* (1948) and *Flames of Sunrise* (1954), he personified himself as the Archangel Raphael, the protector of Albion, England's otherworldly counterpart. I think it unlikely that anyone will ever go to the trouble of fully identifying Chubb's sources, but from my brief examination of these last-mentioned books it seems obvious to me that he had read and re-read such occult writers as Blavatsky and Eliphas Levi, that the writings of the seventeenth-century alchemist and physician Paracelsus

APPENDIX E

had exerted a strong influence upon him, and that he was not unacquainted with the works of such comparatively obscure late seventeenth-century mystics as Samuel Pordage and Jane Lead. In his *Love in Earnest* Timothy d'Arch Smith has admirably summed up the contents of Chubb's later writings:

> "The heterogeneous mass of occult facts and figures collected . . . embrace numerology, astrology, classical and Celtic mythology, Christianity, the Grail legend . . . and all these various systems are twisted and entwined to shed light on his prophecy of the Third Dispensation, the Advent of the Boy-God. Coincidental dates and minor chance occurrences are interpreted as auguries of his mission."

Chubb died in 1960, an embittered failure with few admirers and even fewer followers. The only recognition he obtained during the last years of his life was from the Lord Abbot of the Order of St. Raphael who conferred upon him an illuminated scroll. Richard Duc de Palatine, the Lord Abbot in question, had originally been a priest of the Liberal Catholic Church under the name of Ronald Powell. At about the same time as he had attained his ducal status he had become the first Bishop of the Pre-Nicene Catholic Church, an organisation which aspired to "co-ordinate the Masonic, Theosophical, Rosicrucian, Hermetic . . . Gnostic and Esoteric Christianity . . . and their relationship to the Eternal Truths of God." I cannot help feeling that a scroll, even an illuminated one received from such an august source, was poor recompense for Chubb's forty years of hard work.

A full account of Chubb's life can be found in Timothy d'Arch Smith's intensely readable *Love in Earnest* (Routledge and Kegan Paul 1970).

APPENDIX F

Crowleyanity in Switzerland

Just as Reuss chartered Aleister Crowley's *Mysteria Mystica Maxima* as a semi-independent British section of the O.T.O. (see chapter 10) so he chartered the *Mysteria Mystica Aeterna* as an Austrian section (under the leadership of Rudolf Steiner) and the *Mysteria Mystica Veritas* as a Swiss section.

The *Mysteria Mystica Veritas* appears to have enjoyed a quiet—almost a dormant—existence until 1943 when a Swiss-German occultist known as Frater *Paragranus* was initiated into it. Within a few years Frater *Paragranus* had become the Chief of the Swiss section of the O.T.O., had entered into friendly relationships with the disciples of Aleister Crowley—notably Karl Germer—and had established a magazine. Subsequently Frater *Paragranus* inherited the chieftainship of Krumm-Heller's *Ancient Rosicrucian Fraternity* and the Patriarchate of the *Gnostic Catholic Church*—this latter dignity he derived from Chevillon, murdered by the Gestapo in 1944, who was himself the successor of Joanny Bricaud. Frater *Paragranus* is also the head of one of the several groups who claim to be the true heirs and successors of the Illuminati of Weishaupt as revived (*circa* 1895) by Leopold Engel.

Over the last twenty years the Swiss O.T.O. have been responsible for the German translation and publication of many of Crowley's works.[1] They have also staged a production of Crowley's mystery-play *The Heart of the Master* and established an Abbey of Thelema in the heart of rural Switzerland.

---

[1] Notably *Book Four* (parts I and II), *Magick in Theory and Practice*, *Eight Lectures on Yoga* and *The Heart of the Master*. German versions of Crowley's *Liber Legis* and many O.T.O. documents have also been produced.

APPENDIX F

In 1971 Liz Miller and I visited the Swiss Abbey of Thelema and were impressed by its almost Shangri-La type self-sufficiency; the Swiss Crowleyans have their own church, complete with bell-tower, their own printing press, their own alchemical laboratory where they engage in the production of 'Paracelsian' remedies, their own hotel, the Gasthof Rose, and even their own paint factory! We found Frater *Paragranus* and his fellow-workers to be dedicated occultists, working extremely hard at their chosen tasks, yet managing to retain that streak of hard commonsense which is lacking in so many esotericists. We attended the Swiss version of Crowley's Gnostic Mass and were impressed by both its beauty and the economy of its performance. The one thing we did *not* find were the type of sexual orgies engaged in by Crowley at his Sicilian Abbey; but, of course, we hadn't expected to!

Selected Bibliography

SELECTED BIBLIOGRAPHY

AVALON, Arthur. *Principles of Tantra* (Madras, Ganesh and Co. 1955)
—, *The Serpent Power* (Madras, Ganesh and Co. 1958)
—, *Shakti and Shakta* (Madras, Ganesh and Co. 1953)
—, *Garland of Letters* (Madras, Ganesh and Co. 1953)
—, *The Great Liberation* (Madras, Ganesh and Co. 1952)
BATHURST, Leila. *Manifesto of the M.M.M.* (London, M.M.M. 1913)
BHARATI, Agehananda. *The Tantric Tradition* (London, Rider & Co. 1965)
BHATTACHARYA, Benoytosh. *Buddhist Esoterism* (London, Oxford University Press, 1932)
—, *Buddhist Iconography* (Calcutta, Firma K. L. Mukhopadhyay, 1959)
BLOCH, Ivan. *Sexual Life of Our Time* (London, Rebman, 1908)
CAVENDISH, Richard. *The Black Arts* (London, Routledge and Kegan Paul, 1967)
CHUBB, Ralph. *Manhood. A Poem* (Published by the author, 1924)
—, *The Sacrifice of Youth* (Published by the author, 1924)
—, *A Fable of Love and War* (Published by the author, 1925)
—, *The Cloud and the Voice* (Published by the author, 1927)
—, *The Book of God's Madness* (Published by the author, 1928)
—, *Woodcuts* (London, Andrew Bloch, 1928)
—, *An Appendix* (Published by the author, 1929)
—, *Songs of Mankind* (Published by the author, 1930)
—, *The Sun Spirit* (Lithographed and published by the author, 1931)
—, *The Heavenly Cupid* (Lithographed and published by the author, 1934)
—, *Songs Pastoral and Paradisal* (The Tintern Press, 1935)

—, *Water Cherubs* (Lithographed and published by the author, 1937)
—, *The Secret Country* (Lithographed and published by the author, 1939)
—, *The Child of Dawn* (Lithographed and published by the author, 1948)
—, *Flames of Sunrise* (Lithographed and published by the author, 1954)
—, *Treasure Trove* (Lithographed and published by the authtor 1957),
—, *The Golden City* (Lithographed by the author and posthumously published by his sister, 1961)
CROWLEY, Aleister. *White Stains* (Supposedly Amsterdam 1898, but may well have been produced in London by Leonard Smithers)
—, *Snowdrops from a Curate's Garden* (Privately printed, circa 1904, Brussels(?))
—, *Collected Works* (3 vols. in one) (Boleskine, S.P.R.T. 1907)
—, *Bahg-I-Muattar* (London, privately printed, 1910. Probsthain acted as distributors)
—, *777* (London, Neptune Press, 1951)
—, *Book of Lies* (London, Wieland and Co. 1913(?))
—, *Magick in Theory and Practice* (Paris, Lecram, 1929)
—, *Confessions* (London, Cape, 1969)
(See also under EQUINOX, *a periodical largely written by Crowley*)
CULLING, Louis T. *Complete Magic Curriculum* (Minnesota, Llewellyn, 1969)
D'ARCH SMITH, Timothy. *Ralph-Nicholas Chubb: prophète et pédéraste* (an article in Arcadie, March, 1963, pp. 137-44)
—, *Love in Earnest* (London, Routledge and Kegan Paul, 1970)
DASGUPTA, Shashibhusan. *Obscure Religious Cults* (Calcutta, University Press, 1946)
—, *Introduction to Tantric Buddhism* (Calcutta, University Press, 1950)
DAVENPORT, John. *Aphrodisiacs and Antiaphrodisiacs* (London, Hotten(?), 1869)
DAVID-NEEL, Alexandra. *Initiations and Initiates in Tibet* (London, Rider and Co. 1932)
EQUINOX, THE. *Volume I, Number 1* (London, Simpkin Marshall, March, 1909)
—, *Volume I, Number 2* (as above, but September, 1909)
—, *Volume I, Number 3* (as above, but March, 1910)
—, *Volume I, Number 4* (London, Published by Aleister Crowley, September, 1910)

SELECTED BIBLIOGRAPHY

—, *Volume I, Number 5* (As above, but March, 1911)
—, *Volume I, Number 6* (London, Wieland and Co., September, 1911)
—. *Volume I, Number 7* (As above, but March 1912)
—, *Volume I, Number 8* (As above, but September, 1912)
—, *Volume I, Number 9* (As above, but March, 1913)
—, *Volume I, Number 10* (As above, but September, 1913)
—, *Volume III, Number 1* (Detroit, Universal Publishing, 1919)
—, *Volume III, Number 3* (*The Equinox of the Gods*) (London, O.T.O. 1936)
—, *Volume III, Number 4* (*Eight Lectures on Yoga*) (London, O.T.O. 1939)
—, *Volume III, Number 5* (*The Book of Thoth*) (London, O.T.O. 1944)
—, *Volume III, Number 6* (*The Book of Wisdom of Folly*) (California, Thelema Publishing Co. 1961)
EVANS-WENTZ, W. Y. *The Tibetan Book of the Dead* (London, Oxford University Press, 1928)
—, *Tibetan Yoga and Secret Doctrines* (London, Oxford University Press, 1935)
—, *The Tibetan Book of the Great Liberation* (London, Oxford University Press, 1954)
FULLER, Jean Overton. *The Magical Dilemma of Victor B. Neuburg* (London, W. H. Allen, 1965)
GARDNER, Gerald. *Witchcraft Today* (London, Arrow Books, 1966)
GUENTHER, H. V. *Life and Teachings of Naropa* (Oxford, Clarendon Press, 1963)
HOWARD, Clifford. *Sex and Religion* (London, Williams and Norgate, 1929)
JENNINGS, Hargrave. *The Rosicrucians, Their Rites and Mysteries* (London, John Camden Hotten, 1870)
—, *Phallicism, Celestial and Terrestrial* (London, Redway, 1884)
KING, Francis. *Ritual Magic in England* (London, Neville Spearman, 1970)
KNIGHT, Richard Payne. *Essay on the Worship of Priapus* (London, Hotten, 1865)
LAVER, James. *The First Decadent* (London, Faber and Faber, 1954)
LEVI, Eliphas. *History of Magic* (London, Rider and Co. 1968)
LUK, Charles. *Taoist Yoga* (London, Rider and Co. 1971)
MOSSIKER, Frances. *The Affair of the Poisons* (London, Gollancz, 1970)

SELECTED BIBLIOGRAPHY

NETHERCOT, Arthur. *The Last Four Lives of Annie Besant* (Chicago, University Press, 1963)
OLIVER, George. *History of Initiation* (London, privately printed, 1829)
REGARDIE, Francis Israel. *My Rosicrucian Adventure* (Minnesota, Llewellyn, 1971)
—, *Golden Dawn* (4 vols. in 2) (As above, but 1969)
—, *Tree of Life* (New York, Weiser, 1969)
—, *Art of True Healing* (Toddington, Helios Books, 1964)
—, *Philosopher's Stone* (Minnesota, Llewellyn, 1970)
—, *Eye in the Triangle* (as above)
—, *Enochian Dictionary* (Texas, Sangreal Foundation, 1971)
REICH, Wilhelm. *The Sexual Revolution* (London, Vision Press, 1952)
—, *Mass Psychology of Fascism* (New York, Orgone Institute Press, 1946)
—, *Function of the Orgasm* (London, Panther Books, 1968)
—, *The Cancer Biopathy* (New York, Orgone Institute Press, 1948)
—, *Ether, God or Devil* (Maine, Orgone Institute Press, 1951)
—, *Cosmic Superimposition* (Maine, Orgone Institute Press, 1951)
—, *The Oranur Experiment* (Maine, Orgone Institute Press, 1951)
—, *The Murder of Christ* (Maine, Orgone Institute Press, 1953)
—, *Contact with Space* (New York, Core Pilot Press, 1957)
—, *Selected Writings* (London, Vision Press, 1961)
RHODES, H. F. T. *The Satanic Mass* (London, Arrow Books, 1965)
ROHMER, Sax. *Romance of Sorcery* (New York, Paperback Library, 1970)
RUSSELL, C. F. *Znuss is Znees* (California, privately printed, 1970)
SEABROOK, William. *Witchcraft* (London, Sphere Books, 1970)
—, *Magic Island* (New York, Harcourt Brace, 1929)
SMYTH, Frank. *Modern Witchcraft* (London, Macdonald Unit 75, 1970)
STEIGER, Brad. *Sex and Satanism* (New York, Ace Books, 1969)
SUMMERS, Montague. *The History of Witchcraft and Demonology* (London, Kegan Paul, 1926)
—, *The Geography of Witchcraft* (London, Kegan Paul, 1927)
—, *The Discovery of Witches* (London, Cayme Press, 1928)
—, *The Vampire, His Kith and Kin* (London, Kegan Paul, 1928)
—, *The Vampire in Europe* (London, Kegan Paul, 1929)
—, *The Werewolf* (London, Kegan Paul, 1933)
—, *A Popular History of Witchcraft* (London, Kegan Paul, 1937)
—, *Witchcraft and Black Magic* (London, Rider and Co. 1946)
—, *The Physical Phenomena of Mysticism* (London, Rider and Co. 1950)

TUCCI, Giuseppe. *Theory and Practice of Mandala* (London, Rider and Co. 1961)
WALKER, Benjamin. *Sex and the Supernatural* (London, Macdonald Unit 75, 1970)
WATTS, Alan W. (editor). *The Two Hands of God—The Myths of Polarity* (New York, G. Braziller, 1963)

INDEX

Abra-Melin, see *Sacred Magic*
Alchemy, Chinese, 37–46
Allegro, John, 95
Anus, blocking with bun, 45
Aphrodisiacs, 40
Ashbee, H. S., 11*n*, 19*n*, 159*n*
Athame, 4, 175–6
Aveling, Edward, 99

Bagshawe, Bishop, 137–8
Beatles, 169
Bernard, Pierre, 155–7
Besant, Annie, 123*n*, 124*n*, 128, 129–36, 139
Bharati, Agehananda, 32*n*, 34*n*, 36, 169
Blavatsky, Madame H. P., 123, 124, 192
Book of the Law, see *Liber Legis*
Book of Lies, 102, 187*n*
Boullan, Abbé, 74*n*, 180–5
Bo-yang, 38, 39
British Israelites, 139*n*

Cantharides, 68, 72*n*
Cat, spiritually evolved, 141
Charvoz, Abbé, 178, 179
Chasteuil, Captain de, 66–7
Chubb, Ralph, 122*n*, 190–3
Copulation and astrology, 116–19
Crowley, Aleister, 8, 52*n*, 63*n*, 98*n*, 101–14, 115, 119, 120, 122, 135, 143, 144, 145, 146, 154, 157*n*, 158, 162, 164, 168, 169, 186, 189
Crowleyanity, Swiss, 194 *et seq.*
Culling, Louis, T. 146–7, 148–9

Dalai Lama, 30, 32
d'Arch Smith, Timothy, 9, 193
Dennis, Helen, 125
Dennis, Robin, 125, 126
Dildo, 3, 173–4
Dilettanti Society, 75
Drugs, hallucinogenic, 36*n*, 118
Duality, 50

Elephant, sacred Tantric baby, 156
Enochian *Aires*, 108

Five Ms, 25, 35, 36
Folklore Society, 4–5
Fortune, Dion, 122, 123, 141
Fourier, 142
Freemasonry, 95–7
Fullerton, Alexander, 125, 126

Gardner, Gerald, 4–5, 6–7, 163, 168, 175
Garter, Order of the, 81–6
Geoffroi, 178, 179–80
Germer, Karl Johannes, 119–21, 154
"Godwin", see *Russell, C.F.*

INDEX

Golden Dawn, Hermetic Order of, 101, 109, 162, 167–8, 186n
Gozzoli, 179–80
Graves, Robert, 59n, 175–6
Guibourg, Abbé, 69–74

Hecate, 54–5, 56
Heimsoth, Karl-Guenther, 115
Herbert Breakspear, 12
HICE, 186–7
Holy Ghost, Mass of, 66
Homosexual Magic, 109–12, 113, 114
Homosexuality and astrology, 115, 118
Hubbard, L. Ron, 149n
Huysmans, J. K., 182–4, 192
Hyndman, H. M., 99

Inpenetrable, 167–8
Isis, see HICE

Jennings, Hargrave, 9, 80–1, 86n, 87
Jones, C. S., 143, 146n
Jones, George Cecil, 101
Jung, C. G., 46n

Kautsky, Karl, 99
Kellner, Karl, 96, 97, 99
King, Bishop Robert, 139
Krishnamurti, J., 128, 129–36
Kuntzel, Martha, 189

Lao-Tse, see Bo-yang
La Bosse, Marie, 68
La Vey, Anton, 149–53
La Voisin, 66, 68–73
Lead, Jane, 193
Leadbeater, Charles, 122–36, 139–41
Le Sage, 66, 68, 69
Levi, Eliphas, 178n, 181, 192
Lewis, H. Spencer, 144
Liber Legis, 103n, 114, 186n, 187n
Liberal Catholic Church, 136–41, 193
Life, Qabalistic Tree of, 187n
Lodge, Lunar, 154

Magicians, Battle of, 181–5
Makara, see Five Ms

Mansfield, Jayne, 149–53
"Marian", 3, 4, 7, 8, 163, 164
Mariette, Abbé, 66, 69
Marlowe, Christopher, 191n
Marpa, 30–1
Marston, Commander, 107
Marx, Eleanor, 99
Marx, Karl, 99
Masturbation, 41, 43, 98, 107
Mathers, S. L. MacGregor, 101–2, 120n, 168, 176
Memphis and Mizraim, 96–7
Milarepa, 31
Montespan, Marquise de, 66, 70–4
Monvoisin, Catherine, see La Voisin
Morris, William, 99n
Murray, Margaret, 57–9, 63n
Mysteria Mystica Maxima, 102, 113, 186

Neuberg, Victor B., 103n, 108–12
Nyack, 155–6

Olcott, Colonel, 123, 124n, 125n, 127, 128
Old Catholic Church, Dutch, 137–8
Oom the Omnipotent, see Bernard, Pierre
Ordo Templi Orientis, 8, 96–100, 102–3, 143, 147, 149, 154–5, 164, 186, 189

Payne Knight, Richard, 10, 75, 79, 80
Pettit, Douglas, 124–5, 126n, 127
Pisanus Fraxi, see Ashbee H. S.
Pordage, Samuel, 193
Pornography, 167–8
Powell, Ronald, 193

Randolph, Paschal Beverley, 97, 143
Recnartus, Frater, 114, 115, 119
Regardie, F. Israel, 120n, 158
Reich, Wilhelm, 158–62
Reuss, Theodor, 97, 99–100, 102, 113, 114, 143
Reynie, Nicolas de la, 67–70
Rose-Croix, Kabalistic Order of, 181–2
Russell, C. F., 144–8

INDEX

Sabbath, Witches', 60–4
Sacred Magic of Abra-Melin the Mage, 61–2
Saint Duncan, Book of, 5–6
Sanders, Alex, 164–7
Satan, Church of, 149–54
Saturnus, Frater, *see* Germer, Karl Johannes
Sellon, Edward, 9, 10–29
   commences regular course in fucking, 11,
   invigorating effect of Carbonell's old Port upon, 15,
   becomes driver of mail coach, 16
   sets up as fencing master, 16
   enjoys rural life with wife, 17,
   teaches school-girls hide and seek, 18,
   copulates in railway carriages, 20
   is laid in tomb of blood, 21,
   misinterprets Tantric philosophy, 22
   fails to understand *Mudra*, 25
   unusual beliefs regarding boats, 53n.
Semen, 31, 35, 40–2, 68, 73, 98
Shakers, 142
Siddha cult, 36–7
Star Ruby, Ritual of, 187n
Stokes, H. N., 122, 123
Summers, Montague, 56

Tantricism, 8, 30–6, 37, 52n, 143n, 155–7, 169
Temple, Order of, 91–4
Thomas, Dylan, 103n
Time, nature of, 50–1
Tom-tom, 107
Trotsky, Leon, 57n
Trotskyists, 58n

Ups and Downs of Life, 10

Vanderbilt, Mrs. W. K., 156
Vanens, Louis de, 67
Vestments, remarkable properties of, 140
Vintras, Eugene, 177–81
Von Hammer, Joseph, 92–4

Wedgwood, James, 139–41
Weishaupt, Adam, 103n, 186n
Willoughby, F. S., 138, 139
Witchcraft, contemporary, 3–8, 163–8
Witchcraft, traditional, 54–64
Wright, Thomas, 10, 79–80, 92, 174

Yab-yum, 33n
Yoga, sexual, *see Tantricism*

also available from feral house

APOCALYPSE CULTURE II
Edited by Adam Parfrey
WE'VE BEEN TOLD THAT THE ORIGINAL **APOCALYPSE CULTURE** RUINED MARRIAGES, CREATED FISTFIGHTS, AND INSPIRED PEOPLE FOR LIFE. REVIEWERS CLAIMED **APOCALYPSE CULTURE** WAS "THE NEW BOOK OF REVELATION" AND "THE TERMINAL DOCUMENTS OF OUR TIME."

"ADAM PARFREY'S ASTONISHING, UN-PUT-DOWNABLE AND ABSOLUTELY BRILLIANT COMPILATION, **APOCALYPSE CULTURE II**, WILL BLOW A HOLE THROUGH YOUR MIND THE SIZE OF JONBENÉT'S FIST."—JERRY STAHL, AUTHOR OF *PERMANENT MIDNIGHT* AND *PERV—A LOVE STORY*

6 X 9 • 470 PAGES • FULL COLOR SECTION
ISBN 0-922915-57-1 • $18.95

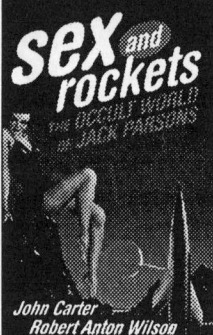

SEX AND ROCKETS
The Occult World of Jack Parsons
John Carter, Introduction by Robert Anton Wilson
"THE FIRST IN-DEPTH AND LONG OVERDUE LOOK AT THE LIFE OF JOHN WHITESIDE PARSONS – PIONEERING ROCKET SCIENTIST, AND ARDENT DISCIPLE OF THE NOTORIOUS MAGUS, ALEISTER CROWLEY. . . . WHAT MAKES THIS BOOK ALL THE MORE FASCINATING IS THE SHIFT IN FOCUS THAT TAKES PLACE THROUGHOUT, AS THE AUTHOR DEMARCATES BETWEEN JOHN PARSONS THE BRILLIANT ROCKET ENGINEER, AND JACK PARSONS THE FAILED MAGICIAN, WHO IN HIS ATTEMPT TO CROSS THE ABYSS, FELL INTO IT INSTEAD, FULFILLING A FIERY DEMISE, WHICH PARSONS HIMSELF PROPHESIED."
—ADAM GORIGHTLY, *THE EXCLUDED MIDDLE*

6 X 9 • 256 PAGES • CLOTH ORIGINAL • PHOTOS
ISBN 0-922915-56-3 • $24.95

THE GATES OF JANUS
Serial Killing and its Analysis by the "Moors Murderer," Ian Brady
Introduction by Colin Wilson, Afterword by Peter Sotos
"THE MOORS MURDERS," THE CASE OF IAN BRADY AND MYRA HINDLEY AND THEIR GLEEFUL TORTURE AND MURDER OF A CHILD AND TWO TEENAGERS IN THE EARLY '60s, ARE THOUGHT TO BE THE MOST APPALLING CRIMES EVER COMMITTED IN ENGLAND. **THE GATES OF JANUS** IS A FULL-LENGTH WORK BY BRADY HIMSELF, WRITTEN AFTER COLIN WILSON SUGGESTED THAT HE ANALYZE SERIAL MURDER AND COME TO TERMS WITH THE CRIMES HE COMMITTED 40 YEARS AGO. BRADY'S WORK IS BOTH PSYCHOLOGICAL AND PHILOSOPHICAL, BASED UPON HIS READINGS, OBSERVATIONS AND LIFE STORY, REMINISCENT OF NOTHING LESS THAN THE MARQUIS DE SADE. A REMARKABLE, ONCE-IN-A-LIFETIME WORK.

5.5 X 8 • 312 PAGES • CLOTH ORIGINAL • ISBN: 0-922915-73-3 • $24.95

TO ORDER FROM FERAL HOUSE: DOMESTIC ORDERS ADD $4.50 SHIPPING FOR FIRST ITEM, $2.00 EACH ADDITIONAL ITEM. AMEX, MASTERCARD, VISA, CHECKS AND MONEY ORDERS ARE ACCEPTED. (CA STATE RESIDENTS ADD 8% TAX.) CANADIAN ORDERS ADD $9 SHIPPING FOR FIRST ITEM, $6 EACH ADDITIONAL ITEM. OTHER COUNTRIES ADD $11 SHIPPING FOR FIRST ITEM, $9 EACH ADDITIONAL ITEM. NON-U.S. ORIGINATED ORDERS MUST BE INTERNATIONAL MONEY ORDER OR CHECK DRAWN ON A U.S. BANK ONLY. SEND ORDERS TO: FERAL HOUSE, P.O. BOX 13061, LOS ANGELES, CA 90013